Harvey Girls

Kit

Finding Freedom and Love

Katherine St. Clair

ISBN: 978-1546834533

Printed in the United States

MAPLEWOOD
— PUBLISHING —

FOR CHARLOTTE

CHAPTER 1

Summer, 1895

Kit Pridgeon hated fish. She was not just annoyed by fish or slightly irritated by fish – she *hated* fish. While the fish were swimming in the creeks and rivers, the harbors, or the sea they were fine; she was alright with them. Once they were caught in a net and brought up from the briny deep, fish became her problem.

In this part of Bridgeton there was simply no escaping the smell of fish. She'd been born and raised here, in a clapboard house just off Main Street, and like any other native, she should have been used to the smell. But she wasn't used to it, and she wasn't sure she ever would be. It was just one more sign that she didn't belong in Bridgeton.

Bridgeton was a small town on the coast of North Carolina that boasted three churches, a small grocery, a hotel, a library, and a fishing fleet. Everyone she knew was a fisherman, was married to a fisherman, or worked in a cannery.

There were people in Bridgeton who didn't have to fish for a living, but Kit didn't know any of them, personally. On Saturday afternoons, she would see them on Queen Street in their fancy clothes coming and going from the

1

restaurant at the hotel, or attending a show at the small theater. To them, she was just another girl from the part of Bridgeton they called "Fish Town."

It was a beautiful summer day and she had only a few minutes left on her lunch break from the cannery. She sat on the dock with her feet dangling over the side. She was trying to eat her cold chicken sandwich but the smell of rotting fish was overwhelming.

Hunger won out over her repulsion, so she finished the sandwich in three bites.

"You ate that sandwich like a hound dog eats table scraps, you didn't taste n'are a bite, did ya?" asked Letty Harper.

Kit looked at her best friend and smiled. Letty was the kind of girl who fit right in here. She was down to earth, kind, and her greatest ambition was to marry a man who owned his own fishing boat. Kit and Letty couldn't have been more opposite if they had worked it out on paper, but they'd been friends since they were little kids.

Letty had just barely learned how to read and write and do arithmetic, but Kit had excelled at her studies. She was disappointed when she reached the sixth grade and her parents pulled her out of school, but that was how it was in Fish Town. As her Pa had said, "Wont no sense teaching a girl that wont never going to need it."

Kit tried to explain to Letty about the sandwich, but she knew it was no use. "I ate it fast because if I didn't, I wouldn't eat it at all. Not with that godawful fish smell."

"What smell, the leftover pile? I can hardly smell it at all. You going to eat your pie?"

Letty looked down at the slice of pecan pie her mother had packed with her lunch. It was her favorite. Normally she wouldn't part with it, but today she couldn't stomach any more food – not with the smell of dead fish perfuming the air.

"No. Here, you can have it."

"Thanks. You going to the social this Sunday after church?"

Kit shrugged. "I don't know, maybe. I haven't really thought about it."

2

"I am, you can bet on it. Come on Kit, it'll fun. My brother told me to ask you," she added, with a twinkle in her eye.

"Jacob asked if I was going to be there?"

"He sure did! If you want to know the truth, I think he's sweet on ya."

Kit blushed. She'd always liked Jacob but he never seemed to notice her. She was surprised he'd ask about her.

"Why Kit Pridgeon, you are turning just as red as can be."

"Come on Letty, we don't want to be late, Mr. Howard will dock our pay if he catches us lollygagging again."

Kit stood and helped her friend to her feet. As they headed back inside, Kit hung back and turned to look at the view from the dock once more. It was a beautiful here. The water sparkled on the water of the harbor and the reeds at the water's edge swayed in the summer breeze. She hated fish but she loved the water; she just didn't know if she could spend her days gutting fish and canning them for the rest of her life.

Reluctantly, she returned to work.

It was after dinner when Kit's two oldest brothers, Thomas and Samuel, walked through the kitchen door. Kit and her younger sisters were helping their mother clean the kitchen after dinner and Kit greeted Thomas like she did almost every night.

"There's a plate on the stove for each of you. Thomas, how was it today? Did you meet anyone interesting?"

"I don't know what you call interesting, but I call any man what pays me to take him fishing *interesting*. Now what's for dinner? I'm starved."

Thomas and Samuel sat down at the kitchen table and Kit brought their plates. Her sister, Sarah, poured two glasses of lemonade and brought a basket of bread. Kit watched her brothers eat and wondered what their days must be like.

They owned their own boat and made a living chartering fishing trips for the rich people at the hotel. Other times, they fished on their own and set out crab pots. They spent their days on their boat, and she was sure that if she had been born a boy, she would have been right there with them, on the water every day. It was better than facing the monotony of the cannery.

Her brothers finished eating and Kit and her sisters were finally able to finish their chores for the evening. There was only an hour left of daylight and freedom before she would have to get to bed. She was normally up before dawn and started work by 7:00 every morning. That made for a long day and she needed plenty of rest to get through it.

Kit climbed the stairs to the bedroom she shared with Emily, who at seventeen was only two years younger than her. There was a book she wanted to finish reading and she only had an hour left to do it – it was due back at the library tomorrow. She washed her face and hands and changed into her nightgown. She crawled into her bed with her book and for just a few minutes was transported to a world that did not revolve around fish.

The next day, Kit arrived at the cannery well before she was scheduled to begin work. It was Saturday, and if the work was finished after lunch, the boss would let everyone leave early. Saturday afternoons were the only time she had free to go to the library, and today she hoped there would be time to get there after work.

Kit tried to work as fast as she could. Looking around the cannery floor, it seemed everyone was on the same page. The work was tough and the hours were long. She worked six days a week and the only days off she could count on were Sundays, Christmas, and Easter. The prospect of a Saturday afternoon free was enough to motivate her (and all the ladies she worked with) to go as fast as they possibly could.

Luckily, it paid off. The cannery closed at 3:00 that day. That gave her just enough time to go home, take a bath, and get to the library before it closed. Letty wanted to talk about the social the next day, but Kit didn't have time. The book was due that day and she had another secret reason for wanting to go the library, a reason that she had never shared with anyone, not even Letty.

She apologized to Letty and rushed home as fast as she could. She bathed and dressed in a hurry. Her hair was still damp when she braided it and put it up in a bun. She grabbed the library book from the bedside table and raced out the door before her mother or her sisters could stop her or slow her down.

4

She was halfway to the library when she finally caught her breath and stopped running. It would not do, she told herself, to be seen running down Main Street at the age of nineteen. She was sure that she already looked like she was from Fish Town with her plain clothes and simple straw hat, but she didn't need to act like it, too.

She arrived at the library a half hour before closing. At the front desk, she was met by the town librarian, an older lady with grey hair who went by the name Mrs. Cates, although she had never married.

"Mrs. Cates, I need to turn this book in, and I was wondering if you could recommend something with adventure and faraway places, may be with a heroine who is smart and funny?"

Mrs. Cates' eyes sparkled. "Are you looking for a book to read, or are you planning an escape?"

"Both. Did you get the paper from Raleigh yet?"

"I did; I've got it right here for you. You're the first to see it this week"

The older woman handed Kit the newspaper as she walked to the stacks to find Kit a book. Kit carried the newspaper to a reading table and unfolded it. The date read July 12, 1895. The paper was only two days old which, to Kit, was practically brand new.

She turned the pages so quickly they made a swishing sound as she searched for the section that listed correspondence courses. The secret hope that Kit harbored in her heart was to one day become a teacher and go somewhere far away from the little town of Bridgeton.

She wanted to go somewhere no one had ever heard of a place called Fish Town, where people didn't talk about fishing night and day, and where the smell of dead fish didn't linger in the air. If she could become a teacher, then she could travel anywhere in the world where they needed teachers. That sounded like a good life to her, and she had been saving a little money from her meager wages every week so she could afford to take the classes she needed to pass the teacher's exam.

She looked at the classes offered in the paper, from educational institutions as far away as New York. She thought about how much money she had saved up and realized it was not quite enough. At this rate, it would take her another year, or maybe more, to save enough for the classes, and then there was no guarantee she would pass the exam.

Her heart sank as she flipped through the pages of the paper. There was nothing else in Bridgeton she could do to earn money. The rich people had servants but that didn't pay very well, and they didn't hire people from Fish Town. Other than the cannery, there were no other options. It was a hopeless situation.

Or was it? She thought about a city the size of Raleigh. She had never been to a town that big, but it was the state capital, there must be something there that paid good money? She turned the page to the help wanted section and looked at what was available in the capital. It wasn't where she wanted to go, but it might be a step in the right direction, especially if they paid more and she didn't have to ever gut another fish.

She looked at several listings for domestic help, posts for teachers and governesses, and a few listings for shop assistants. Kit was about to close the paper when an advertisement caught her eye.

Intelligent women of strong character wanted for the position of waitress at the Harvey Restaurants opening in Kansas and destinations in the West. The ideal candidate is between the ages of 18–30, is clean, courteous, and efficient. A generous salary will be provided to those selected for employment. If interested, please apply in person at the Carriage House Hotel, Raleigh, on the 21st of July at 10:00 a.m.

Kit could hardly contain her excitement; she was intelligent, courteous, and possessed a strong character. It wasn't a teaching positon like she had dreamed of, but it was a chance for an adventure. The advertisement mentioned Kansas and destinations out west, so it would be an opportunity for her to go on an adventure, but there was just one problem – how was she going to get to Raleigh by the 22nd?

"Mrs. Cates?" Her voice rang out loud in the empty library.

"Yes, Kit, I'm still looking for a book for you."

"Don't worry about that one, what do you have about the West?"

The older woman answered as she stepped out from the stacks. "The west? What would you want with a book about the west?"

"Can you keep a secret?"

"Kit, as many years as we have known each other, you must know that I can."

Kit had not realized it until that very moment, but Mrs. Cates had been the closest thing to a real confidant she had in that town. Letty was her friend, but there was so much that Kit could not talk to Letty about, like her thirst to see the world and have adventures. Mrs. Cates had always listened to Kit and had never once told her that she needed to get her head out of the clouds, like her mother said at least once a week.

"I am thinking about applying to be a waitress."

"A waitress? That would be a change for you from the cannery, but I didn't think they had waitresses at the hotel, only waiters."

"Not here, somewhere out West. In Kansas."

"What are you talking about?"

"Take a look at this advertisement in the paper." Kit showed the paper to Mrs. Cates.

Mrs. Cates read the advertisement and commented, "You want to work for that Harvey fellow. Seems to me I read an article about him. He was opening restaurants and wanted to find young women to work in them."

"You have heard about it, then? Do you think it's respectable?"

"It seems to be; I can't think why they would have featured it in the paper, if it wasn't. The Raleigh paper wouldn't take an advertisement from someone looking for saloon girls."

"You're right about that. But how am I going to get to Raleigh?"

"I suppose you'll have to take the train. The advertisement said the Carriage House in Raleigh, that is one fancy place. If you're going, better wear your Sunday best."

Kit had less than a week to make a decision that would affect her entire life. The first thing she needed to do before she became too excited about the whole thing was to find out when the next train was leaving, and how much the ticket was going to cost. If she didn't have enough money for the ticket, then there was little point in getting her hopes up.

She left the library and headed straight for the train station. She had never traveled by train before, and even by wagon, never more than five miles from Bridgeton. She had always dreamed of adventure and the places she saw in the books she read, but this was the first time she was on the verge of having an adventure herself. She tried to contain her rising sense of optimism as she walked the three blocks to the train station.

The Bridgeton train depot was a small station in the middle of town. It catered to rich people who came for fishing and boating, it transported fish from the town to destinations all over the state, and it brought in the mail. In a station that small, she quickly found the ticket office.

Mr. Quinn, who managed the station and ran the ticket office, didn't know her by name. She was thankful that he didn't know who her father was, or else she would have a lot of explaining to do.

"Good afternoon Miss, what can I help you with on this fine day?"

"Sir, I was wondering if you could tell me when the train runs to Raleigh. I need to be there by the 21st."

"Well, let me see," he said, as he turned in his swivel chair and reached for a schedule. He handed the schedule to her and said, "It looks to me like the train to Raleigh runs two more times before the 21st. Monday and Friday."

"If I take the Friday train, what time will I be arriving in Raleigh?"

"It arrives at 1:10 p.m. – dinner time."

"It looks like the tickets cost a lot of money."

"Those tickets are for first and second class. You could ride in third class with the mail, but you would have to bring your own meals."

"I could do that. Thank you."

"You're welcome, Miss. Be sure to get here early. That train leaves promptly at 8:00."

"Yes sir, thank you again."

Kit left the train station with a plan. If she rode in the mail car, she would not have to spend all of her money. She would have enough left over to stay in a hotel. One thing was for sure – if she left Bridgeton, she was either going

8

to become a Harvey girl, or she was going to stay in Raleigh. She would be done with fish once and for all.

There was only one problem with her plan: Jacob Harper.

Poor Letty was so excited about the social tomorrow, and Kit had abandoned her. She felt guilty now, especially if she was about to leave Bridgeton. She stopped by Letty's house, hoping she would be home.

She walked through the garden gate and knocked on the back door. The screen door was unlatched. When she put her hand on the handle, she heard a familiar voice.

"Hey there Kit, you must be looking for Letty," said Jacob.

Kit opened her mouth to say something and found that she was unable to say a word. Jacob was the most handsome man she had ever seen. He had dark eyes, dark hair, and he looked the way she imagined a pirate must have looked – even down to the smirk.

She brushed a wisp of blonde hair out of her eyes and tried not to blush.

He smiled knowingly, which only made the problem worse. "Come on in; I'll get Letty."

She nodded and stepped into the kitchen. Leaving Bridgeton would be so much easier if it wasn't for Jacob.

"Kit, where did you get off to today? Doesn't matter, do you want to go get some ice cream?"

Kit thought about her limited funds, but then remembered this might be the last time she went to the ice cream parlor with her best friend. "Sure, why not?"

"Good, I'll get my hat."

From the moment the screen door closed, Letty chattered incessantly about the social. It did not take long for Kit to discover the reason for her friend's excitement.

"Kit, do ya think yer family's going be there tomorrow?"

"Yes, I suppose so. Ma and Emily are baking pies to take, and I think there may even be a cake as well."

"That is good to hear, but do you think all them are going to go?"

Kit looked at her friend and realized that Letty was asking for a reason. "Letty Harper, what has got you so interested in whether or not my family is going to be attending the social, or should I say who?"

"Kit, I ne'er could keep a secret from you. It's your brother."

Kit rolled her eyes. "Yes. But which one?"

"Thomas. I've had my eye in him for a good while, who is he sweet on?"

"Letty, I don't know that he's sweet on anyone, but I got another brother if Thomas is taken."

"I don't know, there's just something about Thomas."

"Yes, Letty, he will be there."

When they arrived at the ice cream parlor, it was full of the children of the rich people in town. Kit and Letty were the only ones from Fish Town standing in line. As Kit watched the children dressed in their everyday clothes nicer than anything she had ever owned, she thought about the first time she had ever had ice cream from an ice cream parlor. It was after she had started working at the cannery, when she had a little extra money to spare. The people in Fish Town didn't waste their hard-earned money buying ice cream for their children.

As Kit and Letty placed their orders, Kit was acutely aware of the stares they were receiving from the well-dressed ladies in the parlor. She ignored those looks as she had always done, but she knew that if she stayed in Bridgeton, she would have to endure those same stares for the rest of her life.

Letty, as always, seemed oblivious to the looks from the rich women, the same way she was to the smell of fish. Kit, on the other hand, found it difficult to bear. The signs had been there all along. She needed to leave Bridgeton behind her and make her own way in the world. Now, if she could just convince her heart that she could live without Jacob, she could leave Fish Town and never look back.

10

The church social was an event that nearly everyone in Fish Town looked forward to for weeks. It was held on a Sunday after Church at the park across the street. There was delicious food, games, and even a little courting, as young couples went strolling along the footpaths lined with rose bushes. The gazebo was a popular destination for many of the young men and women, and Kit and Letty were no exception.

Kit was overcome by mixed feelings when she looked around at all the familiar faces at the social. These were people she had grown up with and known her entire life. Bridgeton was not a bad place, and Fish Town was full of good, honest people who worked hard and made a living from the sea – but it was tough work and there was never enough money.

Everyone she knew was poor just like her family, although she was proud that her brothers owned a boat and so did her father; the boats were all they had to call their own. There was nothing fancy about a working fishing boat, nothing glamorous.

She sometimes felt guilty because she wanted more in life than to live and die here beside her family and friends, but it was a spark that had always been there, in her heart. It had not dimmed like girlish dreams often do – instead, it had grown brighter and more vivid with each passing year. At the age of nineteen, she could hardly contain the flame, the yearning that was unquenchable and burned deep inside her.

She was lost in her thoughts when Jacob Harper came walking up to the gazebo. Letty elbowed her in the ribs. He brushed his dark wavy hair back from his face, and leaned on the railing.

"Kit, I was hoping ya might want to take a walk with me."

Kit could feel her heart beating wildly as she looked into his dark eyes. She stood up and her legs felt weak. She held on to the railing for support and answered, "Yes, I would like that."

He held out his hand to her. She put her hand in his and she could feel her pulse race. She looked around the gazebo and realized that everyone had stopped talking, and all eyes were on them. She turned red as Letty winked at her.

Jacob held her hand as she walked down the stairs, and then he politely withdrew it. If he held her hand in public for any length of time, word would get around that they were courting and he had not asked permission from her Pa to do that. Kit's heart pounded just thinking about that. If he wanted to court her, what would she do?

She had liked Jacob Harper ever since she was ten years old, and now here he was asking her to go walking at the social. It was like a dream come true…except she planned on leaving town forever in less than a week.

They walked in silence for a few minutes. Kit didn't know what to say and Jacob was the quiet type, like most of the men in Fish Town. He didn't believe in speaking unless he meant what he said, or it had something to do with fishing.

The silence between them grew as Kit waited for him to say something, anything. Kit had never been alone with Jacob before, and now she didn't know what to say or do. She looked at this strong man at her side, and was struck by his demeanor – he was calm and stoic and didn't express how he felt. She wondered what lay beneath the exterior.

"Jacob, how have you been?" she found the courage to ask.

"Well enough."

Kit waited a few more minutes. They were in the shade of a majestic oak tree, and a bench beckoned just ahead.

"Jacob, can we sit for just a little while?"

He glanced around, and Kit know he was making sure they were in plain sight. "I don't see why not."

Kit sat beside the man she had dreamed of for years. He was honest, he worked hard for his living, and he was ruggedly handsome. She had thought of this moment and what it would feel like to be his girl. Now that she was with him, she realized they didn't have anything to say, – or at least *he* didn't have anything to say. It was awkward, and Kit realized that while Jacob may be handsome, there was nothing between them.

The goosebumps and pulse pounding she felt was from her girlish notions of Jacob, but the reality was quite a bit different. She decided to plunge ahead and see just how different they really were.

"Jacob, tell me something. What do you want out of life?"

"You don't waste no time`, do ya?" He gave her a crooked half-smile.

"No, I don't have any to waste."

"Well then, I want a fine boat, a sturdy house, and a good wife."

"That's all you want out of this life? Just what you can get here in Bridgeton?"

"What more would I want? I got the sea, all the rest will come in due time."

"Didn't you ever dream of leaving here, of finding out what was out there in the world?"

"Why would I do that? On a boat, I can go to sea and I'm as free as any man can be. Rich or poor don't matter when you're captain of your own boat."

Kit nodded. "I think you've helped me answer something that's been bothering me for a while."

"I have, and how is that?"

"For a man, living here's hard but you have the sea; you have the ocean. I love the water, same as you, but I'm stuck here on land. I can watch the tide come in, but I'll never ride it out to the ocean in my own boat. I want adventure, and you have adventure every day."

Jacob stared at her as though she was speaking a language he'd never heard before, "I wouldn't call it adventure. If you think it's fun, then you don't know a thing about it."

"No, I know it's not fun. I know it's dangerous and the sea can kill you fast as look at you, but out there you are free. Here, I will never be."

"Letty told me you were one for the books and your pretty head was filled with odd notions."

"Letty was right. I am one for books and I suppose my head is filled with odd notions, for a girl."

"Still, you're a sturdy and good looking woman, you'd make a good wife."

Kit had to laugh at that, but she felt sad. "Jacob, I have longed for you to say that for years, and it's not easy for me to tell you this, but I think you'd do better with a girl who is content to spend her days in Bridgeton. Take my sister Emily, she's like Letty. She couldn't be happier here."

"Hmm. I might have to study on that."

"You study on that, Jacob. What do you say we get back?"

"Or we could just sit here for a spell and enjoy the shade."

"Or we could do that, too."

Jacob reached for hand and she let him have it. It felt nice, even though she knew there would be no future for them. He held her hand on the bench and neither of them spoke a word. Butterflies fluttered in the rosebushes and a warm breeze was filled with the scent of flowers for once, and not fish.

CHAPTER 2

The train rumbled out of the station and Kit sat on a bag of mail. It was not comfortable, but she would make do. She dabbed her eye with a handkerchief. This was it; she really was leaving everything and everyone she had ever known behind. It was a happy day, but there was a bittersweet quality that she couldn't shake.

Her family and friends didn't know she had gone, at least not yet. She would send them all letters as early as she could. The only person in Bridgeton who knew she was leaving was Mrs. Cates. The librarian had slipped her a little money and box of peppermints to take with her on the trip.

She felt guilty that she had left without saying goodbye, but she didn't think she had a choice. If her parents had suspected she was going all the way to Raleigh by herself, they would have forbid her. If she had told them she wanted to go all the way out West they would have been furious, maybe to the point of locking her in her room. They were old-fashioned and Kit knew they would never understand.

Leaving Letty was the part that hurt the most. She had wanted to tell her best friend she was leaving so many times in those final days, but she just could not risk Letty saying something to her brother or her parents, even by accident. As bad as she felt about it, sneaking away was the only way she knew she could leave without being hindered or forced to face ridicule and anger.

A porter came into the mail car to check on Kit. It was unusual for a woman to be riding third class and she thought he must be concerned for the young lady sitting on a bag of mail, crying. She thanked him for his concern and took a book out of her lunch basket. It was one of the only books she owned, and she had read it so many times that the pages were dog-eared. It was an old worn out copy of Pride and Prejudice that Mrs. Cates had given to her years ago. She read the inscription and the tears stared falling again.

To Bridgeton's own Elizabeth Bennet,

Be brave and strong like Lizzie and you will surely find happiness. Always follow your heart.

Adelaide Cates

Kit knew she was following her heart, that finding the advertisement was providential, and she just needed to be brave. This was an adventure; she was finally the heroine in her own story. Wherever she going, she would never have to gut another fish ever again. She had made an important decision: no matter what happened at the Carriage House Hotel, she was going to leave her tears behind in the mail car of the train.

She had spent a lifetime with people who thought all she would ever be was a cannery girl or a wife. This was her chance to lead a life that was not defined by one single other person. This was *her* moment. She looked around at the sacks of mail and vowed that when she got out of this mail car, she was going to live life to the fullest and never settle for anything less than her dreams.

Finally, the train pulled into the station in downtown Raleigh. Kit had grown accustomed to the constant rumbling of the wheels on the track just beneath the floor. When the train came to a stop, it took a few minutes to adjust. The porter opened the door and helped her down the stairs onto the platform. He held her arm until she had her bearings.

She walked to the ticket master's office to ask about a place to say for the night. He recommended a boarding house run by a Christian woman two blocks from the station, on Elm Street. As she walked to the boarding house she was amazed by the buildings she could see only a few blocks from the train station. She had never been to a city as big as Raleigh and she was not used to seeing buildings over three stories tall. There were several here that she guessed must have been six or seven stories high.

16

Mrs. Taylor ran the boarding house and had one room left. She welcomed Kit to stay. Kit was tired from the journey and she could barely hold her eyes open as she walked up the stairs to her room. Mrs. Taylor took pity on her and brought a dinner plate to her room.

"My dear," said Mrs. Taylor, "You look like you've been traveling for weeks; what brings you to Raleigh?"

"I want to be a Harvey Girl."

"A Harvey Girl? You mean like the Harvey Hotels that are so popular nowadays?"

"Yes, ma'am. I came here all the way from Bridgeton. I have to get to the Carriage House Hotel tomorrow morning; do you think I can walk there from here?"

"You will do no such thing, I will take you in my carriage."

"Mrs. Taylor, I don't have enough money for a carriage ride."

"Stuff and nonsense, what kind of Christian would I be to let some poor girl walk the streets of this town alone? What if you were to get lost? What were you going to wear; did you bring anything nice?"

Kit opened her carpet bag and looked at her skirt, shirtwaist, and jacket. They were all a wrinkled mess. She felt frustrated. She couldn't go see about getting a position as a Harvey Girl in these wrinkled clothes. "I was going to wear this. I didn't know it would get so wrinkled on the train – do you have an iron I can use?"

"Child, you leave that to me, now, and just get your rest. I won't ask where your family is, or who let you come away on this fool's errand, but now that you're here, I'll help you."

Mrs. Taylor had brought Kit a bowl of beef stew with a dinner roll. Kit ate every mouthful and then she could fight sleep no more. She leaned over in the bed and instantly went to sleep.

～

The next morning, Kit woke with a start. She was in a strange bed in a place she didn't recognize. For a few minutes, she was disoriented, until she remembered where she was and why she was here. It was the 21st and she needed to be at the Carriage House Hotel well before ten. The sun was up and for a moment she was frantic; she couldn't find her Sunday suit.

A knock on the door and a bright cheerful voice eased her anxiety, "Dearie, it's Mrs. Taylor, I have your suit all pressed and ready for you."

Kit opened the door and there stood Mrs. Taylor with her suit. It was crisp and presentable. Mrs. Taylor had something else for her as well. "I thought you might want to wear my new hat, I just bought it and it will look very smart with your light hair."

"Thank you so much! I only just met you, and you've been as wonderful to me as if you were my own mother." Actually, quite a bit nicer, though Kit thought it would be unkind to say so. Her own mother had many people to care for, and little time or money with which to do so.

"God sent you to me to look after, that's all there is to it. I think it's dangerous for young ladies to leave home, but here you are, and you seem determined. The Harvey Girls have been in the newspaper, so if you are bound and determined to do this, then let's get you ready for your big day. Now what are we going to do about your hair?"

Mrs. Taylor sat Kit down and with a hairbrush and few hair pins arranged her hair in a more fashionable updo. It wasn't quite a pompadour, but it looked much better than a simple bun at the back of her head. She helped Kit get dressed and pinned the hat on her head.

Mrs. Taylor stood back to admire her work, "The suit is a little plain to my eyes, but that hat sets off the color of your hair and you are a pretty girl. I don't think you have a thing to worry about. Just smile and be polite...oh, let's see those hands."

Kit held out her hands, and Mrs. Taylor shook her head, "My girl, you have been working for a living, haven't you? Never worry, I have a pair of lace gloves that will hide those hands until they heal."

Mrs. Taylor went to her bedroom to fetch the gloves. She returned and rushed Kit out the door and downstairs to the waiting carriage. As they rode through the streets of Raleigh with the carriage top down, Kit stared at the rows of two-story houses and brick building that seemed to touch the sky. Oak trees lined the streets and everywhere she looked, women and men were dressed in the latest fashions. She felt as though she was living a dream.

They arrived at the Carriage House Hotel at half past nine. Mrs. Taylor promised to meet her after luncheon, as she had a few errands she wanted to run downtown. Kit walked inside the hotel and was directed by a staff member to the atrium.

She was surprised by the number of women who were already there. She smoothed her skirt and tried to fight her nervousness. She didn't know how many ladies they needed to fill the positions, but she didn't think they needed as many as she saw in the lobby.

Kit joined a line that had formed at a table with two men and a woman seated behind it. They were all impeccably dressed and they did not smile. Girl after girl went before those three, and only one or two were sent to the next table, farther back in the room. Kit guessed that these three made the decision of who would even be considered. She had never been on an interview for a position like this and she had no idea what to say.

She tried to remain calm as she waited for her turn. This was her adventure and she had nothing to lose, so she would give it her best. Finally, she was the girl standing in front of the table.

"What is your name, age, and where are you from?" asked one of the men.

"Katherine Louise Pridgeon, nineteen, Bridgeton, North Carolina."

"Bridgeton? Where is that?" asked the other man

"On the coast."

"Do you have family in Raleigh?" asked the first gentlemen

"No sir, I do not. I came to Raleigh to become a Harvey Girl."

"Young lady, are you telling us that you traveled all the way from wherever you said you were from, just to work for Mr. Harvey?"

"Yes sir, I spent my savings to get here, that is how much this means to me."

"I'm impressed by your dedication, but tell us, have you ever served a meal before in a restaurant?"

"I have not, but I am intelligent, possess strong character, and I am courteous."

19

"And resourceful, I would say."

"If we were to offer you a position, are you aware that you would enter into a contract for a year, during which time you could not date, court, or marry? That you would live in the west where there may not be all the modern conveniences you are accustomed to?"

"Sir, if you knew where I came from, you'd know that I am not used to the modern conveniences now."

"Very well, you're the right age, and you're articulate and attractive. Please see Mrs. Appleton at the next table."

Kit was beaming with delight; she had made it through to the next table.

Mrs. Appleton introduced herself. She was the matron of the Harvey House in Topeka, Kansas. Kit answered her questions about her background, family, and education. Kit was truthful and despite not wanting to admit it, told Mrs. Appleton about working in a cannery.

"Miss Pridgeon, you are one of the most determined ladies I have met, and I can tell you are no stranger to hard work. We pay $17.50 per month. Your lodging, laundry, uniforms, meals, and travel expenses are all covered by the Harvey Company. Your contract would not permit you to leave our employment for a year. There are strict rules and guidelines that must be followed at all times. Any hint of less than wholesome behavior will result in your immediate termination. Would you be willing to agree to these conditions?

"Yes ma'am, I sure would!"

"Very well. Congratulations, you are now a Harvey Girl. Your employment begins at this moment. Your conduct and manner are all a reflection on the name of Mr. Harvey himself. You will be fitted for your uniform on Monday and we will be leaving for Topeka on Wednesday. Please see Mr. Fenton at the next table; he will need your information."

"Thank you, Mrs. Appleton. Thank you so much!" exclaimed Kit.

"Yes, congratulations Miss Pridgeon. I will see you bright and early on Monday, 8:00 a.m. sharp, in the lobby."

CHAPTER 3

The train rumbled out of the station, and this time Kit was not sitting on a bag of mail. She was sitting in a coach car with eight other girls and the matron, Mrs. Appleton. They were leaving Raleigh for Topeka, Kansas. She wore her Sunday best and was pleased that this time, she could see out the window, rather than stare at bags of mail. It was a wonderful change.

Mrs. Taylor packed a hamper of goodies for the trip. Kit was sorry to leave Mrs. Taylor; the woman had taken her under her wing and in only a few days' time had become as close as family. Kit wrote letters to her family and Letty, and one to Mrs. Cates. Now that she knew where she was going she didn't want them to be worried.

Mrs. Appleton wasted no time getting the girls trained to the Harvey standards. Every day on the train, she spent hours drilling them in the rules and standards. They practiced setting tables and taking each other's orders. It was fun, and Kit looked forward to her new position.

Along the way, Kit made friends with the other girls hired in Raleigh. Of all the girls she met, she liked Maggie Lawson from Raleigh the best. Maggie was a pretty girl with flame red hair and a milk white complexion. She was nice, but she had a wicked sense of humor that Kit enjoyed. They were inseparable from the first.

Maggie even knew where Bridgeton was. She had been there with her parents and stayed in the hotel. She was educated, and her father owned a general mercantile. Kit could not understand why a girl like Maggie would venture out West, but it soon became obvious that she, like Kit, had a love for adventure. Kit had never met another woman who shared the same restless spirit until she met Maggie.

The journey to Topeka took several days, and Kit and Maggie were amazed at the sights that passed by their window. They crossed the Appalachian Mountains and both nearly fainted when they looked down as the train crossed the railroad bridges in the sky. They saw cities that were even bigger than Raleigh, and saw fields and forests that stretched for miles. They crossed the Mississippi and all of the girls cheered, even though Mrs. Appleton frowned at them. They were officially in the West. Kansas was one state away.

As they approached Kansas, Mrs. Appleton explained in great detail about the training they would receive. It would last thirty days and they had to be quick and pay very close attention. Only if they could demonstrate that they were sufficiently trained to the stringent Harvey standard could they remain employed; otherwise, they would be sent home. Kit and Maggie looked at each. For Kit, failure was not an option.

On the final day of their journey by train, Kit shared the last of the cookies that Mrs. Taylor had made for her. They would be arriving in Topeka within the hour. Kit gazed out the window while she ate. She had never been this far from home, and she had never been this far from the sea. But the wheat in the endless fields of Kansas moved in waves as the wind blew, and it reminded her of the waters near Bridgeton.

For the briefest of moments, she felt homesick for the lush green of the pine trees and the blue shimmering waters of the ocean, but she soon overcame that feeling when she looked at the big open sky and the fields that stretched all the way to the horizon. She was moved by the rugged beauty of this land.

"Have you ever seen anything like this?" Kit asked.

"No, never. We wanted adventure," said Maggie, as she looked out the window alongside Kit.

"And we sure did get it. Do you think we will be able to pass the training?"

"I do. Just smile, do what they tell you, and work hard. We will be just fine."

"I wish I had your confidence," said Kit who was trying not to be nervous.

"There's nothing to it. I heard there were over a hundred girls that day who wanted to be in our shoes. They must have seen a quality in you and me that they were looking for."

"When you put it like that, I feel better already."

"You should! I don't think they made any mistakes."

Kit watched as the train entered the station. There was a row of Harvey Girls standing in a perfectly straight line waiting to meet the train. They looked so professional and fashionable in their black skirts, black shirtwaists, and crisp white aprons. Kit was excited. Soon, that would be her, standing at the station waiting to greet hungry travelers on the Atkinson, Topeka, and the Santa Fe rail line.

When the train came to a stop, Mrs. Appleton led the girls to the platform. Porters unloaded their luggage onto a cart, and Kit saw her sad carpet bag sitting beside suitcases. She suspected that she had been the poorest girl to have been chosen in Raleigh. She smiled when she realized that from this day forward, it didn't matter where they were from or how much money their families had, they were all equal – they were all Harvey Girls.

The matron formed them into an orderly group and led them across the street from the train station to a three-story building. Kit was impressed by the station at Topeka. It was a large, modern building, bigger than the train station in Raleigh. The street was wide and bustling with wagons and carriages. Topeka seemed like a busy place.

Two glass doors with polished brass handles were opened by men in crisp uniforms. The girls followed the matron into the lobby and were met by a receptionist at the front desk. The lobby and the marble staircase looked as nice as the Carriage House Hotel in Raleigh. Kit and Maggie looked at each other and smiled.

"Ladies, this is Miss Pierce; she manages the dormitories," said Mrs. Appleton.

"How are you all? I hope your ride was a pleasant one," said the lady, who appeared to be in her thirties. She wore a crisp black uniform and her hair was in a neat pompadour without a hair out of place. She spoke in a southern drawl, "I want to welcome you to the Harvey Company Dormitory. This building will be your home when you are not working at the restaurant.

Good manners and decorum are expected to be followed always and the doors are locked at ten every night. There are no gentlemen callers allowed in the building. All of your mail will be received here at the front desk. I know all of you are new, and I want to congratulate each and every one of you on being selected to become a Harvey Girl."

Kit and the girls greeted Miss Pierce and then turned their attention back to Mrs. Appleton. She led them up the stairs and then up another flight to the third floor.

"This building is known as the dormitory. There will be two girls to each room. The necessary rooms are located down the hall and will be shared. Your luggage will be arriving any moment in the downstairs lobby. You will have a few hours this afternoon to rest and get unpacked. Dinner this evening will be in the dining room on the ground floor. Tomorrow your training begins."

"Mrs. Appleton, when do we get our uniforms?"

"You have all been measured for your uniforms; they will be arriving in two weeks. Until then, should you need anything, there are a number of good dress shops in the city and a department store only a few blocks from here. These are the dormitory assignments."

Kit listened for Mrs. Appleton to call her name, and wondered who she would be rooming with.

"Miss Pridgeon, you will be in a room of your own until the other girls arrive form Atlanta," said Mrs. Appleton.

"Lucky," whispered Maggie.

Kit had never had a room all to herself. Even if it was only for a few days, she was going to enjoy every second of it. She thought about her luggage downstairs and her clothes. All she had was her Sunday clothes, and two plain skirts and shirtwaists that she wore to the cannery. She would be embarrassed if anyone here saw her old and somber dark clothes.

She opened her purse and looked at the money she had left. She thought she could make do with her skirts, and if she could buy a crisp new shirtwaist she would feel less conspicuous. She knew she should save the money she had left, but she really wanted something nice to wear like the other girls had. She didn't want to look like she was going to work in a cannery and be terminated on her first day of training.

Mrs. Appleton finished with the room assignments and dismissed the girls until dinner. Kit turned to Maggie and asked, "What are you going to do with your free afternoon?"

"I don't know, maybe read or take a nap, something like that."

"I hate to admit this, but all I have is my Sunday best suit and the clothes I wore to work. I was thinking about going to that store Mrs. Appleton mentioned. Do you want to come along?"

"I sure do; it will be much more fun than what I was going to do."

"Maybe you can give me some advice. I've never purchased clothes from a store before; my mother always made everything at home," said Kit, who then whispered, "except for my petticoats and my corset."

Maggie giggled at the mention of the word petticoat, "Come with me, young woman. It will be my pleasure to escort you on this shopping expedition."

"Thirty minutes. That is all the time the passengers of the Santa Fe railroad have to eat a wholesome and delectable meal. Remember that, thirty minutes. These are the most important two words you can take away from this training. Remember them and repeat them every day when you rise, when you are polishing the brass in the dining rooms, and before you lay down at night, after your prayers," said Mrs. Appleton as she addressed the nine young ladies at 8:00 in the morning.

"If you are too slow, the passenger you are serving may miss his train, and that would be unacceptable. Mr. Harvey himself guarantees all the patrons of his restaurants a four-course meal, prepared by the finest chefs, served on fine china, in the thirty minutes of a whistle stop. This is our promise and this is what we must do each and every time."

"Mrs. Appleton, what about our customers who are not from the train?" asked a young lady.

"The same rule applies for each and every customer, every time, no exceptions."

Kit had a lot to learn, a lot more, she feared, than the other girls. She had never been a waitress before, and had never set foot in a dining room or restaurant as fancy as the Harvey Restaurant in Topeka. The tablecloths and napkins were made of the finest European linen and were without blemish or stain. The napkins were folded precisely the same way at each table, for every customer.

The silverware was difficult at first for a girl who was only used to a knife, fork, and spoon. She had not been aware that there were different utensils for different foods. The possibilities were bewildering. She nearly laughed when she beheld a grapefruit spoon and a soup spoon.

The glasses were the highest quality available. The plates and cups were all made of china that bore the Harvey logo. Her family had never had anything half as nice. The closest she had ever come to such quality was at the ice cream parlor in Bridgeton, and when she stayed with Mrs. Taylor.

Kit refused to let being born poor in Fish Town stop her. She paid attention to everything Mrs. Appleton said, and then she watched the other girls. When she was in way over her head, she asked Maggie.

It soon became apparent that what Kit lacked in knowledge of a well-set table, she more than made up for in speed and efficiency. She was the fastest waitress in training. She could take the order, serve the meal and pour coffee in twenty-five minutes or less. Mrs. Appleton praised her ability and Kit thanked Saturdays at the cannery.

The thirty days' training was tough and the hours were long, but Kit was able to handle the rigorous schedule with ease. Mrs. Appleton compared it to being in the army, and the girls were to be properly trained and drilled. They were becoming a force unlike any the West – or the world – had ever seen; they were going to be the best-trained wait staff that had ever graced a restaurant.

Day after day, Kit learned, studied, and practiced such skills as how to juice the oranges without making a mess, how to pour just the right amount of coffee for cream, how to serve on the left and remove plates on the right. She memorized the menu and knew how long it would take to cook a steak to medium or well and what to suggest as a side dish.

All her training took place in a Harvey training facility located at the dormitory. It was a fully functioning Harvey restaurant built for one purpose only: to train the girls in thirty days to work in any restaurant along the Santa Fe rail line.

26

In two weeks, Kit and the rest of the girls received their uniforms. There were three skirts, three aprons, and three shirtwaists. Two white bows came with the uniform to be worn on the top of the head with a pompadour hairstyle. A pair of shining black boots came with the ensemble. Kit was nearly in tears, she was so happy.

"Ladies, you have now received the official uniforms of a Harvey Girl, and starting tomorrow you may wear them. You have worked hard and you have earned it. Your uniform must always be pressed and your apron starched. There can be no stains on the apron even while you are working. You are to wear no jewelry or makeup while you are in the dining room. Hair is to be neat and tidy and nails and hands must always be clean. Congratulations."

The next morning, Kit arrived to training first. She was so excited, and she felt like a real Harvey Girl. The skirt, shirtwaist, and boots were of better quality than her own Sunday best. She felt like a she had received the most wonderful Christmas present. She was admiring her reflection in the mirror by the door when she heard a whistle.

"Don't you look nice? You'd better be careful or some passenger may try to take you with him," said Maggie, as she walked in.

"Maggie, you look beautiful. You look like a girl from a magazine."

"I'll say, and so do you."

"Is it true what they say about this company? That after a year if you do well, you get to wear a tie and get a raise and a promotion?"

"That's what I heard from Ruth; she's been with here eight months."

"Oh, can you believe it? We could get a raise and be promoted? I never thought it was possible."

"It's possible, alright. So, you are thinking about making this a career?"

"Yes, I think so, Mrs. Appleton says they plan to open ten more restaurants in the new year, maybe as far away as California. They're going to need staff; can you imagine going to California?"

"That would be an adventure, would it not?"

"You want to come?" asked Kit.

"I wouldn't miss it." Maggie giggled.

Kit and Maggie were soon joined by the other girls. Everyone looked lovely in their uniforms. When Mrs. Appleton came in to greet them, she had a special surprise – Mr. Harvey himself. He addressed the young ladies.

"Ladies, Mrs. Appleton has told me how impressed she is with this class, so I wanted to come and welcome you to my company, personally. I want to say just a few words before I leave you to finish your training.

"Every one of you have come out West just like the pioneers, but your job is different. You are not here to tame the land; you are here to tame the heart of this rugged country. You bring civility and courtesy, a cheerful smile and a delicious meal at any of our restaurants. When we open a restaurant and you arrive with your pressed uniforms and high moral standards, civilization is not far behind. My promise to you is this: if you work hard and uphold our standards, there is boundless opportunity for each one of you. Thank you for making the decision to come west, and welcome."

The girls clapped, and Mr. Harvey shook hands with each one of them before he left. Kit looked at Maggie and smiled. She was on an adventure, and boundless opportunity awaited.

CHAPTER 4

Christmas was only a week away, and Kit Pridgeon had not seen her family since she'd left Bridgeton in July. She had only received a few letters from home, and most of them were from her dearest friend Letty and Mrs. Cates the librarian. In only a few months, her old life at home seemed like it was very far in the past.

Letty's older brother Jacob, whom she had once thought she was in love with, had been courting her younger sister Emily, and to everyone's delight would be marrying her in the new year. Letty had hopes that Kit's own brother Thomas would soon be hers, as they'd been attending church together on Sundays since October.

Kit sent Mrs. Cates postcards from the gift shops of Topeka, which showed all its modern buildings and fancy department stores. Mrs. Cates sent newspaper clippings and all the news from home. Kit realized as she wrote her Christmas letters to the folks back home that she had not heard much from her own family.

Her closest new friend Maggie told her she shouldn't be so surprised they didn't write, considering how she had left them. She did leave Fish Town to pursue a way of life they neither supported nor wanted for her, and she'd done so without a word of explanation, or even a goodbye. It was sad to think that one decision had driven her family to practically disown her, but that was the unfortunate truth. She'd love to have a letter from her mother, but it didn't look like that was going to happen.

However, if she had to do it over again, she knew she would do the same. Being out west, wearing nice clothes, and earning a respectable wage was a far better life than she could ever have dreamed possible in the part of Bridgeton she was from. She wrote home regularly, trying to explain, and telling them about her new life. She hated that her family couldn't understand that a woman could be so much more than just a fisherman's wife. Perhaps one day they would come to see that this was the right decision for her, and until then she sent them her letters and hoped they read them.

With Christmas quickly approaching, she mailed a letter to the nice woman from Raleigh who had been such a godsend, Mrs. Taylor. The packages of homemade cookies that Mrs. Taylor sent were a treat that she and Maggie looked forward to at least once a month, and sometimes more.

It had been nearly four months since she and Maggie had become Harvey Girls, and the time had gone by so quickly. Working in the Harvey Restaurant six days a week, for ten or more hours a day, meant that their schedules were always full. What little down time the girls had was usually spent seeing to their laundry, resting, attending church, picnicking along the Kansas River, or attending lectures at the college.

Topeka was the capital of Kansas and the headquarters of the Atkinson, Topeka, and Santa Fe Railroad Company. It was booming, large, and growing. Kit could not imagine a more thrilling city to be in than this capital on the edge of the Wild West.

Working in the restaurant was exciting, with travelers coming out west from the east coast and all over Europe. Only this past week, she'd had the pleasure of serving people from Germany, Russia, and even Turkey.

When she thought about the adventure that she was now part of, and the history of the nation that was unfolding before her eyes, being trapped in a tiny town back east seemed like a bad dream that she had somehow managed to escape.

With hard work and her cheerful disposition, she was finding the world to be stimulating and she enjoyed her position as a waitress. Mrs. Appleton, the matron, was pleased with Kit and Maggie. Kit had heard her say that of all the new girls from Raleigh, those two stood out for their dedication to the company and their embodiment of the standards that Mr. Harvey had set for all his wait staff.

Kit, Maggie, and Anne from Smithfield had been selected to be photographed for the Harvey House Postcards. There was some good-natured teasing from the other girls, but even early on, Kit could not help but notice that two kinds of girls worked for Mr. Harvey. There were the girls like herself who were dedicated to making a career, and the girls who were hoping to find husbands.

Girls like Meg and Beulah were hard-working and dedicated, their work ethic unquestioned. It was their attitude to the rules, the curfew, and what they did during their time off that set them apart. It was against the rules to court, date, or socialize with men in any way that would suggest romance, and these girls pushed the boundaries of those rules.

Kit and Maggie could hardly blame them. They were young, beautiful, and far away from home, where they would have been under the watchful eyes of fathers and neighbors. Even more tempting, in the west there were far more men than women. It was only natural that eligible, attractive young women garnered the attention of many of Topeka's leading gentlemen, and in some cases, not so leading, like the cowboys and occasional outlaws.

The number of secret meetings and romances that were happening under Mrs. Appleton's nose was astounding, although Maggie was not so sure that it was as unnoticed as the girls supposed. After all, if they terminated every young woman for meeting a gentleman for a secret stroll, or accepting small tokens of innocent affection from regular customers, then they would have no staff left!

Even Kit had garnered a rare trinket or flower from the occasional traveler as he ate his lunch in the thirty minutes allotted for the whistle stop. She kept these tokens in a cigar box hidden under a floorboard in the closet. Inside the box was a coin from faraway Egypt, a small brooch, more than a few hastily penned poems and notes expressing affection and admiration – and one marriage proposal. A dried rose completed the hidden cache. She suspected that she was not the only Harvey Girl to receive a profession of undying love from a man in only half an hour. She often joked that a steak cooked to perfection would do that to any man.

As exciting as those trinkets and the polite attention she received was, it was not as exhilarating as the prospect of being promoted or being transferred to some wild place. Kit loved Topeka and couldn't imagine any place better, but there was still a part of her that longed for somewhere that was uncivilized, just to see a place in this vast world that was yet untamed.

That was a dream that for now would have to wait. And anyway, Mr. Harvey was giving a Christmas party for his staff. With so many of the girls away from home for the first time, he wanted to give them a wonderful Christmas.

Mr. Harvey had given the girls one afternoon off before Christmas, so Kit and Maggie had visited their favorite department store. Kit had never seen a store decorated for Christmas. There were toys, candies, red ribbons, and greenery in the windows. Being in the store put her in the Christmas mood, especially since this was the first year she actually had money she could spend on store-bought presents.

The choices were overwhelming; there were hair combs and brushes, bottles of perfume, and leather gloves. It was like a dream come true, as she selected a gift for Maggie and one for Mrs. Appleton. She bought small gifts for each of the girls who had come to Kansas with her from North Carolina, and she bought an embroidered lace handkerchief for her new roommate Lucy Barrows, who hailed from Richmond.

She felt like St. Nicholas himself with all the presents she had bought. She'd even purchased a treat for herself, a new set of hair combs. She couldn't wait to try them out, and she thought the Christmas party would be the best time to wear them. When the girls returned to the dormitory that afternoon, they were both so laden down with packages that it looked like Christmas had come early. Mrs. Appleton shook her head and laughed at her two star employees as they passed her in the hallway.

Everything was going well until Kit opened the door to her room and found Lucy on her bed, crying. She quickly closed the door and put her presents down on her bed.

"Lucy! Are you well; what's the matter?"

"It's George," the girl sniffled. "He says he's tired of waiting."

"George?" asked Kit.

"Yes, George, the man I am going to marry. He sent me this letter – here, you can read it for yourself." She thrust the crumpled paper toward Kit.

"Lucy, dear, don't cry. I'll help you if I can, now tell me all about George." She smoothed the paper out, but didn't trouble to read the messy scrawl on it.

"I met him through the mail; he lives out near Wichita. He has a farm and needed a wife. He didn't have the money to send for me, and I didn't have the money to buy a ticket, so I became a Harvey Girl. I don't know what to do now, I have to work for a whole year before we can be married."

"You've never met George, yet you're crying over him?"

The girl sat up and wiped her eyes. Her face was puffy and red from crying, but she was still beautiful. Her black hair was the perfect complement to her pale skin and her long lashes framed pretty gray eyes. Kit shook her head at her roommate. Lucy was the prettiest girl in the dormitory and she was crying her heart out for a man she'd never met, who lived on a farm and couldn't even afford to buy her a train ticket. It was inconceivable to Kit.

"Yes, I am. George is the first man who has ever wanted to marry me."

"Lucy, you're far too pretty – and far too smart – to be crying over man you don't even know. I promise you that this George character is *not* the man of your dreams."

"How do you know?"

"The right man won't make you cry. The man of your dreams wouldn't be threatening to break off your engagement. He wouldn't make you pay to go to him, and then complain that you're taking too long."

Lucy stared at Kit and said, with a southern accent that seemed to get deeper the more she cried, "I suppose you might be right. Of course you are."

Lucy had only recently arrived from Virginia. The matron had said she was from Richmond when she introduced her, but Kit suspected Lucy came from somewhere not unlike Fish Town.

"Lucy, did I ever tell you where I'm from?"

"Are you from Charleston? A lady as stylish as you must be from somewhere nice. Atlanta?"

Kit laughed. She hated to destroy the lovely image her roommate had of her, but she decided it would do the poor girl some good.

"No, I'm from a poor town in the middle of nowhere. Not many people know this, but I used to work at a cannery, where my job was gutting fish."

Lucy stopped crying and stared at Kit, "You're telling me a fib. A fine lady like you; I don't believe it!"

"Believe it. I came from a family that was poor, just like yours."

"My family wasn't even good enough to be poor! The people in the county I'm from thought we were trash."

"I know that feeling."

"Do you? My father picks cotton for a rich farmer. I'm the only person in my family who can read and write worth a darn."

"Lucy, out here no one cares where you and I are from. They aren't judging us by our families, or how much money we have. We have an opportunity to do something with our lives, to go places no one has been, and to make something of ourselves."

"What about a husband and children; don't you want to get married?"

"Someday, but not to a man who doesn't appreciate me. When I get married, I want a husband who works as hard as I do and values me – and what I've accomplished. Don't you want that?"

"I don't really know what I want. My whole life, I was told I was supposed to marry and have kids."

"Me too. But Lucy, why did you become a Harvey Girl? Was it just to come out here to Kansas to marry George?"

Lucy chewed her lip. "If I'm telling God's honest truth, yes it was, but I like it here and I like the clothes we get to wear. Do you really think I'll meet a man who will appreciate me, and want to marry me?"

"Lucy, as pretty as you are, I'm sure you will have no trouble meeting a man who will want to marry you. Now stop crying over that fool George, or else I will give your Christmas present to some other girl."

"You bought me a present?"

"I did, but you can't have it yet. You have to wait until Christmas." Kit sat on the edge of Lucy's bed, and watched as Lucy tucked her hair behind her ears and dried her face. "Did you ever think about making this a career, at least for a little while?"

"Not really. I'm barely getting through the training."

"If you promise to leave George behind and work hard, I'll help you as much as I can."

"You promise?"

"I promise; now let's get you fixed up. We don't want anyone to think you're not happy here."

"No, we sure don't."

It was the first time Kit had ever been called stylish by anyone, and she had never been mistaken for a lady from a big city before today. It was true that opportunities abounded for those women who were intrepid enough to take advantage of them, and she was one of those ladies. She had Mr. Harvey to thank for this chance and she intended to repay that kindness by making good on her promise to help dear Lucy become a true Harvey Girl!

Christmas was over far too quickly and the girls in Topeka settled into a winter routine. It was too cold for picnics and strolls. Shopping, church, and visits to the library were the only outside pursuits that anyone cared to do. Most free time was spent indoors by the fireside of the parlor in the dormitory. Card games were popular, and so was knitting and crocheting.

The illicit romances that had begun in earnest when the weather was warmer now cooled off or were in danger of being discovered. Gentlemen callers were not allowed in the building and more than one girl had been nearly undone by a love interest who could no longer stay away. Some of these men had begun to show up at the restaurant, always getting a table in a certain girl's section.

Kit was worried about one girl in particular, and that was Anne. Anne was pretty, almost as beautiful as Lucy. Several members of the staff remarked that the two girls resembled each other so closely that they could even be sisters.

Anne was the eldest daughter of a Baptist preacher. Her father had recently died, leaving the family nearly destitute. Anne went to work as a Harvey Girl and sent all her money home to her mother to help support her brothers and her little sister. Of all the girls who came to Kansas from North

Carolina, Anne was the most serious and quiet. She could be found attending church, bible study, or praying in her spare time.

Kit found it strange that it was Anne who was in danger of getting into serious trouble – and possibly even losing her positon. Anne had the weight of the responsibility of her family on her narrow shoulders, and she was in grave peril when it came to an illicit romance.

Kit and Maggie had both noticed that an older gentlemen had come into the restaurant on more than one occasion and always sat in Anne's section. At first, they thought nothing of it. Anne seemed to be the sensible type, and they were sure she could easily spurn the unwanted attentions of a man if it became necessary. It was only after they saw her climb out of his carriage that they became concerned.

It had happened last Sunday, after church. The weather was freezing, and the wind made it even worse. Kit's teeth were chattering as she and Maggie hurried to get back to the fireside in the dormitory's parlor. They were only a few blocks down Main Street when they witnessed Anne stepping down out of the carriage. They both saw the man in the seat of the carriage as it drove past them.

They had hardly spoken to each other about the incident, and hoped that no one else had seen, or Anne would be terminated on the spot. Harvey Girls were supposed to maintain the highest standards at all times, and never behave in a way that would appear immoral or give the suggestion of impropriety. Riding in a carriage with a man who was not a blood relative and without a chaperone was definitely not proper.

In the weeks that followed, they could no longer ignore the fact that the older gentleman was becoming a fixture and seemed to be showing up at the restaurant at least once a week. Anne was always pleasant with her customers, but with this strange man she seemed to be more outgoing, even lively.

It was a transformation that only happened in his presence. Kit was certain that if she and Maggie both saw this stunning change come over Anne, that others must see it as well. They discussed it after church one Sunday.

"Maggie, what about dear Anne? I am not trying to gossip, but that man keeps stopping by the restaurant."

36

"I know. I've seen him and it doesn't seem possible that others haven't noticed him, if we have."

"I wouldn't worry so much about it if weren't for that day when she stepped out of his carriage."

"She must have known she was taking a terrible risk. If she had been seen by one of the other girls, they may have told Mrs. Appleton, or even spread gossip about her."

"I don't want to upset her by asking about him. It's not our business what she does; I just don't want to see her make a mistake that might result in her termination."

"Do you think we might be interpreting this all wrong? The man is practically old enough to be her father. What if he is a kindly older man who is like a father to her? Wouldn't she be insulted and her feelings hurt if we made the suggestion that it...wasn't innocent?"

It was a tough decision to make, but one Kit thought was entirely necessary. "She has always been such a good girl, and she's never given anyone reason to doubt her morals or her character. If we ask her about her actions she might be insulted, but it's a chance that we may have to take for her own good."

"After all she's been through, I don't want to add to her grief or make her feel like we're talking about her behind her back."

"You mean, like we are at this very moment?" asked Kit with a mischievous smile.

"Just like we are at the present moment, yes."

"If we did nothing and she was terminated I'd feel awful, knowing her family is desperately in need of her help."

"That makes two of us. It looks like we've made a decision."

They decided to invite Anne out to dinner with them, so they could speak in private. They wanted to speak with her as caring sisters, and try to help her without offending her, if they could.

Kit was glad that Anne had agreed to have dinner. She just didn't know quite how to ask about Anne's romance without seeming rude or intrusive. In truth, Kit and Maggie barely knew the young woman, and this was the type of question most young ladies would hesitate to ask anyone but a close friend or sister.

As Maggie ordered the soup course, Kit could think of no way to approach a topic so delicate without sounding insensitive. She would just have to risk seeming forward and rude. The waiter left to put in the soup order, and the young women were alone at the table. Maggie looked at Kit and raised an eyebrow. Kit knew what that meant; it was time.

Kit took a deep breath and began with the usual pleasantries. "Anne, I can't tell you how pleased we both are that you joined us for dinner."

"Thank you for the invitation. I don't ordinarily have money to spend on myself like this," said Anne.

"How are your mother and your family back home?" asked Maggie.

"Mother is still not well but she is trying to manage. My brother William has quit school and found work on a farm, but my other brother and sister are not old enough to work yet."

"I am sorry to hear that your brother had to leave school. I understand how difficult that can be; my family made me quit when I was young," said Kit.

"He writes that he hopes to go to the seminary and become a minister like our father was, but there isn't enough money."

"What are your plans? Do you plan to keep working?" asked Maggie.

"I have to. I can make more money out here than I ever could back home," answered Anne, as she looked down at her napkin.

The waiter brought their soup and bread. While the girls were enjoying the soup, Kit knew it was time to take the plunge. "Anne, if I may, I need to ask you a question and I don't want to upset you."

Anne put her soup spoon down and looked at Kit with a quizzical look on her face. "I don't get upset easily; please, ask."

"I know that you are working very hard to send money to your family, and believe me when I tell you that I consider you to be the best of us on morals and character. Yet, there is something I have noticed that may seem at first glance to give quite a different impression."

"What are you talking about?" asked Anne.

"There is a gentleman, an older man, who visits the restaurant."

"There are lots of older gentlemen who visit to restaurant," said Anne, as she sat up in her chair.

Kit looked at Maggie and realized that this conversation was not going very well, but she no longer had the option of backing away from subject. "There are lots of older gentlemen," she said gently, "but this is the same man we saw you with one Sunday afternoon, when you were climbing out of his carriage."

Anne folded her napkin and put it on the table. She looked at Kit and then Maggie. "Is that what you think? That I am behaving like a...a... I can't even say it! Like a woman without morals?"

Kit was horrified that Anne thought she was suggesting something so scandalous. "No, my dear, not at all! That thought never even crossed my mind. I thought you might have found a man who had fallen in love with you, or was perhaps like a father to you – I never would have suggested anything else."

The indignant look on Anne's face softened, and a tear fell down her cheek. All three young women sat in awkward silence as the waiter removed the soup bowls. Maggie ordered a main course and still Anne stared at the table in front of her.

Kit reached into her purse and pulled out a handkerchief, offering it to Anne.

"Thank you," she said, as she dabbed at her eyes "I'm sorry I thought you were implying that I was that kind of woman."

"It was my fault if I gave you that impression. I should have been blunt and not tried to be delicate," said Kit.

"Anne, if you are unwell, we can go back to the dormitory," Maggie suggested gently.

"I'm fine, I'm just so emotional these days, since my father died and I am so far away from home. If it was not for my faith in God, I don't know what I would do." Anne spoke quietly.

"Please, Anne, understand that I didn't mean any harm. I just don't want anyone to get the wrong impression and have it jeopardize your job."

"I know that now, and it was a sweet gesture. It must have taken courage for both of you to approach about me about Mr. Simpson."

"Mr. Simpson?"

"Yes, the man you've seen at the restaurant. He is a pastor of the church here in Topeka. His wife died many years ago, and he's been alone ever since. I've been going to his church. The day you saw me getting out of his carriage, he insisted on bringing me home so I would not catch a chill. It was so cold."

"Is he your beau?"

"Oh my, no! He wants to meet my mother. I've been trying to save money to send for her and my family to come to me here, but it's hard to save anything *and* send them money to live. I think Mama and Mr. Simpson would make such a good match. He's a good man, and I believe my father would have liked him; he reminds me of him in so many ways. I've been praying that God would find a way for them to be together."

"I'm not trying to be rude, but why does *he* not send for your family?" asked Maggie.

"He's offered to pay what he can, but he doesn't make much, you see, being the pastor of a church."

"And when he stops by the restaurant, what about the money he's spending then?" asked Kit.

"Oh, he never orders anything more than a cup of coffee and piece of pie. He comes by to check on me and make sure I'm doing well. He's worried about me, living so far from my family."

"Anne, just be careful. If we noticed this, then the other girls – or even Mrs. Appleton – may have as well. We don't want to see you get in trouble or lose your position," warned Maggie.

"I'll be careful, now that you have mentioned this to me. I didn't know it looked that bad, but I can see it would be easy to get the wrong impression."

"It would. Anne, let us help you. If there is anything we can do, please let us know," said Maggie.

Kit now felt guilty about the money she'd spent on hair combs at Christmas. If she known Anne needed to bring her family to Kansas she would gladly have given her the money instead. "Anne, after the pastor pays what he can, how much do you need?"

"Oh, Kit, I couldn't let you do something like that."

"No, I insist. You have too much on your shoulders. If we could bring your mother and your family out here, it might do them some good, especially if your mother and Pastor Simpson were to be married."

"That would be a dream come true. Smithfield is a not a big town, and there isn't a lot of work available. Out here, my brother may find a job that pays more, or even find a way to go back to school." Anne's face was even prettier when she was having hopeful thoughts.

"It's settled then. Tell the Pastor we will find a way to help."

"Thank you! This means so much to me."

That night, back at the dormitory, Kit and Maggie both agreed that speaking to Anne had been the right thing to do, and that it had been tense when Anne thought they were accusing her of loose morals.

"Honestly Kit, I thought she was going to throw the soup at you," said Maggie with a laugh.

"Me too – did you see the look on her face, poor girl. I'm glad that turned out well."

"Kit, I want to help out with Anne. My family doesn't need me to send money back home and I never spend my whole salary every month."

"Oh Maggie, would you? That would be wonderful. Maybe her family can be out here by the spring if we work hard and save our tip money."

"Kit, I believe that with you around, anything is possible."

41

That night, Kit went to bed warm and still full from dinner. The cold wind howled outside the window, but she was safe knowing that she was right where she belonged. Maggie's words were a comfort to her and she went to sleep wondering what else she could do, if she just set her mind to it.

~

Kit and Maggie worked hard to earn as much tip money as they could. They smiled, laughed, and raced around the restaurant at top speed to make sure their patrons never had to wait for a refill of coffee or an extra napkin. They had taken their usual level of superior customer service to an even higher level, and all for a good cause. They nearly had enough money to bring Anne's family out west.

Kit didn't realize how much of a difference she and Maggie were making to the restaurant until they were approached by Charlotte Greene and Melanie Herring. Charlotte and Melanie were two of the most light-hearted girls in the dormitory. They had joined the ranks of the Harvey Girls solely for the purpose of finding husbands, and were not at all happy about being compared unfavorably to Mrs. Appleton's star employees.

Kit and Maggie were downstairs in the parlor, sitting with Anne. They were discussing the cost of renting a house for Anne's family and how much they would need to pay the monthly bills until her brother could find work. It was a lot, and Kit and Maggie were trying not to let Anne see that they were uncertain whether they could meet their goal of having the family come in the spring. They were surprised when Charlotte and Melanie came into the room and approached them.

"Anne, if you don't mind, we need to have a private conversation with Miss Pridgeon and Miss Lawson," said Charlotte.

Anne stood to leave, but Kit stopped her. "Charlotte Greene, I don't know what you intend to speak with us about, but Anne doesn't have to go anywhere."

"I was just trying to be polite, Anne, because this does not concern you. If you insist on staying, then suit yourself," Charlotte said with disdain.

"Well, go ahead, we're waiting," replied Maggie.

"You two are giving us a bad name," accused Melanie, as she pointed at Kit and Maggie.

"A bad name? Neither of us has ever said a word against you."

"I know you haven't," Charlotte put in, "but you two must overdo everything, and it makes the rest of us look like we're idle. Mrs. Appleton remarks on it all the time. I'm tired of it."

"Maybe you should work harder and spend less time trying to find a husband," said Maggie.

"Do be honest," Charlotte rolled her eyes. "Mr. Harvey didn't hire any ugly girls, did he? He would never have hired all pretty girls if he didn't intend for us to find husbands."

"I doubt that he invested so much in each of us, solely for the sake of finding us husbands," answered Maggie drily.

Kit could stand no more. "If you cared about your job half as much as you do about a bunch of silly men, you wouldn't have to worry about Mrs. Appleton."

"Hold on, are you saying it's *my* fault Mrs. Appleton thinks I'm lazy and idle compared to you two Polly Perfects?"

"Yes, I am," Kit said, as she stood up.

Maggie followed her to her feet, and soon the two girls were standing nearly nose to nose with Charlotte and Melanie. Kit knew that at any moment this was about to change from an argument to a fight, but she didn't care. The tension was palpable as Lucy, who had been passing the door, came over to stand with Kit and Maggie. Charlotte opened her mouth to say something but was interrupted by Anne, who had been sitting silently at the table.

"Wait, stop. Everyone listen to me," Anne spoke in a voice that commanded attention.

The girls all stared at her; she was always so quiet and studious that they had not realized she could have such quiet authority. There was silence as the girls waited for her to speak.

"Charlotte and Melanie, if you must know, Kit and Maggie have been working hard to help a family in need. If you want to keep being lazy that is up to you, but leave them alone."

"Are you calling us lazy?" asked Charlotte as she took a step closer to Anne.

"Hold on," said Melanie, as she put a hand on Charlotte's arm. "What do you mean, they are helping a family in need?"

"Anne, you don't have to do this," said Kit.

"Yes, I do. My father died last year and my family is going through a tough time; they are barely able to put food on the table. The family in need is mine," said Anne, with quiet dignity.

Melanie looked at Charlotte. Charlotte still looked like she wanted to fight, but Melanie put her hand on her friend's arm. "Anne, I didn't know about your family. I just thought Kit and Maggie were trying to make us all look bad. Is there anything we can do?"

"Yes, anything," said Charlotte, a little less enthusiastically.

"Just don't be angry with Kit and Maggie," answered Anne.

"Done." For a moment it looked like Melanie was going to leave the room, but she tilted her head to the side and continued. "So, by my observations, it looks like you girls are raking in the tips. Is it money you need?"

"If you must know, yes," said Anne as she looked at the floor, flustered.

"You've embarrassed her; I hope you are happy," Maggie said to Melanie.

"Anne, don't be embarrassed. It's not your fault your family is going through a rough patch. If you need money...there's nobody better at convincing men to part with their money than us," said Charlotte, with a sly gleam in her eye.

"And their hearts," said Melanie.

"That, too," answered Charlotte.

"Thank you, this means so much to me."

"Kit, it looks like you and Maggie have got some competition." Once again, the girls faced each other across the parlor. The spirit now was quite a bit friendlier, though it still had a slightly adversarial edge they could all detect.

"If it's for a good cause, I welcome it," she answered.

"Then it's agreed; we all are going to help out Anne and her family?" Maggie asked.

"Yes, we sure will!" answered Charlotte, her eyes still on Kit.

The clock in the parlor rang ten, and the girls made their way upstairs to bed. Kit was almost asleep when Lucy whispered, "Kit, are you still awake?"

Kit wanted to answer no, but she answered, "Yes, what is it?"

"It's about Anne. I want to help out, like you other girls, but I don't know how much money I can afford to spare."

Kit bunched up her pillow and rested her chin on it. "I know your family doesn't have a lot of money. Do you send money back home to them?"

"I do; I have to. I didn't want to say anything about it, downstairs."

"No one has to know how much you give, and you don't have to give a penny if you can't. My contribution can be from both of us."

"That wouldn't be right. I just wanted to tell you, so you wouldn't think I was being stingy."

"I would never think you were being stingy."

"I promise I will give what I can spare – it just may not be much, that's all. When I think about it, my father is still alive. If anything happened to him, my family would be in deep trouble, just like Anne's. I don't mind giving, because I might need it myself someday."

"Thank you, Lucy, goodnight.

"Goodnight, Kit."

Kit still could not believe that Charlotte, Melanie, and Lucy were all going to help Anne and her family. It seemed that they may actually get them out to Kansas soon after all.

~

Mrs. Appleton was astonished at the change that spread through the staff at the restaurant in Topeka. Girls she had written off as being only 'short-termers,' the ones who stayed for just a year and were lucky to make 12 months, had shown vast improvement.

The manager of the restaurant, Mr. Crawford, no longer came to her with reports of idleness. In recent conversations, he gave only glowing recommendations of the girls he had previously described in less than favorable terms. It was a remarkable turn of events, and she wondered if it was somehow engineered by her favorite girls, Kit and Maggie.

Mr. Crawford had been the manager in Topeka since the very first day. He had seen a number of girls come and go. Some made careers in the company, and others did not, but this staff was by far the best he'd ever had the pleasure of managing, he told Mrs. Appleton. With so much positive attention on the staff in Topeka, it eventually came to the notice of those closest to Mr. Harvey himself.

In the last few weeks of winter, he made several unannounced visits to the restaurant and was impressed. The service had always been top notch, but there was something a little different in the formula than he had seen before. He was not sure what that could be, although he did have to wonder about the recent additions to the staff, and the reports he had heard from his employees.

He spoke with Mr. Crawford and Mrs. Appleton and decided to have an informal meeting with some of the new staff members. He invited them to afternoon tea at the office, so he could have a casual conversation with them. If he could determine what was different about this new group, he could make improvements to his hiring process and ensure that all of his customers were given the opportunity to experience this level of service.

The meeting was unprecedented, according to Mrs. Appleton, as she delivered the invitations to Kit, Maggie, and Melanie. The girls squealed in delight and promised the matron they would not brag or boast of this great honor. They all agreed, and even Melanie managed to remain discreet about being selected.

On the following Thursday afternoon, a carriage sent by Mr. Harvey arrived, and the girls, together with Mrs. Appleton – all impeccably dressed – climbed inside. Only Mrs. Appleton had been to the office before. Kit was excited and nervous. This was the first time she was to meet with Mr. Harvey in such a small social group; she hoped she would not sound too ignorant or unrefined.

"Girls, I know I don't have to tell you this, but I feel a few simple reminders would be best. At a formal tea, your saucer is always with your tea cup, and don't forget to eat small portions. Be dainty and feminine; do *not* gobble up the cakes and sandwiches like common field hands," instructed Mrs. Appleton.

"Yes, Mrs. Appleton," the girls chimed in and then erupted into peals of laughter.

"This is important; you must act as ladies," the matron said, trying to hide her smile.

"We will, I promise, Mrs. Appleton," said Kit, as she elbowed Maggie. Melanie rolled her eyes and smiled.

The office was in downtown Topeka and occupied a three-story brick building. They were met by a staff member who introduced herself as Mrs. Brogden. She showed the ladies into the building and to Mr. Harvey's office. Mr. Harvey was at his desk when they arrived.

He greeted the ladies and invited them to be seated. Several comfortable chairs and a table had been arranged by the fireplace at the end of the room. Kit had never seen a room owned by a single person that contained so many books. His office gleamed with polished wood, and had bookshelves that extended from the floor to the ceiling. His desk was large and covered in a neat assortment of papers and ledgers. There was a carpet on the floor, and a marble fireplace in the seating area. If this was his office, she wondered about his home, as she sat down by the fire.

Mrs. Brogden returned with tea on a silver tray. There were sandwiches and cakes, just as Mrs. Appleton had warned. Kit looked at Maggie and tried hard not to giggle with nerves. Mr. Harvey joined the girls and explained his reason for the invitation as they carefully sipped their tea.

"Thank you for accepting this invitation. With the rapid growth of this company, I often find myself in new territory, and this is no different. I am sure you must be curious why I have selected you to come to tea."

Kit carefully set her tea cup and saucer down on the table and folded her hands in her lap. She hoped they were not in any kind of trouble. They had been collecting a large amount of tips lately, and she was sometimes concerned it may appear suspicious, or draw critical attention.

"Ladies, as you are aware, this company is growing and new opportunities are created each and every day. Of all the members of the staff here in Topeka, I see real potential in all of you. I have prided myself on the ideals and quality of service at our restaurants but here in Topeka, you and the other new employees have managed to surpass even my own high standards. I want to know what makes you ladies different, and how you have succeeded so admirably. I confess, I am impressed."

Kit, Maggie, and Melanie looked at each other, and at first, no one said a word. Surprisingly it was Melanie who spoke first.

"Mr. Harvey, sir, I appreciate the invitation to tea today, but I think Kit and Maggie need to answer that question."

Kit tried not to be nervous. She knew Anne was the reason, but she wasn't sure she wanted to speak about Anne and her family situation without Anne's permission. Unsure what to say, she thanked Mr. Harvey and said, "Mr. Harvey, working for you has been a dream come true. You have given me a chance to make something of myself and I am grateful."

Maggie looked at Melanie and then at Kit. She smiled at Mr. Harvey and answered his question. "Sir, I hope I'm not speaking out of turn, but we have all been working hard at the Topeka restaurant because we have a common cause, a goal."

Kit's eyes opened in surprise; she was not expecting Maggie to tell him the truth.

"And what would that be?" asked Mr. Harvey.

"Sir, I am not at liberty to say, but it is a good one and we have all been pitching in to help."

"I give you my word, ladies, you may speak with me openly about any matter concerning my restaurants or your employment. Your words will not be repeated."

Kit took a deep breath and replied, "There is a family that is starving and poor back home. We have been working to bring them to Kansas so they can start over and make a new life."

Mr. Harvey looked at Mrs. Appleton. She looked back with a quizzical expression.

"So, what I'm hearing is that you have improved the efficiency and customer satisfaction at one of my busiest restaurants…for charity."

Kit, Maggie, and Melanie all nodded their heads and looked sheepish. "Sir, we hope you're not angry with us," said Kit.

"On the contrary, it just goes to prove my theory about hiring girls with good character and morals. I am proud of each and every one of you. Tell me about this family. Are they relatives, or someone that you know?"

"Not exactly our relatives, but they are related to one of the girls at the restaurant," Melanie offered.

Mr. Harvey looked at each of the girls in turn. "I see. You ladies have all pulled together as a team to offer assistance to a coworker's family. That is admirable. Is there anything I can do to help, anonymously?"

Kit spoke up, "Actually, sir, it's been more difficult than we thought at first. We've managed to save up enough money for the train tickets, but getting together the necessary money for rent and furniture has proven to be much harder than we expected."

Mr. Harvey stood and walked to his desk. He removed a small key from his pocket and unlocked a drawer. He pulled out a ledger book and silently sat at his desk, writing. The office was quiet, except for the crackling of the fire in the fireplace and his pen on the paper. A clock on the mantle ticked the time away as the girls waited to see what he was going to do next. He returned a few moments later with a check for $200.

He handed it to Kit and said, "I hope this is enough. If there is anything else you need, please do not hesitate to contact me."

"Mr. Harvey…oh thank you!" she exclaimed. "Yes, this is enough."

"Ladies, I am impressed with your dedication to my company and to your colleague. You have all three demonstrated leadership skills and initiative; I hope you will consider making this a career. I can promise you that in the coming years, there will opportunities available for which I will need exemplary employees such as yourselves. I look forward to speaking with you again, and I am sure this will not be our last meeting. Thank you for coming today."

"Thank you, sir, for your generosity," said Kit.

49

"You're welcome; it was my pleasure."

For the next half hour, he talked with them about the work environment they had created at the restaurant, and he was very interested in how they had improved their efficiency. Then they said goodbye, and thanked him for the tea.

The girls waited until they reached the carriage to react to the check.

"Have you ever seen a check for that much money?" asked Kit.

"No, I haven't. Not personally," said Melanie.

"What now? We have enough to find a house and buy a table, maybe some chairs, and a couple of beds."

The girls were so excited they had forgotten about Mrs. Appleton. "Girls, if I may offer a suggestion, there are large churches that offer second hand furniture for the poor."

"Mrs. Appleton, what a great idea," said Melanie, and the girls spent the carriage ride planning how to spend the check from Mr. Harvey.

With Mrs. Appleton's help, they found a small bungalow that was priced in their budget and just needed a good cleaning and some fresh paint to make it livable. Kit and the girls spent every minute of their free time working to make it perfect.

Mrs. Appleton found a few pieces of good second-hand furniture, and Mr. Simpson fixed up the yard and painted the porch. He was nearly brought to tears by the generosity of the girls Anne worked with. His congregation was small and what little money he had he often gave to those in need.

Kit liked Mr. Simpson and could understand why Anne wanted her mother to meet him in person. They had begun a correspondence that Anne was confident was going in the right direction. Kit had a good feeling about Mr. Simpson, and hoped Anne's mother would see him in the same light.

She had never met a pastor so dedicated to his own congregation that he often went without so children could eat or a have a roof over their heads.

She even started going to his church, and found she felt more at home in the smaller congregation.

It was the end of March, and the house was ready. Anne was overjoyed with the results and even said that it was nicer than their previous home. Her family had packed everything they could carry in trunks and sold what few possessions they still owned. They were scheduled to arrive on the afternoon train in three days, and Anne and Mr. Simpson could not be happier.

For Kit, all this was more than just helping Anne and her family, it was her way of giving what she could to help others change their lives, just as she had done. If it had not been for the generosity of Mrs. Cates, Mrs. Taylor, and the opportunity to come west, she would still be working at a cannery for a fraction of the wages she received as a Harvey Girl. She made a promise to herself that she would never forget that, and to help others whenever she could.

Three days passed quickly and Anne was more animated than Kit had ever seen her before. The serious, quiet girl was happy, smiling, and at times even jovial. The transformation was incredible and Kit tried not to tease her too badly about it. Maggie had chosen to go a different route, and engaged in a bit of good-natured teasing about who the new girl was and what had happened to Anne. Anne took it in stride.

On the day the train was scheduled to arrive, Mrs. Appleton had given the girls special permission to take a few minutes and greet Anne's family. She sent a basket of fresh bread, cold cuts, and lemon pie with Anne to the station for her family.

Mr. Simpson stood with Anne, Kit, Maggie, Charlotte, Melanie, and Lucy as they waited at the station for the train. The girls were dressed in their pressed uniforms and starched aprons, and Mr. Simpson wore his Sunday suit. Kit looked at their delegation and thought they made a cheerful welcoming committee.

It was Melanie who saw the train first, and then Anne. A wave of excitement swept over the girls as the moment had come at last. All of their hard work was about to make a difference in the lives of one family. Mr. Simpson smiled and the girls lined up just like they did when they greeted passengers arriving at the restaurant.

The train came to a stop and the doors opened. A woman stepped onto the platform, followed by two teenaged boys and a girl. Anne broke ranks, ran to

51

her mother, and embraced her. There were happy tears as the family was reunited.

Kit wiped away a tear of her own, and so did Maggie. Mr. Simpson was all smiles as he waited patiently for Anne to beckon them over. As Kit approached the family, she was amazed at how beautiful Anne's mother was as she introduced herself as Easter Smith. The lady was in her forties but she appeared to be much younger, with skin as pale as alabaster and the same dark hair as Anne. Her smile was warm, and she greeted Mr. Simpson and all the girls with heartfelt gratitude.

Kit looked at Mr. Simpson and could tell that he was smitten. From the smiles and the easy laughter, it appeared that the feeling was mutual. She turned to Maggie with a raised eyebrow and Maggie nodded. It was obvious to anyone at the train station that afternoon that everything was off to a good start between Mrs. Smith and Mr. Simpson.

Kit smiled to think about Easter as being a time of beginnings, and the arrival of spring. With Easter just around the corner, it seemed a good sign to Kit that Anne's mother was named for the holiday.

Anne's family settled into the bungalow and immediately everyone began referring to it as the Smith Cottage. The small but welcoming residence had become a second home for the girls in Topeka. Anne still stayed in the dormitory, since that was required in her contract, but most evenings she could be found at her family's house until curfew.

Easter Smith had invited the girls from the Harvey Restaurant to make her house their home away from home, since so many of them were far away from their own families. It was not unusual for a small crowd to have lunch on Sundays after church at the small kitchen table, or sit around the fireside knitting and crocheting together.

William, Anne's slightly younger brother, was sweet on Maggie. Charlotte and Melanie helped Anne's sister, Ella, with her homework, and Kit and Lucy played board games with Anne's brother Avery. Mr. Simpson was a regular at the cottage and often brought fresh fish that he had caught at the river for dinner. Kit could not remember ever being so happy. It was like being part of a family once again.

It was after Easter that Mrs. Appleton passed along a message that Mr. Harvey would like to speak with Kit and Maggie the following afternoon at his office. Kit and Maggie spent the remainder of the day trying to figure out what could have warranted a private meeting with Mr. Harvey. Neither one could think of anything, and so they were forced to be patient.

The following day, the carriage arrived to pick them up, just as it had before. Mrs. Appleton joined the girls and this time she gave no instructions regarding tea. The matron appeared to be forlorn. Kit wondered if she and Maggie were getting sacked.

Mrs. Brogden met the ladies at the door and escorted them to Mr. Harvey's office. Mr. Harvey greeted them warmly. His demeanor was in contrast to Mrs. Appleton's somber mood. Kit was confused, and tried to hide her rising sense of anxiety. He invited the ladies to be seated in chairs arranged at his desk, and did not mention tea.

"Ladies, this is not a social call, I have invited you both here to discuss business."

Kit swallowed hard and tried to remain calm.

"With the continued success of this company, there is also continued growth. As you both recall, I mentioned that there would be opportunities for hard workers such as yourselves. Your dedication and character are what I am looking for when I establish a new restaurant."

Kit could hardly believe her ears, maybe they were not getting sacked after all!

"As the railroad expands, there are new towns, new places in the west that can benefit from the civility and progress that we at the Harvey Restaurants represent – that *you* represent. Some of these places are still wild and uncivilized, but with the coming of the railroad and the opportunities for commerce and expansion, these wild places will soon be like main street anywhere in America, with churches, banks, stores, and even theaters. But it will take work and dedication to get there, just like what you two ladies have shown these past few months in Topeka."

"Sir, if I may? Are you telling us that you want to send us to another town?" asked Kit.

"Yes, Miss Pridgeon, I am. The town I have in mind for you and Miss Lawson, I must be honest with you, is not for the faint of heart. It will be a

53

challenge but one I am sure you are both capable of meeting. Your tenacity and determination to help your colleague is just the kind of initiative I am looking for."

"Where is this town?" asked Maggie.

"Holbrook, Arizona," said Mr. Harvey.

"I have never heard of it," said Maggie.

"I would be surprised if you had. It is a brand new town, just established fifteen years ago. It's on the edge of the frontier. Not to alarm you, but there are still cowboys, cattle barons, and the occasional outlaw who calls that patch of desert home, and it is one of the newest stops of the railroad."

"Is it safe?" asked Mrs. Appleton.

"Not entirely, but we will have measures in place for your protection. Although I must warn you there are no churches yet, there is a sheriff and a deputy. Ladies, I know this sounds shocking, but if you want to see the wild west before it slips away into the pages of history, this is the place. I will give you both generous raises – and there's more."

"More?" asked Kit.

"Yes, if you can go to Holbrook and help make the restaurant a success, I will promote you both to positions as head waitresses in the new restaurant I have scheduled to open in California in the coming year."

Kit and Maggie were both speechless. It was a lot to consider.

"Mr. Harvey, may we have some time to think about it?" asked Kit.

"Yes, of course. How much time do you need? A few days?"

Maggie answered, "Ten minutes at the most."

Mr. Harvey and Mrs. Appleton left the girls in the office. Kit could hardly contain herself, "Oh Maggie! California! At last, he's promised us California!"

"Hold on a minute, you did hear the part about Holbrook – a town that is no doubt lawless and uncivilized?" asked Maggie.

"I did. How exciting. Cowboys, outlaws, and then California!"

"He wants to send us to a town that is smaller than Bridgeton. There will be no stores, no church, nothing."

"I know, but what an adventure! We get to meet real cowboys and then, if we do a good job, we get to go to California! After Fish Town, I can live almost anywhere."

"I don't know, I'm not used to small town life. I like churches and department stores," said Maggie.

"Come on, where is your sense of adventure? There is no more Wild West – this is it, don't you want to see it before it disappears forever, and then go to California?"

"When you put it like that, I guess so. I did come out here for an adventure, didn't I?" asked Maggie.

"Yes you did. Come on, I don't want to go by myself, and be alone with a lot of strange girls. Please?" pleaded Kit.

Maggie sighed and smiled at her friend. "You've talked me into it. When I am old and gray at least I can say that I had a grand adventure," said Maggie.

"We both can! Topeka has been great and we will never forget it, but Holbrook needs us and there are travelers who need a hot meal in a nice restaurant."

"You know what they say, no matter the weather, no matter the circumstances, the passengers of the Atkinson, Topeka, and Santa Fe must be fed!"

"And we are just the girls to do it!" said Kit.

Mr. Harvey and Mrs. Appleton came back to the office and Kit told them both the news. She and Maggie were up to the challenge and could not wait to start their new jobs in Holbrook, Arizona.

CHAPTER 5

The sun was blazing overhead as Kit and Maggie stepped off the train in Holbrook, Arizona. Kit wasn't sure what the temperature was, but it was the hottest day she had ever experienced in her life.

Kit wiped the sweat from her brow in a manner that was not ladylike and remarked, "Maggie, I don't know about you but I thought I knew a thing or two about hot, coming from North Carolina, but this is how a biscuit in the oven must feel."

"Is now a good time to remind you that this was your bright idea? We could have said no and still be back in Topeka at a candy counter right now, a bowl of strawberry ice cream in one hand and a sweet tea in the other."

"I give you permission to remind me as often as you like. Not to be indelicate, but in weather like this, I wonder if anyone would notice if we stopped wearing crinolines?"

Maggie covered her mouth as she gasped. "Kit, I hope no one heard you," she said as she looked at the deserted platform. "But while we're on the subject, I wish I wasn't wearing this heavy corset or these stockings. It's positively indecent to make us wear all these clothes in the desert."

"Maggie! I am shocked at you. No I'm teasing, you know you could never say anything to shock me too horribly. I was raised around fisherman, after all – but this long-sleeved jacket is more than I can stand."

Kit looked at the platform and the station. It was a simple stone building that lacked embellishment or decoration of any kind. There was no one to meet them from the restaurant or the company. Kit was curious if they were at the right place on the right day, but their travel had been arranged in Topeka, so that should all be in order.

"What do you think?"

"I think it's too hot," answered Maggie as she fanned herself with her hand in an attempt to cool down.

"Shouldn't someone be here to meet us?" asked Kit.

"Oh that, I suppose. Maybe they do things differently in Holbrook," answered Maggie.

Kit and Maggie were debating what their next move should be when a man with a thin mustache and dark hair came out of the station.

At first glance, Kit thought he might be the station master, but his uniform and immaculate grooming told a different story; he was connected to the Harvey Company.

He approached them with a pleasant smile. "Ladies, do I have the honor of addressing Miss Kit Pridgeon and Miss Maggie Lawson?"

"Yes, that is us, and who are you, sir?" asked Kit.

"I am Mr. Beauregard Tate, the restaurant manager. It is a pleasure to make your acquaintance."

Kit noticed that Mr. Tate spoke with a pronounced southern accent, almost with a drawl. She was not sure what part of the South he was from, but it was somewhere deeper in the magnolias and pines than Fish Town.

"Pleased to meet you, but is there no one else to meet the train? No other Harvey girls, I mean," said Maggie.

"That is not surprising, as you two are the first. The rest of the girls will be arriving within the week."

"Mr. Tate, we didn't see a porter. We have two trunks; is there anyone who can assist us?"

"Staffing here in Holbrook is woefully inadequate, at least for the time being. I intend to change that. I will see to it that your trunks are delivered to the residence. If you'll excuse me, I'll make those arrangements with the station master now. I will be back momentarily."

Kit looked at Maggie and said, "Did you hear that? We are the very first Harvey girls in Holbrook! Isn't that exciting?"

"Exciting? Look, little miss optimist, for the last time, are you sure you want to do this? We can be back on this train when it heads out of town and no one would say a word."

Kit looked around them at the brown landscape. There were only a few scrubby trees and almost no green at all. There were rocks, boulders, and mountains in the distance. It looked like an unforgiving sort of place, not for the weak or delicate. She took a deep breath as hot wind blew across the platform. It was desolate and unlike anywhere she had ever been, but she had signed up for an adventure and she knew she would get one here.

"Let's give it a chance. If we hate it in a month, we can go anywhere in the world you want to go. I promise, anywhere – China, New York, England, anywhere. You know we have a knack for saving money and here in Holbrook there is no place to spend it anyway. We could buy a ticket to anywhere in the world, you just name the place."

Maggie smiled at her best friend. "You are sincere about making this a success, aren't you? I can see it in that silly expression on your face." Her voice was full of affection. "Alright, you've talked me onto it. We'll try it out and see what happens. Besides, Mr. Tate is a dish, isn't he? With that sweet Alabama accent of his."

"Maggie, you are simply too wonderful for words. We have a duty to Mr. Harvey and his company; there are travelers who are going to need a nice place to have lunch and a good cup of coffee."

"I doubt anyone needs a hot cup of coffee today; maybe a glass of cool lemonade would be better," muttered Maggie.

Mr. Tate returned from the station master's office with a smile. "Ladies, if I may escort you to your residence."

Maggie looked for a carriage and didn't see one, "Mr. Tate, where is the carriage?"

"There is no need of a carriage, it is just a short stroll from the station," he answered.

Maggie and Kit exchanged glances. Maggie leaned in close to Kit and whispered, "Still want to give it a chance?"

~

The residence for the Harvey girls was a two-story stone and wood house located, just as Mr. Tate had said, a short stroll from the station and the restaurant. It was square, sturdy, and cheerfully trimmed in red with red shutters. There was a small yard enclosed by a low stone wall, complete with a wrought iron gate.

Mr. Tate removed a large key from his pocket as Maggie and Kit enjoyed the shade of the porch. A porch swing and two rocking chairs were invitingly arranged on the wide boards, and Kit thought about sitting down in one and melting into a puddle.

"This will be your home while you are in Holbrook, employed by the Harvey Company. The rules will not be challenging for you ladies as there is very little to do in Holbrook except visit establishments that ladies of your strong moral character would never choose to frequent. No men are allowed at the residence, except myself if necessary. The doors will be locked at nine here in Holbrook, rather than ten.

"Mr. Tate, why nine? The rule book clearly says ten," said Kit.

"It is only a safety precaution. Holbrook is not Topeka, and it is the decision of the management that it would be better if our girls were safe at home by nine, as this town does play host to a different class of people than I am sure either one of you is accustomed to."

The heavy wooden door opened into a foyer with dark wood floors and a high ceiling. A staircase and a small desk shared the austere but clean space. It was surprisingly comfortable inside the residence and Kit breathed a sigh of relief that it was several degrees cooler inside. She hoped the bedrooms upstairs would be just as cool.

"Sir, to what class of people are you referring?" asked Kit.

Mr. Tate sighed, and fiddled with the key. "I will try to put this as delicately as possible. Holbrook is a town that depends on cows and cattle ranches. Some sheep are raised nearby, but mostly it's cattle ranches, as far as the eye can see. Here in town, there are the owners of the ranches, a genteel though rugged sort, and then there are the cowboys, and sometimes the cattle rustlers."

"You mean there are rich folks and the men who work for them? Is that what you mean?" asked Maggie.

"Let me see, I may have to be a little clearer in my explanation, if you will forgive me. There are no churches in town, but there are several saloons. Does that help? You ladies will be ambassadors of class, civilization, and a genteel way of life that is presently unknown here in this part of the West."

"Saloons? You mean like dance halls?" asked Kit.

"Yes, Miss Pridgeon, that is exactly what I mean. The sort of people who frequent such places will be our customers and we must treat them with respect, but I doubt we will be engaging socially with them."

"I have yet to meet the matron, is she at the restaurant? I am surprised she didn't meet us at the train station," Maggie said as she looked around the empty space.

"Mrs. Clarke was supposed to be your matron, but unfortunately she has taken ill. The doctors are not certain she will be returning to work anytime soon. She is still in Wichita and was unable to make the journey."

"Are we to have no matron, then?' asked Maggie.

"You will not have one, at least for now. I intended to address this matter at a later time, but since you have brought up the subject, we may proceed with a discussion regarding the details of this unforeseen turn of events. You ladies come highly recommended by Mr. Harvey himself. I am confident you will be epitome of respectability at all times and with the new staff arriving soon, that you will both take on the role a matron would fill. I have been instructed by Mr. Harvey to increase both of your salaries by three dollars a month to compensate for your additional responsibilities."

"A raise, that is good news. Are we both being promoted?"

"If you are able to take charge of the new girls coming in and bring this restaurant's service up to the Harvey standard, yes, promotions will be in your future in only a short time. If I may introduce you to the cook and the housekeeper. The housekeeper will be in charge of your laundry as there is no reliable service in Holbrook.

Mr. Tate gave them a tour of the house and introduced the girls to Mrs. Hill, the house cook and Mrs. Garner, the housekeeper. Both ladies looked to be in their fifties and were as opposite as they could be, Mrs. Hill was pleasant and short and Mrs. Garner appeared to have much more serious disposition and was as tall as Mr. Tate.

Kit and Maggie were surprised that they each had their own rooms without a roommate. Kit's room was small and narrow with a brass bed, a desk, a chair and a wardrobe. It was small but it was all hers and she couldn't be more delighted.

The walls were painted white and the floor was the same dark wood as in the rest of the residence. A tall window with lace curtains opened to a view of the mountains in the distance. Kit opened the window to let the fresh in as Mr., Tate finished his tour.

The trunks arrived from the station and were brought upstairs by two men that Kit was certain must work for the restaurant. She discovered that she was not wrong as Mr. Tate introduced Mr. Joshua Smith the head cook and his assistant, Mr. Percy Bryce.

"Ladies, these two men are in charge of the kitchen at the restaurant, a finer pair of cooks you won't find anywhere else west of the Mississippi," said Mr. Tate with pride.

"It's about time you girls decided to join us, we open the restaurant in two weeks and it sure was getting lonely with just each other to talk to," said the younger man, Mr. Bryce.

Mr. Bryce was about Kit's age maybe a little older, his easy manner and gregarious personality reminded her of her friend Letty back home. Kit was convinced that Mr. Bryce had never met a stranger.

"We are glad to be here, aren't; we?" said Kit as she nudged Maggie.

"Yes, we are, thank you both for bringing up our trunks, it was very nice of you," said Maggie as she smiled in the direction of Mr. Smith.

Kit noticed that Mr. Smith returned her smiled and then looked away. He was tall, slender and exuded a farm boy charm but was dressed in a big city fashion. Kit watched as Maggie gazed at the head cook surreptitiously. Unless she missed her guess, it looked like Maggie was smitten.

Construction on the restaurant was completed, it just need to be fully staffed. That was good. The bad news was that it was small and could only accommodate a limited number of customers, which meant speed would be even more important in Holbrook than it ever had been in Topeka.

As Mr. Tate led them on a tour of the restaurant that afternoon, he suggested that they drill and practice over the next few days. Maggie and Kit were in agreement that a little practice never hurt anyone.

Kit whispered to Maggie during the tour, "Do you think he realizes that we hold the speed record for serving in Topeka?"

"Probably not, we will have to surprise him."

The kitchen was the most impressive part of the restaurant; the ovens, stoves, kettles, pans, and all manner of cookware stood gleaming and ready for customer orders. It was obvious that Mr. Smith and Mr. Bryce were happy with their preparations; they beamed like proud parents as they showed the girls all the modern conveniences and latest technological gadgets for making delicious meals as quickly as possible.

Maggie asked a lot of questions about cooking and Mr. Smith answered them all in detail. Kit had never seen Maggie so interested in how to cook a steak before now. She thought about teasing her best friend, but she decided to wait until they were alone.

After the tour, Mr. Tate escorted them back to the residence, where he suggested they remain for the night. They would have the house all to themselves as Mrs. Hill and Mrs. Gardner did not live on the premises.

"If you need us, I and the kitchen staff will be nearby. Our residence is next to the train station."

"Mr. Tate, do you think we'll be safe, staying here all alone?" asked Maggie.

"I do. Mr. Harvey would never have allowed you to come here if he thought you were truly in any danger. I did not mean to alarm you; I just

63

prefer to be cautious. This town can be a bit rowdy after dark, so I'd suggest an early evening."

Mr. Tate left Kit and Maggie standing in the parlor of a residence that was not far enough away from the saloons to suit either of them. With the closing of the front door, they both realized that they were truly in for an adventure.

Before Mrs. Hill left for the evening, she fixed two bowls of beef stew with fresh bread and peach pie for the girls. Maggie and Kit sat at the long wooden table in the dining room all alone.

"You don't suppose this place is haunted, do you?" asked Kit as she watched the shadows growing with the setting sun.

"How can it be? This house is new. No one but us has ever lived here before, so that means no one has died here," answered Maggie.

"Yet Mr. Tate seemed anxious about our safety."

"He did seem a bit concerned, but I wouldn't worry. He is a manager; it is customary for a man in his position to fret over the details. Our safety and the smooth management of all the affairs of the restaurant must surely fall into that category."

"If you say so, but I still think this place is haunted," said Kit.

"Silly goose! If it's haunted, it's haunted by two tired, hungry girls all the way from North Carolina who can't figure out for the life of them how they ended up out here in cowboy paradise," Maggie said with a smile.

Kit conceded and finished her slice of peach pie in three bites. "One thing is for certain: if that Mr. Smith can cook half as well as Mrs. Hill, our customers will be in for a treat!"

"That pie *is* delectable. Say, if we're the only ones here, that means we can raid the kitchen. I bet there's more pie in the pie safe," said Maggie.

"I don't know where I'll put it, but I sure would love another slice. Last one there is a wet hen!" said Kit, as she raced to the kitchen.

Maggie caught up with her as they reached the doorway. It was soon agreed that it was a tie, and the remainder of the peach pie was located. Maggie cut another two slices as Kit sat down at the kitchen table and lit the kerosene lamp.

The girls laughed and joked as they ate more peach pie than either should have been able to. The sun was down and the only light was from the lamp as they cleaned up the dishes and put them away. It was the least they could do since they had raided the pie safe, they decided.

Making their way to the parlor, Kit could hear melodic strains of music. She stopped and listened and then asked Maggie, "Do you hear it?"

"I do; it sounds like it's coming from down the street."

"Maggie, you don't suppose it's from a dance hall or a saloon, do you?"

"I would say that's exactly where it's coming from. It sure doesn't sound like any choir music or classical symphony I've ever heard."

"Are you certain? It doesn't sound like it's that far away – perhaps we should go out on the porch and see?" asked Kit.

Maggie shook her head. "I wouldn't do that, not after dark." They walked into the parlor and lit another kerosene lamp. The glow of the two lamps made the room seem less gloomy and lonely.

Kit sat down on the settee and asked Maggie, "*Is* it dangerous? Do you think we're safe?"

Maggie settled beside her with a tired sigh. "I didn't want to tell you this, because you were so happy about coming out here, but I did some research before we left Topeka. Holbrook's history is violent and colorful."

"Really, how so?"

Maggie spoke in a serious tone as she described what she had discovered. "They say it's not a town for women or churches, and it's known for its lawlessness. Only a few short years ago, there was a shoot-out on Main Street over a dispute involving *cows*. I read that it was quite a feud. A little war, some said."

"We can't be the only women here besides Mrs. Hill and Mrs. Gardner," said Kit.

"Well, we know there are women here who work in the saloons, but we may be the only ladies, if you take my meaning."

Kit's eyes twinkled. "No wonder the men at the restaurant were so glad to see us, there can't be many other girls in town to talk to!"

"I bet the cattle ranchers have their wives and daughters out here but they probably aren't staying in town. Yes, ma'am, a shoot-out right here in beautiful downtown Holbrook. For all we know it could have happened right outside our front door," said Maggie.

"Then this place might really be haunted with the ghosts of dead cowboys or cattle rustlers."

"I'd be less worried about the dead cowboys and more worried about the living ones, from what I read. Let's just say I'll be checking to make sure we've locked the doors tonight before we retire."

Where Kit had grown up, there had never been a need to lock the door. Listening to the raucous laughter and wild music from just down the street, she decided that it was time to establish a new habit.

Despite being a little scared, Kit slept with her window cracked open just so she could enjoy the evening breeze. The desert changed temperature rapidly as soon as the sun set, and the cool night air was a welcome change after the oven-like temperatures of the day. She remembered the warnings about the night air and catching her death, but after being about to burn up, she decided she would take that risk.

She fell asleep to the tinny sounds of saloon music and a fight in the early hours of morning. The next day at breakfast she felt like she needed to say something to Maggie to ease her guilt.

Maggie was already downstairs enjoying a cup of coffee, fried eggs, and sausage. Kit joined her and after taking a sip of good, strong coffee, she said quietly, "Maggie I didn't realize what this town was like when I made you feel like you had to come with me. I apologize for getting you into this jam."

Maggie turned to Kit and answered, "Kit, my dear, I knew what I was getting into before I ever set foot on that train. I didn't have to agree and I could have changed my mind, but I couldn't let you come out her all alone, now could I?"

"Yes, you could have – and knowing what I know now, I can't say that I would have blamed you. We can leave if you like, I can make arrangements today.'

"No, no, no! We're not going anywhere. This place is dangerous and there is nowhere to spend my salary, but I do like the fact that we are the only ladies in town. Do you know what that means? If one of us should meet a handsome man who is well off, then there isn't anyone else to distract him." Maggie speared a piece of egg in a most unladylike fashion.

"But what about California? Aren't you going to California with me?" asked Kit.

"Of course I'm going to California with you – if we manage to survive Holbrook. But I may have a little fun along the way. I do have to warn you, if a dashing young cattle baron asks for my hand in marriage I may have to say yes."

"What about our contracts?" asked Kit.

"There are up this fall. By then I could be a wealthy woman with a grand house somewhere," answered Maggie.

"Or be working at the side of that handsome cook right here in Holbrook."

"Kit!" Maggie protested, and set down her fork with a clatter. "What do you mean?"

"Maggie, I suspect the only reason you're even considering staying in this dusty, dangerous town is because of a certain Mr. Joshua Smith."

Maggie blushed a deep red at the mention of his name. "You are silly; I've only just met him. I would not impulsively fall for a man in such a short period of time; it would be unseemly."

"Hmmm. Perhaps not so very unseemly, if it was love at first sight." Kit leaned closer to her friends and whispered, "I don't think you were by yourself – he looked like he was suffering from the same ailment as you. Either that, or you were just both incredibly interested in how to make dinner rolls when he showed you his kitchen yesterday."

"Kit, I am not having this conversation. I'm sure Mr. Smith was just being courteous."

"Sure. I'll bet he was more courteous with you than with any other woman in Holbrook."

"Well, that's not much of a challenge," said Maggie with a smile.

"No it's not," Kit laughed, and wiped her mouth with her napkin. "We'd better hurry or we'll be late for practice and drills. Remember what I said, Mr. Tate has no idea how fast we are and we want him to be impressed."

"Right you are, just let me have one last sip of coffee; I'm going to need it!"

Maggie and Kit left the residence and walked up the block to the restaurant. On the way to work, Kit looked back down the street, in the direction where she had heard the music coming from the night before. She was overcome with curiosity and thought about convincing Maggie to take a peek at the saloons while they were closed during daylight hours.

The impulse surprised her. She knew she could get in a lot of trouble if she went anywhere near a saloon, but she told herself there was no harm standing in front of one while it was closed. She'd never been so close to a real bar before – her father was a devout Christian and would have whipped her with a belt if she'd ever done such a thing back home. But these saloons were a part of the Wild West she'd only read about, and she wanted to see one before they disappeared forever.

CHAPTER 6

Impressing Mr. Tate was woefully easy. He was expecting the Harvey standard of meals served in just slightly under thirty minutes. Kit and Maggie both performed brilliantly and in the smaller restaurant, were able to do a practice drill at twenty-five minutes without so much as breaking a sweat. Kit even bragged that they may shorten it to twenty-three minutes if the customer was in a hurry.

In the following days, Kit and Maggie met the remainder of the kitchen staff, which included several young men to chop, wash dishes, bus tables, and bake. Kit struck up a friendship with Mr. Bryce, and Maggie continued to find innocent reasons to go and spend time in the kitchen.

The nightly concert of yelling, laughter, and music came to be just part of life in Holbrook as Kit and Maggie settled into a routine. Some nights were not so bad, as the cowboys and farm hands didn't come into town every night of the week, just sometimes. Judging from the sounds of brawling and drunken singing, these men more than made up for the time they spent away on the cattle ranches.

It was Tuesday afternoon, and Kit and Maggie had been in Holbrook a little over a week when the remaining Harvey girls were due to arrive. It was Maggie's idea that everyone, including the kitchen staff, line up at the station and give the new girls a real Harvey welcome. Mr. Tate thought that would be a fine idea, and ordered the staff to be turned out in pressed uniforms when the train arrived at the station.

Kit and Maggie were excited to be meeting the new girls. This was their first time being in charge of anyone, and they hoped to make a good impression on these young ladies. Mr. Tate told Kit and Maggie that these girls were fresh out of training and had never worked in restaurant before. This would be their first real assignment, and Kit hoped she and Maggie would be able to lead by example and make Holbrook the finest and fastest Harvey Restaurant of them all.

Standing on the platform in the sweltering heat, Kit and Maggie smiled their most pleasant smiles as the train came to a stop. The doors of the train opened and out stepped four fresh arrivals from Kansas. With their hats, jackets, and long skirts, they looked just as unaccustomed to the heat as Kit and Maggie had only the week before. Kit was glad she had urged Mrs. Hill to make sweet tea and lemonade to have on hand when the girls arrived at the residence, as a welcome.

"Ladies, welcome to Holbrook. I am Mr. Tate." The manager introduced himself to the four young ladies.

Kit watched as four young faces turned to face Mr. Tate. The girls were all pretty, fresh faced and dressed in the latest fashion – all but one. A young, red-haired woman was wearing a plain jacket and an unembellished skirt. Her hat was just as plain as her clothes.

Kit could tell right away that this girl was just like her. She'd come from somewhere poor and was here to make something of herself. Kit suspected this girl would probably work harder than all the other girls combined.

As they were introduced, Kit made sure to remember that the girl in the plain suit was named Hattie Schultz and she was from Pennsylvania. The other ladies were all from big cities back east – Annie Blyth was from Boston, while Henrietta Solomon and Emma Berkowitz both hailed from New York. Emma was funny and outspoken and Henrietta seemed every bit as candid. Kit knew there was never going to be a dull moment now that the new girls had arrived.

Mrs. Hill met the young ladies with tea and lemonade at the residence. Kit could tell from their grateful reactions that a cool drink and warm welcome was the way to make friends in Holbrook. She and Maggie showed the new girls around the residence and gave them an education about the town and the rules. They seemed to take it in stride. The only young lady who looked a bit nervous was Annie Blyth from Boston.

Annie wore her hair in a blonde pompadour with pearl drop earrings and a pearl ring to match. A strand of pearls complemented the ivory suit she wore, which was delicately embroidered with yards of lace. She was the most fashionably dressed of all the new arrivals, a fact that was not lost on Maggie, who made mention of it to Kit when they had a few minutes alone. "Did you see her skirt and that hat? I know material and fashion, and that outfit cost more than any dress I have ever owned, maybe even my whole wardrobe."

"Does it? It's very nice; she looks like a woman from a society page in the newspaper."

"I bet that's it, she may have run away from a scandal, or maybe her family insisting that she marry a man twice her age," said Maggie.

"Maybe she just wanted to come on an adventure?" asked Kit.

"I doubt it; girls like her don't go on adventures. I bet you anything that her family up north in Boston doesn't have the slightest clue where their daughter the heiress has gone, she simply vanished. There may be a reward," giggled Maggie.

"A reward, can we split it? No, that wouldn't be right. Maybe she was just tired of being rich, you know all that money can't buy you happiness," answered Kit.

"I may have to disagree with you – I would sure be willing to give it a try," said Maggie.

That evening at dinner, the residence became a home and Kit no longer joked that it was haunted. There was life and energy with every laugh, giggle, and new friendship that began that night. Kit and Maggie agreed that if they were to be in charge, they were very lucky. They couldn't have asked for a better group of girls. Kit could envision her and Maggie boarding the train to California in record time.

~

In less than a week, Kit and Maggie had the new girls performing their duties like veteran Harvey girls. The new girls were eager to please, and everyone – even the kitchen staff –encouraged them. Kit couldn't help but notice that the staff in Holbrook was becoming a large family, encouraging each other to be better, often with cheers and applause.

Back in Topeka, the staff was friendly and everyone worked well together, but here in this small town, the staff acted like brothers and sisters, except for the occasional innocent flirting, when Mr. Tate was not paying attention. Maggie and Mr. Smith were never far apart, while Mr. Bryce had taken a shine to Hattie, as they used to say in Fish Town.

Mr. Tate never flirted with anyone, or acted in any way that was not strictly in line with the rules and regulations of the Harvey Company, but Kit noticed that he spent more and more time addressing concerns he had in regards to the restaurant with Maggie. If Kit didn't know any better, it would appear that Maggie had two beaux, and at work, nonetheless.

The new girls were working out wonderfully, and just as Kit suspected, Hattie was the hardest worker of them all. In a conversation with Kit, she confessed that the suit she wore that day on the train was the nicest one she owned. She was the only daughter in a family of mill workers, and she refused to spend one more day in a factory when she knew there was more to life. Kit understood completely and offered to help her in any way she could.

The grand opening of the restaurant was timed with a new service being offered on the rail line that would bring travelers to Holbrook four times a week. Already in the little town there was interest in the restaurant. Rich cattle barons were requesting reservations on the opening day and the local sheriff, a widower, asked about securing a lunchtime table. Kit could feel that it was going to be a success, or at least she hoped it would be. On more than one occasion, they had turned away drunken cowboys or ranch hands who stumbled into the establishment thinking it was a bar.

The night before the grand opening she could hardly sleep. There was a lot riding on the success of the restaurant. If it went well and good news got back to Topeka, then her career would be assured. Lying awake in bed well past midnight, Kit heard a creaking sound and steps on the stairs. She strained to listen in the dark, and heard the creaking sound again.

She sat up and quietly made her way to her bedroom door. She wasn't sure if someone was sneaking up the stairs or sneaking down. She thought of all those drunken cowboys in town, and hoped there wasn't someone in the house who meant them any harm, or was there to rob them.

Kit opened the door and snuck out of her bedroom and towards the stairs. She hoped it was just one of the girls going downstairs for a midnight snack, and not an intruder. Not armed with a gun or weapon, she wasn't sure what she would do if she found a cowboy in the house. Making her way to the stairs, she could smell the scent of roses – whoever was sneaking around the house was wearing a wonderful smelling perfume.

Kit walked down the stairs, taking care not to make them creak, and was almost to the last one when the stairs groaned under her weight.

A voice from the darkness whispered, "Who's there? Show yourself this instant."

"Maybe I should say the same thing to you," said Kit in a low voice to the figure in the darkness.

"Hold on, let me turn on the lamp," the female voice said.

"Don't, do that, or we'll both be in trouble. It's well past lights out, and we don't want to get Mr. Tate's attention, do we?"

"I apologize, although for me that really shouldn't matter," said the unknown woman.

Kit stepped closer to the figure, and in the pale light of the moon streaming through the windows in the foyer, she could see who she was speaking to.

"Annie, why are you up at this hour? Where were you going?" Kit asked. It felt strange to be questioning someone, but as matron it was her duty to see that the girls behaved properly – and this was not proper behavior.

"If you must know, I'm leaving. I plan to be on the first train out of here."

"Annie, tomorrow is the grand opening – you can't leave!"

"Yes, I can. I don't know what I was thinking. Oh, why did I come out here?"

"Does your family know where you are?"

"Not exactly."

"By not exactly, do you mean they don't, or they do?"

Annie sighed and confessed, "They don't. I ran away. It seemed like a romantic adventure, something fun, a lark, but now I regret that decision. This place, this town is not what I signed up for."

Kit sighed and tapped her fingers on the hall table, thinking. "Alright. But before you go, come with me. The train won't be here for hours anyway, and it's not safe to be out on the platform by yourself. Come with me," said Kit.

Annie followed Kit into the kitchen. The kitchen was at the back of the house and the lamp would be unseen from the street. Kit lit it, and put the kettle on for tea. She opened the pie safe and found the remnants of the pecan pie Mrs. Hill had served at dinner. Cutting a generous slice, she put it on a plate and handed it to Annie. She made a pot of tea and sat down with the young woman.

"From the start, I could tell that you came from a wealthy background, but out here none of that matters. Tell me the truth; why did you really want to be a Harvey Girl?"

Annie ate a bite of the pie and looked at the table. Even in the lamplight she had the bearing and beauty of an aristocrat. There were a few minutes of awkward silence and then she answered. "I think it all began as a dream. I saw the advertisement in the paper. My brother had recently invested in the railroad and the large cattle ranches that are prevalent in this part of the country. I listened to him talk about his trips out West and how exciting it was. I think I wanted to have experiences like that."

"Why didn't you just accompany him when he came out here?"

She shook her head. "My family would never have allowed such a thing; it wouldn't be proper for a young lady of marriageable age to go traipsing around the wilderness. I remember asking my mother and father at dinner one night, and the reaction I received was as though I had asked to go on stage, or something as scandalous as that. I never brought it up again."

Kit looked at the young woman and understood what it was like to feel frustration with the limited choices in life. She took a sip of tea and said, "Annie, you ran away from Boston, searching for adventure and a new life, and now you're running away from Holbrook because this is more adventure than you expected. If you get on that train tomorrow morning, you'll never know what could have happened, or what life you could have led. You know what waits for you in Boston: duty, rules, marriage, and more duty. Why don't you give this a try? Even if you decide not to stay, you can go home with a few stories of your own."

"I'm not sure what I should do," Annie said in a quiet voice.

74

Kit stood up and suddenly felt tired enough that she knew she could go to sleep. If she went now, at least she would be able to get a few hours in before the dawn.

"Annie, you are talented and smart, and I would love to see you helping us open the restaurant tomorrow. You've worked hard to become a Harvey Girl and it is an honor given to very few. If you must leave, I wish you all the best and a safe journey, but I sure hope you stay – not for me or the restaurant, but for yourself. Goodnight."

"Goodnight,' said Annie, drawing circles in the syrup from her pie with one tine of the fork.

Kit walked back up the stairs in the dark. She stifled a yawn as she crept back down the corridor and to her room. She was asleep as soon as her head hit the pillow.

The next day, Kit was pleasantly surprised to see Annie wearing her black waistcoat, skirt, and crisp white apron. It was good sign, she thought, as the girls stood in a row on the platform to welcome the train as it arrived. The customers from the train were to be the first served in the restaurant, and then it would be open to the public.

The travelers climbed down from the train and in only a few minutes the little restaurant was bustling with activity. There was orange juice to serve, coffee cups to fill, and steak and potatoes with all the trimmings to be eaten by hungry men who had been traveling by rail for hours. Kit looked around the restaurant and was pleased with how smoothly it was running.

As the travelers finished their lunches, the doors were opened to the public and a stream of well dressed men, the sheriff, and a few disheveled cowboys came parading through the door demanding to be fed.

The cowboys were rugged and their language was occasionally coarse. They objected to being made to wear jackets in the heat of the day, but Mr. Tate assured them he would not allow them to be served until they dressed and acted as gentlemen. Like recalcitrant children, they donned the complimentary jackets and curbed their more colorful phrases as they sat at the counter waiting for service.

The girls were not sure what to do about the cowboys. It was their first time interacting with them, even though they had been in the same town for a few weeks. The cowboys were equally unsure how to act in a restaurant with clean white tablecloths, no bar, and well dressed women. Kit and Maggie volunteered to serve them, and hoped for the best.

Kit approached a tan fellow with a scar on his face and wide smile. As she came near he said, "Well dawg gone it, ain't you pretty. How about a dance, little lady?"

"Sir, may I bring you a cup of coffee, or may I suggest a glass of fresh lemonade?"

"How about a bottle of a whiskey and you and I..."

"Sir, the steak is delicious but we also have roast chicken with all the trimmings, sole, trout, and pork chops fried to perfection."

The cowboy looked confused. Kit was being polite but not acknowledging his bad behavior. He took his hat off and looked at the menu for a moment before saying, "Look I ain't the best at reading all this writing. I'll have whatever you think is good."

"Very well, I suggest starting with the cream of celery soup, a green salad, the pork chops with roast potatoes and carrots, and then end with rhubarb pie. We have delicious sweet tea only available here at this Harvey House."

"Yes ma'am, I'd be much obliged."

Kit walked away from the man and entered the kitchen to the sound of subdued applause.

"How did you do that? That was well done," said Emma, who seemed to be speaking for everyone.

"I gave him the service we are known for. Ladies, try that and see if being polite works. If they get forward, let me know and we will ask them to leave. Who wants the next one?" Kit poured the tea, put the soup in a bowl, and grabbed a basket of fresh dinner rolls.

She returned to the cowboy and sat his food and drink down in front of him. He smiled and dug into the rolls as though he hadn't seen food for some time. Then she retreated to the side of the restaurant, and watched as Emma tackled the next one.

The Harvey girls scored a victory that day. In only twenty minutes they had some of the roughest men in Holbrook saying thank you and using silverware. Kit looked at Mr. Tate and he was beaming. It was a good day, and Kit knew she was going to love the challenge of working in a restaurant that had such a colorful cast of characters.

The opening week was filled with similar scenes playing out over and over as the town of Holbrook was treated to a novelty it had never experienced before: a civilized restaurant where good food and good service were always on the menu. Kit was honestly astonished that in that week, only a small handful of men had to be asked to leave. For a town with the reputation of Holbrook, that was quite an accomplishment.

A month had come and gone so quickly that Kit hardly noticed. They sat in the parlor of the girls' residence, enjoying a much-deserved day off, drinking tea and eating the chocolate cake that Mrs. Hill made the night before.

Kit was sprawled out in a very unladylike fashion on the settee, reading a newspaper that a traveler had left at the restaurant. It was from Denver and only a week old. Kit had not realized until just then how isolated they were in Holbrook; there was no newspaper and the only way to communicate was through the post or the telegraph service.

Kit was devouring the newspaper when she saw a news story in the corner of the society section about a missing Boston heiress; she knew that was Annie. She decided she would convince Annie to send her family a letter when the young woman returned to the residence that evening.

Maggie was reading a novel and suddenly announced to Kit, "It will be autumn soon. It's almost be a year since we became Harvey girls."

Kit looked up from the paper, "Hmm, so it has. I will be content with some cold weather, personally."

"Kit, do you realize we've been here for a month?"

"That's right! We have, haven't we?" Kit sat up and folded the paper, placing it on her lap. "We need to talk about what we are going to do, don't we?"

"You mean that promise of yours? Kit, I wouldn't let it worry you. I'm content to stay in Holbrook. This town doesn't hold much in the way of entertainment for us morally upstanding young ladies, but it's been more fun than I dreamed it would be that day we stepped off the train."

"Do you mean that? I was being sincere – I'll be happy to go anywhere in the world you want to go, except for Fish Town."

"My dear Kit, I promise you, if I was given the choice of places to travel in this world, Fish Town would not be on my list."

"Mine, either." Kit hesitated. "Maggie, are you staying because of Mr. Smith?"

Maggie riffled the pages of her book thoughtfully. "I don't want to admit it, but he might be part of it – that, and you seem so happy here. The way you make those cowboys behave like gentlemen, I never get tired of watching that."

Kit was unsure where the cook and the housekeeper were in the house, so she lowered her voice and asked, "What about Mr. Smith, has he given you any indication that he has affection for you? It would appear that he does, but has he said anything?"

"Not exactly. I think he values his position too much to jeopardize it. If I weren't working for the company, I believe he'd be more forthcoming in his affections," replied Maggie.

Kit thought about that, and it dawned on her what her best friend was suggesting. "You're not seriously considering leaving the company after one year, are you?"

Maggie looked down at the book in her hand and couldn't look Kit in the eye. "I am considering it. I don't want to lie to you, so yes, it has crossed my mind."

Kit was shocked that sensible Maggie would even think of making such a rash decision without any proof that her intended meant to pursue matrimony.

"He hasn't said or done anything to indicate that he loves you and wants to marry you, yet you're considering leaving when your contract is up? I sincerely hope he feels the same for you as you do for him, but what if he doesn't? Then what would you do?"

Maggie bit her lip and looked at Kit. "I suppose I'd go home and work in my father's store. Maybe I'd get married to someone from Raleigh or be a spinster."

Kit frowned. "How can you risk your future on a man whose intentions you don't know? Please tell me you'll find out what those intentions are before you do something rash."

Unexpectedly, Maggie became defensive. "Kit, why would be so horrid about Joshua? He loves me; I just know it. I won't need to worry about what to do after I resign, because I'm certain he will marry me. You're just jealous of what I've found."

Kit was hurt by Maggie's words and retorted, "Jealous? Why would I be jealous of your affection for a cook in a restaurant in Holbrook?"

"You're just jealous that I'm happy with my life, while you have to go searching for yours! That's what California is all about for you, isn't it? Trying to get as far away from your Fish Town roots as you can get?"

"Maggie! That's not true; you take that back." Kit stood, tears welling in her eyes.

"I will do no such thing; I'm hurt that you're saying he doesn't love me."

"I didn't say that! I only want you to be happy, and that has nothing to do with me, or California. I only want what is best for you. I wish you a good day."

Kit ran upstairs with the paper in her hand. She rushed to her bedroom and closed the door with a slam. She threw herself on her bed and wept, not only for the things Maggie had said, but just knowing that Maggie was letting her heart do all her thinking. Kit really did hope for the best for her friend and couldn't imagine going to California without her, but she was afraid that Maggie was about to make a horrible mistake and she could do nothing to stop it.

Desperately in need of a friend, she sat at her desk and wrote a letter to Lucy Barrows, her roommate back in Topeka. It had been a week since she'd received a letter from Lucy and she felt terrible that it had been this long before she responded. As she wrote the letter she thought about Lucy and realized she missed the girls back in Topeka. Tears fell down her face as she signed her name. Kit felt lonely and didn't know what she would do if Maggie left.

Although they tried to hide it from everyone, the rift between Maggie and Kit was obvious to the other girls in the house. It didn't affect their work, but there was tension that had not been there before their argument. Hattie, Annie, Henrietta, and Emma knew something had happened but none of them knew what, and none of them were forward enough to ask, even Emma.

Now more than ever, Kit wished Holbrook had one church she could walk into and pray. At this point, she wasn't even picky about the denomination, Catholic, Baptist, she didn't care. All her life she had attended church regularly and it was a big part of her life. Now, there was no church or chapel, not even a bible study group. She needed to hear a sermon and sing a hymn to feel like everything was going to be fine.

She had prayed about her crisis and the lack of a church many times before she went to sleep at night. She was surprised when one of her prayers was answered one day, and in a way she was not expecting.

Kit was working in the restaurant. It was the end of the lunch rush, and there were several empty chairs. She felt as though she could relax and catch her breath, and had just sat down when a man walked in who looked like a cowboy. He was wearing the clothes of a ranch hand, yet his manner and way of moving set him apart. He came in, reached for a complimentary jacket from one of the hooks by the door, then took his hat off and hung it on the hat rack.

He asked to be seated at a table and Kit found herself captivated by his calm demeanor and pleasant manners. Putting on her brightest smile, she walked to the man's table, not sure what to expect.

She handed him a menu and said, "Welcome to the Harvey Restaurant at Holbrook, what can I bring you to drink?"

"Ma'am, if it's not too much trouble, I'd like whatever you have that is cold."

"Yes sir, I will bring you a fresh squeezed glass of orange juice," she said, as she turned to walk away.

"Thank you," the man answered.

Kit walked to the counter and as she squeezed the oranges, her eyes kept straying back to the man sitting at the table, studying the menu.

She brought him the glass of juice and placed it on the table in front of him. He drank it in two gulps and smiled.

"I can bring you another, if you like. Have you decided on a selection for a starter?"

"This menu looks so good, I want to order one of everything. What do you suggest?"

The steak and potatoes are always good, but the cook does a glazed duck that is one of my favorites."

"The duck sounds good. For dessert, may I have a slice of that lemon meringue pie?"

"Yes sir, right away."

Kit brought out a light vegetable soup and bread rolls, and squeezed another glass of orange juice for her customer. Underneath the grime and dust he was handsome, with blue eyes and light brown hair. She suspected he was only a few years older than her, but he could be older. Intrigued by his genteel manners, she broke a cardinal rule of the Harvey girls, and asked him a question about himself.

"Sir, your main course will be out in a few minutes. If I may be so forward, do you work around here?"

"I do, for Mr. Landry, although I must admit ranch work is not my first calling."

Kit smiled. She was nervous about being so bold, but decided if she was in for a penny, she was in for a pound. She might as well continue. "What is your first calling?"

He folded his hands together and bowed his head as she placed the bowl of soup in front of him. "I'm a minister."

The man began to pray quietly, and was still for a few moments before he took up his spoon. It was something Kit had never seen before in Holbrook. As she served him the glazed duck, she was curious about why he was working as a ranch hand, but knew she'd asked too many questions already.

He ate his lunch, finished off the lemon meringue pie, and left a generous tip. She hoped she would see him again in the future.

The following day, Kit's heart skipped a beat when she saw the same man come back to the restaurant, but this time she hardly recognized him. He was wearing a light-colored suit and had taken a bath since the previous day. He saw Kit and smiled warmly.

"Welcome back to the Harvey House restaurant, what can I bring you to drink?"

"If I could have another glass of that orange juice, I'd be grateful. I should have introduced myself yesterday; I'm Albert Cleary."

"Good day, Mr. Cleary. My name is Kit. I'll be right back with your orange juice."

Kit returned a few minutes later with a glass of sweet orange juice for her customer. She hoped no one would hear her inviting him to tell her about himself. "You said you were a minister?"

"Yes, I am. Although my ministry is more like mission work."

"Mr. Cleary, we need a church here in this town. Is there any hope we might have one soon?"

"I am working towards that very goal. My work for Mr. Landry helps me save money for a building, but it will be some time. There is a study group I lead once a month when I'm not working on the ranch. We hold meetings at the general store after it closes on the second Wednesday of each month."

"Oh! May I be so bold, to ask if may join your study group?"

Mr. Cleary smiled, and Kit imagined his cheeks tinged just the slightest bit pink. "You're welcome to come study the bible any time. I know Holbrook must seem full of sin, but there are some good people here."

"Thank you, you can count on me. What would you like to order?"

Kit wrote down his order and noticed that today, he looked as clean and handsome as any man she had ever laid eyes on. She was embarrassed that she found a man of God so attractive. She hurried to the kitchen with his order. Stepping inside the pantry, she said a silent prayer of thanks to God. A study group once a month was better than nothing, and the minister was more than she could have hoped for.

She looked at the calendar and saw that the second Wednesday of the month was only a week away. She smiled to herself as she loaded the tray, and making sure to include a few extra rolls and plenty of butter. She returned to the dining room and served his French onion soup and rolls. His blue eyes twinkled, and his smile was ever so slightly crooked. Praying for strength, she finished serving his order. Once again, he left a generous tip and thanked her for a delicious meal and great service.

Kit was elated. She had bible study to look forward to, and the promise of seeing the minister again. It wasn't much, but it was a start. She had just turned to walk back to the kitchen when a well dressed man stormed into the restaurant.

His suit looked expensive and his aristocratic face was red with fury. Kit made an attempt to greet him but he refused to listen to her. Instead, he stood in the middle of the restaurant and demanded, "I am here to see Annie Blyth – my sister. Where is she?"

Kit had known Annie had a brother, but Annie hadn't mentioned that he was so tall, with broad shoulders and a temper. Judging from the fact that he was standing in the Harvey restaurant in Holbrook, Kit assumed that Annie must have contacted her parents.

Annie walked from the kitchen and Kit held her breath, hoping Annie's brother would calm down. He looked dangerous.

Annie was poised and dignified, and Kit was impressed by her courage. "Stewart," Annie said, "I wasn't expecting you. What brings you to Holbrook?"

"You know darn well what brings me to Holbrook! Pack your things. You are going home."

Annie looked around the restaurant; all eyes were on her. She spoke in a quiet voice. "Stewart, you are behaving without any regard for these people eating their lunch. I'm not going home with you. I'm sorry, but that is final."

He looked at the faces staring back at him and said in a menacing tone, "We will see about that."

He left in a huff. Kit ran to Annie and gave her a hug.

Annie was outwardly calm, but this close, Kit could see that her chin quivered ever so slightly. "Kit, that was my brother. I apologize for not introducing you." A tiny gleam of humor shone in her eyes, even though they were brimming with tears.

Kit smiled and squeezed her shoulder. "Don't worry, Annie. I am sure I will have the opportunity to see him again sometime soon."

Annie took a deep breath and returned to serving her customers. Kit watched her and suppressed a feeling of dread. Stewart would be back.

Annie had struggled with her decision to come to Holbrook, but since then she had become so content serving guests as a Harvey girl. She'd begun to shine with inner peace and a new confidence. Kit hoped that the young woman would convince her brother to let her stay.

Kit drank a cup of tea in the kitchen of the restaurant; it was her ten minute break and she could feel a headache coming on. Like a whirlwind, a jumble of thoughts and emotions circled around in her head at a frightening speed. There was so much going on and it seemed as though it was happening all at once.

Annie Blyth's brother was in Holbrook and seemed ready to drag his sister back to Boston at any moment. Annie was standing her ground, but Kit knew that was requiring a lot of courage, and she wondered if Annie could hold out. Then there was dear Maggie, dreaming about the handsome cook Joshua Smith and thinking about resigning her positon. Maggie was still not speaking to Kit except as required, but Kit still cared about what happened to her closest friend. Finally, there was the handsome Albert Cleary, a minister and a ranch hand who was in Kit's thoughts more than she cared to admit.

"Kit, you don't look so good. Can I get you anything?" asked the cook's assistant.

"I'm fine, Percy, thank you. Honestly, I just have a lot to think about."

He nodded knowingly. "Can I do anything to help?"

"You are kind, but I'll be fine," she answered as she tried to smile.

Percy shook his head, "I grew up with a house full of sisters – I know that look. You're being stoic, and that means you're worried sick over something."

Kit smiled. "You remind me of my best friend back home. I won't lie to you, I sure could use a friendly shoulder to cry on."

"If you stay late after the restaurant closes, we can have a chat while the staff finishes cleaning the kitchen. You can talk my ear off if you want," Percy answered with a wink as he returned to stirring the enormous pot of soup on the stove.

Annie burst into the kitchen with a handful of orders, "Kit, we need you, there are cowboys everywhere!"

Kit drank the last sip of tea and straightened her crisp white apron. She welcomed the challenge of a restaurant full of cowboys – at least it would take her mind off her aching head.

Later that afternoon, after the cowboys had eaten their meals and the last customers left for the day, the Harvey Girls, the manager, and the cook, Mr. Joshua Smith, left for the day. Kit stayed behind just as Percy had suggested. She brewed a fresh pot of coffee and waited in the dining room as he gave orders to the kitchen staff.

Kit sat down at a table and for the first time in hours, felt her body relax. Percy joined her, slumping into his chair as he said, "What a day! I tell you, we've served some meals today; there shouldn't be a hungry man left in this town after all the work we did."

"It has been a long day. Thank you for staying to talk with me. I must admit I'm embarrassed that I'm taking your time to listen to my little problems."

"Don't you think on it for a minute. I think of you like a sister, and besides, you're the best thing to happen to this restaurant and I can't let you be unhappy. It wouldn't be good for business," he replied with a mischievous wink.

Kit poured a cup of coffee for Percy and one for herself as she answered. "Everything – wait, that's not entirely true – almost everything I'm worried about it is about someone we know. Can you keep a secret?"

"I can cut my hand with a steak knife and we can swear a blood pact," Percy offered in a conspiratorial tone of voice.

"That won't be necessary; you are too valuable as a cook. Besides, Mr. Tate would murder us for getting blood all over his pristine table linens."

"You make a good point. Since we are in Holbrook, I can say this with a straight face: go ahead and shoot!"

Kit giggled at Percy and his bad jokes. It had been days since she'd smiled and laughed and meant it, and it felt good to do that again.

"If you insist. The first person I'm worried about is our Annie."

Percy leaned back in his chair and whistled. "What a mess *that* could have been, and right at lunch time! I was in the kitchen but I heard every word. Did her brother ever come back?"

"Not yet, though for all I know he could be making her pack up everything she owns at this very second, so he can march her back East."

"I would hate to see her go. Kit, since we're trading secrets, I've got one of my own. I think I'm getting sweet on her. I know that sounds ridiculous. What would a refined lady like Annie see in an assistant cook like me, but if we could convince her to stay, then maybe she might give me a chance. What do you think?"

Kit sighed. "I don't think it's Annie you've got to convince, it's that beast of brother of hers. From what I saw today, he seemed real determined, and I don't think much is going to change his mind."

Percy nodded, and studied his coffee cup. "If anyone can fix things for her it's you; I just know it. You've got a knack for solving problems; I can see that. Mr. Harvey can, too. Before you and Maggie arrived, he sent Mr. Tate a message about you two. Told him to make sure you girls were taken care of, and that you both had a future here in the company. Mr. Tate read that to me and Joshua, so I know it's true."

"I promise to do what I can about Annie, but I'm glad you brought up Maggie. I'm worried about her."

"Maggie? She's been quiet since you two aren't chummy anymore, but she looks like she is doing alright," said Percy, as he stood and walked to a pie stand on the counter. "I could use a piece of pie, you want a slice of apple or peach?"

"Both," she answered.

Percy sliced the pie and brought two plates to the table. With a flourish, he served Kit. "Percy, you may have missed your calling! You would have made a good Harvey Girl."

"The uniforms are not made to my size. Now about Maggie, what has you worried about her?"

Kit bit into a slice of peach and tried to think of how to tell him about her closest friend without betraying her confidence. "I can't say what is going on with Maggie, exactly, because it's confidential, but can I ask you a question?"

"That apple is delicious, my compliments to the chef," said Percy. "Oh wait, that would be me. About Maggie? Yes, you can ask me anything, I'll try to answer it."

"What do you know about Joshua? You two seem to be good friends."

"I thought you were asking about Maggie. Joshua? He's not a bad guy, seems a good sort. What did you want to know about him?"

"It's nothing, never mind. I can't think of how to ask what needs to be asked, it's too embarrassing."

"Are you sweet on him; is that what this is about?" asked Percy.

Kit shook her head, "Me? Good heavens, no. He's a nice man, and a great cook, but no, I am not sweet on him."

"Oh!" exclaimed Percy. "I think I understand what you're trying to ask. It's about Maggie and Joshua, isn't it?"

"Yes, but please, I'm begging you: don't say a word to anyone, not a word. You have to give me your solemn oath, your word as a gentleman."

"I've never been described as a gentleman before, but you have my word. I won't tell a living soul. It does seem like they spend a lot of time talking; she talks to him more than anyone else, doesn't she?"

Kit nodded, "She does. Do you understand what I am trying to say, to ask?"

"I believe I do. I must admit, I never paid it much mind, but I'll keep an ear to the ground and see what I can find out for you, how is that? Will that make you feel better? We can make a deal – you help me with Annie and I'll find out what I can about Maggie and Joshua," Percy said with a dramatic flair.

"We don't have to cut ourselves this time, do we?" asked Kit.

"Not at all. Put 'er there, partner!" he said in his best cowboy accent, as he held out his hand to her.

Kit shook his hand; they had a deal. Finishing her cup of coffee, she wondered exactly how she was going to fulfill her end of the bargain.

Kit hurried back to the house, hoping that she wasn't too late, that Annie hadn't left with her brother. Running through the gate, she dashed along the path and up the front stairs, where Annie met her at the door.

"Kit, I am so glad you're here. You're just the girl I needed to see," Annie said as she stepped outside and closed the front door behind her.

"Annie, am I glad to see you! I thought you would be gone back to Boston by now!"

"Not quite." Annie sat in the porch swing.

"Where is your brother?"

"He's not here. I suppose he's staying at a ranch here in Holbrook, although I must admit it would be funny to think of him in one of those saloons," answered Annie. "He sent word that he wants to have dinner tonight, to discuss my returning home. I don't want to face him alone. Please Kit, may I count on you to join me? I know I have no right to ask, but you could help me convince him to let me stay."

Kit sat beside Annie in the swing. "I don't know how much convincing I can do, but I promise I will try. When I spoke to him at the restaurant he didn't seem to be in the mood to talk."

"Oh, that's just how he is when he doesn't get his way. He is a gentleman, and I promise you he won't treat you so rudely at dinner this evening or he will have to answer to me. Hurry and get dressed; he could arrive at any moment."

Kit rushed upstairs and changed her clothes. She put on her best dress, a lilac confection that was embroidered in ivory thread. The sleeves were in the 'leg of mutton' style that made her waist look narrow and her hips curvy. The color complemented her light hair and blue eyes. Admiring her reflection, she was pleased that she had managed to look presentable in such a rush.

Annie knocked frantically on the door. "Kit, we have to hurry, Stewart is here!"

Stewart stood on the front porch, dressed in a suit that was impeccably tailored and coordinated with his hat. Kit thought that in his expensive clothes, he was as out of place in Holbrook as a fishing dory would be. He greeted his sister in a different tone than the imperious one he had used in the restaurant earlier that afternoon.

"Annie, I'm glad you could join me. And who is this?" he asked as he removed his hat.

"I'm Kit Pridgeon, pleased to meet you. Annie has told me so much about you. We met at the restaurant earlier."

Stewart looked at her with a blank, unreadable expression, and then his eyes widened. "Ah yes, the young lady who attempted to speak to me. Forgive me for not recognizing you. In those drab costumes, you all look alike."

Kit bit her lip. She wanted to tell him that she was proud of her uniform and that it was not a 'drab costume,' but she chose to remain silent and be polite. Annie and Percy had asked for her help, and if she had to be on good behavior, then she was going to do her best. After all, she had given her solemn word.

"Stewart, we have a curfew. We have to be back by nine, and I don't want dear Kit to get in any trouble," said Annie as Stewart escorted them to the carriage.

"We are not going very far Miss Pridgeon, a business partner has recently built a house here and he has offered me the use of the property. It is only a short distance."

"Thank you, Mr. Blythe, for your consideration."

"It is my pleasure. I must confess, Miss Pridgeon, that the transformation you have made this afternoon is nothing short of amazing. If I may be so bold, I detect a southern accent. You are not from out West, are you?"

"No, Mr. Blythe, I am not. My family is from North Carolina."

"Tell me, are they pleased to have their daughter on her own in a town like this, without decent society or gentle people of any sort?"

"In truth, sir, my family didn't think it was fitting for a woman to do anything but stay in the tidy little box they had built for me. I do not think they approve."

"And do they communicate with you, write to you, if I may ask?"

"No sir, they do not. I left home without their permission or their blessing."

"Well then, we understand each other. You must convince our dear Annie to return to her senses and accompany me home to Boston, or she will share your fate." The carriage stopped in front of a grand residence constructed of red stone.

The carriage was met by a well-dressed footman who opened the door so Annie and Kit could step down. Kit had never seen a house as large or as extravagant; the red stone was accented with large wooden beams and adobe, giving the residence the distinct air of a Spanish hacienda or a mission. The footman opened the polished oak door and led the party through a great hall of stone and adobe, into a luxurious dining room.

The footman pulled the chair out for Kit and as she sat down she was astonished to see cut crystal chandeliers, gilt framed pictures, and wine glasses trimmed with gold on the table. She felt alarmingly underdressed in her lilac gown as a pair of footmen served the first course.

"Ladies, let us get down to business, shall we? Annie, if you return with me on the next train, I am certain that we can avoid scandal. There are rumors circulating about your mysterious disappearance, but mother has done much to quell them. Our dearest friends believe you are in France, studying art with Aunt Catherine."

"Stewart, I don't want to be disowned – I just want to have an adventure. You are allowed adventures, so why must I be denied?" Annie asked. "Why does there have to be a scandal? I'm not doing anything wrong and I have not acted in any way that would be damaging to my reputation."

He scoffed. "Do be reasonable. You are working as a waitress; is that not scandalous enough? No woman in our family has ever worked in any capacity. If you insist on lowering yourself to such a position, why did not choose a reputable profession, such as a tutor or a governess?"

"You're being rude. We are not alone and your words are insensitive to my dear friend, Kit."

Kit was too overwhelmed by the wealth displayed in the dining room and the delectable bisque to notice that Stewart was being rude or insulting. At the mention of her name, she quickly snapped back to attention. She had a job to do, and she quietly reproached herself for getting lost in the richly decorated room and the food.

"Miss Pridgeon, I offer you my apologies, but perhaps your family's circumstances were different from those of my sister. You may have been expected to work; that is not uncommon in certain classes. Please assist me as I attempt to convince her to see reason."

Kit put her spoon down and looked at Stewart. "Mr. Blythe, it is true that my family was never rich like yours. I do not come from people who would consider hard work beneath them, as you do, but I will say that my circumstances and your sister's are not as different as you would imagine."

"Miss Pridgeon, I meant no offense by what I said. I meant to suggest—" Stewart began, but his explanation was cut short by Kit.

Kit remembered how the rich people in Bridgeton looked at her in the ice cream parlor, and suddenly she was tired of it. "You were going to suggest what, Mr. Blythe? That since you obviously have money and so does Annie that I – a poor working class girl – should say what I can to save my social superior from a fate such as mine? Is that what you meant to suggest?"

"Miss Pridgeon, wait one minute," he said, as his face turned red.

"No, *you* wait one minute; I don't have to. I don't work for you, and you and your money don't mean a thing to me. I love working and making my own salary, I love getting up every morning never knowing what the day will bring. I was promised adventure and a chance to go to new places when I started working for Mr. Harvey, and he has made good on those promises. Mr. Blythe, if your sister is happy and not being hurt, why don't you and your family just continue to lie to your friends? What harm will it cause? Mr. Harvey runs a decent business and treats us with respect – which is more than I can say for you or my own family."

Annie and Stewart stared at Kit. No one said a word. The footmen returned with the second course and a clock ticked on the mantle.

"Thank you, Kit," Annie said. She turned to her brother. "She is right; Mr. Harvey treats us all with respect. What about you, Stewart? Was that respect today, coming in the restaurant and demanding I go home with you?"

"I can see my arguments are useless. Miss Pridgeon, I apologize if I have caused you offense; it was not my intention. Annie, if you don't come home, you may be disowned. Is that what you want?"

"It's not what I want, but if Mother and Father cannot support me in this, cannot allow me a choice about my own future, then how can you expect me to return home? I'll be treated as though I were a child who needed to be told what to do. I'm an adult – I should have the right to decide what I do, where I go, and whom I marry."

Stewart sighed. "Have it your way. If you choose to stay here in this lawless underbelly of the world, then you will not be allowed to rescind that decision. Is your so-called right to decide your own future worth that?"

Kit watched as Annie looked down at her untouched plate of salmon mousse, tears welling up in her eyes. There was an internal struggle inside Annie and Kit suddenly felt terrible that she had spoken in haste.

Kit put her hand on Annie's shoulder. "Annie, I'm sorry about what I said. Perhaps you don't want to turn your back on your family. If you don't go back to Boston, you won't have a *choice* but to work. At least at home, you could remember that you had a wonderful adventure and still have your grand house and easier way of life. Working is hard, do you want that from now on? My family was poor; I have always worked – but you…you don't have to."

Annie looked at her brother, tears streaming down her face, "Stewart, why can't I have both? You do, why is it different for me?"

"Stop being ridiculous – you are not a child. Women are different than men; you are not equipped emotionally or intellectually for the rigors of life outside the home. Unlike your companion, Miss Pridgeon, you are not suited to work. Women of her class are a different breed altogether."

Kit was stunned by Stewart's casual snobbery; his words cut her to her heart. Tears welled in her eyes, but she was not going to let him see that he had affected her. She pushed her plate away and stood, saying, "Mr. Blythe, if you do not mind, I will see myself out. Annie, I will pack your clothes and send them to the train station. Good night."

Kit walked out of the dining room, wiping away tears that escaped her rapidly blinking eyes. She was almost to the front door when she heard Annie's voice. "Kit, wait for me. I'm coming with you."

Kit tuned around. "Annie! You know what this will mean – no more fancy clothes, no more riches! Do want to give all that up just for a job? Do you really want to be working class, like me?"

Annie wiped away her tears and smiled. "Yes, I do. If my family thinks so little of me, then so be it. I don't need them anyway; I can make my own money. After all, I am a Harvey Girl!"

It was nearly nine when Kit and Annie arrived at home. They were both out of breath and their beautiful dresses were covered in dirt from the dusty roads of Holbrook. As they walked in the door, Kit turned to Annie and said, "It's a shame we didn't get to finish our dinner. I don't know about you, but I'm hungry!"

"I am too. Kit, I apologize for what my brother said to you. I hope you know that I don't feel that way about you, or about anyone."

"I know you don't. Let's raid the kitchen and eat something working class like us, how about a sandwich?"

"A sandwich sounds divine, no more rich people food for this waitress!" said Annie as she smiled and accompanied Kit to the kitchen.

As Kit fixed the sandwiches, she thought about Annie and the strength it must have taken to give up being rich in exchange for independence. For Kit, it had been an easy decision; her family was poor and she didn't have anything to lose, but Annie was different. She had everything to lose.

"Annie, it's not too late to tell your brother you've changed your mind. Are you sure about this?"

"I am. I never realized how awful my family was, how mean they truly are, until today. Stewart insulted you and then threatened to cut me out of the family if I didn't submit to him. That is not how I want my family to be one day. When I have children, I will tell my daughter she can be anything she wants to be, and do anything she wants to do – just like the boys. I won't make her choose."

Kit sat down with Annie at the kitchen table, where they ate their sandwiches in silence, both lost in thought. Kit remembered Percy and thought it might cheer Annie to know she might have a beau. "Annie, do you have a fellow back home, or one you're sweet on?"

"I don't. All the men in Boston were just like Stewart and I have been working too hard to think about it, why?"

"What if I told you that a young man who is handsome, funny, and a great cook may be taking a shine to you?"

"Who would that be? There are so many beautiful girls at the restaurant, I can't imagine a man would notice me."

Kit smiled, and dabbed up a crumb with her forefinger. "Percy."

"Percy, the assistant cook? The one that tells jokes and puts everyone at ease with his pleasant personality, that one?"

"Yes, the very same. He may not be wealthy, but he has a good heart," said Kit.

"He does, doesn't he? I never really thought about it, but now that you mention it, I am flattered that he has – how did you put it – taken a shine to me. He is dashing in an impish kind of way, isn't he?"

Kit finished her sandwich as they talked about Percy's attributes. She was pleased that Annie was going to give the assistant cook a chance. That was all he really wanted, a chance, and now it appeared that he would have it. Climbing the stairs to her bedroom, she was content that it was good ending to a bad night.

Kit remained on edge at the restaurant, expecting Stewart to burst in and make a scene, but as time went by, it became obvious that she no longer had that to worry about. Instead, she focused her thoughts on something far more positive: bible study

It was the second Wednesday of the month and Kit was excited. Tonight, after work, she was going to attend bible study at the general store. To her shock, she wasn't sure what was more uplifting, the thought of attending any kind of church service, or seeing the handsome minister, Albert Cleary, once more. She felt slightly guilty planning so carefully what to wear that night.

After work, she rushed back to the house and chose a simple blue skirt, a white blouse and a crisp striped waistcoat. She left her hair in its pompadour and replaced the white bow of her uniform with a navy blue hat. Grabbing her purse and her bible, she was ready to go in a flash.

The sun was still in the sky as she walked downtown. She was not accustomed to walking in the direction of the saloons and the bars, but it was the only way to reach the general store. She kept her head up and hoped that no one from the restaurant would think she was going to a saloon.

The general store was closed when she arrived. She knocked on the door and was greeted by an older woman with gray hair. "How can I help you? Our store is closed."

"Yes ma'am, I have come for the bible study; I was told you hold it here."

"We do, come on in," said the woman.

Kit was greeted by several kind strangers, and recognized two faces in the small crowd. Mr. Cleary was there of course, and she was surprised to see the cook, Mrs. Hill, in a beautiful green suit.

"Miss Pridgeon, bless my soul, it is good to see one of you young women isn't a heathen, if you don't mind me saying so."

"I don't mind. I thought about telling the girls about this, Mrs. Hill. I don't think they're heathens, I just don't think they know about it, is all."

"You are more than likely right, I didn't mean to call 'em heathens. Forgive me Lord," she said as she looked up.

"It's Kit, isn't it, from the restaurant? How good it is to see you. I'm glad and you came to be with us tonight." Albert Cleary extended his hand.

"Mr. Cleary, I mean Pastor, I am glad you invited me."

"All of God's children are welcome, Kit," he answered with a warm smile.

A circle of chairs and makeshift tables had been created out of planks of wood and sawhorses. The scent of leather, kerosene, and sweet penny candy mingled to create a cozy atmosphere in the small general store.

For two hours, Albert Cleary led the group in bible study and prayer. Her eyes followed him as he spoke and taught the words of Jesus. Spiritually and emotionally, it was much needed nourishment for Kit's soul. By the closing prayer, she knew that she wanted to see him again, to have a real conversation with him. It felt sinful that she was developing feelings for the minister.

After bible study was over, Albert walked across the room to join her. "Kit, Mrs. Hill informed me that you ladies have a long way to walk back home. May I escort you?"

"If it's not too much trouble," she replied.

"No, not at all. It would be my pleasure," he answered with a smile that made Kit's heart flutter.

CHAPTER 7

The weeks passed and summer became early fall. Kit was smitten with the charming Albert, although he gave no indication he felt the same way. His pleasant demeanor was the same for all the members of the bible study group, and she wondered if she was imagining that the feelings she had for him were mutual.

Maggie had grown ever more distant, speaking to her only at the restaurant. Kit grew closer to Annie and her hard working protégé Hattie. Kit worried about Maggie but didn't know what to do to change what had passed between them. She thought of apologizing, but then Maggie's stinging words returned to haunt her.

It occurred to Kit one day as she watched Percy and Annie joke and laugh in the kitchen that Percy had not done a very good job of keeping up his end of the bargain. Kit watched and waited for a moment alone with Percy to remind him.

She was in the pantry of the restaurant kitchen refilling the sugar bowls when he came rushing in for a box of pepper, and it was the chance she was looking for. "Percy, do you remember our pact?" she whispered.

"That's right, I am sorry, Kit. I've had other things on my mind."

"You mean like Annie?" she asked under her breath.

"Like Annie, thanks to you. Love can be so distracting."

"Yes, it can. Now, about your end of the bargain – what do you know?"

Percy looked around and said, "There's not much to tell. There is no question she is sweet on him, and I *think* he feels the same way, but there is something else going on."

"Like what?"

"I can't say, but my gut is telling me that if I was Maggie I wouldn't be planning my wedding just yet. I can't stay right now, but I will find out what I can, I promise." He dashed out of the pantry, leaving Kit alone with the sugar bowls and her thoughts.

During the following day's lunch rush, Percy kept his promise. He slipped a note into Kit's apron and gave her a wink. All through lunch Kit wanted to read the note, but just couldn't find the time until late that afternoon. Slipping into the pantry, she slid the note out of her pocket and read it.

Tell your friend that her Romeo already has a Juliet and doesn't need another one. Sorry!

Crumpling up the note and throwing it into the trash bin, she snuck up behind Percy as he was sautéing vegetables. "Note received," she whispered.

"Good," he answered. "Please hand me the salt."

She handed the salt to him and said in a low voice, "He has a girl?"

"Yes," he replied.

Kit sighed. It was even worse than her suspicions. Not only did Joshua not return Maggie's affection, but he had someone else. She thanked Percy and walked back into the dining room.

It had been several weeks since she and Maggie had spoken like civilized people, so she didn't know why it should matter to her, about Maggie. Maggie was a grown woman who could look out for herself and she had already made it abundantly clear that she didn't welcome Kit's interference in her personal life. Yet Kit felt the pull of loyalty, and didn't find it so easy to abandon.

Dinner was served at the usual hour and the girls sat down to a hearty stew made by Mrs. Hill. All through the meal, Kit tried to catch Maggie's eye but Maggie ignored her. After dessert, Kit was no longer content to be subtle. She stopped Maggie as the other girl tried to leave the dining room.

Maggie turned to face her. "What do you want? I couldn't even eat dinner without you making faces at me."

"Making faces? Maggie, I was only trying to get your attention. I need to talk to you; it's important."

"Is it? What do you have to tell me this time? More reasons why I should stay and be a spinster serving steaks to ranch hands?"

Kit wasn't sure what had happened to make Maggie so bitter. She knew that any sane person would walk away, but she couldn't stand by and let her friend make such a colossal mistake without knowing the truth. Kit lowered her voice and said, "I know you don't want to talk to me, but as your friend, I have some news for you."

"My friend! You're so jealous that I have a beau and you don't."

"Maggie, that is just it; it's about your beau."

"What about him? I'm going to resign in a few days so we can be married. Then you will see how ridiculous you have been," hissed Maggie.

"I wouldn't do that just yet," said Kit.

"That's what you said weeks ago! He loves me and we are going to get married. I am not going to let you poison that with your jealousy."

"Maggie, I am not jealous! You were my friend, and I am trying to help you. He can't marry you – he's not going to. He has someone else. There, I've said it."

"How dare you? That is a lie; who told you that?"

Kit stammered, "I can't tell you, please believe me."

"You can't tell me because it's not true – just wait until he marries me. You can go to California; see if I care! I am going to be happily married!" exclaimed Maggie as she stormed out of the dining room and past the other Harvey girls milling in the hall with shocked expressions.

Kit felt her cheeks turn red as she realized the entire house had overheard their exchange. She ran up the stairs and closed the door of her bedroom. She lay on her bed, curled around her pillow, and listened to the raucous sounds of the saloons down the street. No matter what happened, at least she knew in her heart that she had tried to save Maggie from herself. Unfortunately, it wasn't enough.

Maggie was the first Harvey girl to resign in Holbrook at the end of her year. It broke Kit's heart that Maggie was acting so irrationally but there was nothing she could do about it. She had tried to talk to her former friend, but Maggie was so blinded by her romantic ideas that she couldn't be convinced of anything but her own fantasies.

Maggie agreed to stay on until a replacement could be sent from Topeka. She worked in the restaurant and slept in her room at the house, but her behavior became less refined as she drew closer to her last day at work. The quiet flirtation between Joshua and Maggie had turned into a steamy romance that had the entire restaurant abuzz with gossip when Mr. Tate was not around.

Kit hoped she was wrong about Maggie and Joshua, but she had at least one ally in Percy. Only she and Percy exchanged concerned looks around the couple when Maggie and Joshua would sneak a kiss in the kitchen, or Maggie would make a remark about her wedding dress.

Percy had taken time away from his budding romance with Annie to ask about Maggie one day before the restaurant closed. "Kit, did you tell Maggie about her Romeo?"

"I did, but she wouldn't believe me. Thank you, Percy, you have been a true friend. Is there any chance you could be wrong?"

"Not a chance, Maggie is about to have her heart broken, but at least we tried," he said resolutely.

"Yes, we did."

As Maggie's days as a Harvey Girl ended, she became bolder with each passing moment, even going so far as to brag about her future wedded bliss with regular customers. Kit watched as Joshua smiled each time he overheard Maggie hinting that they were going to live happily ever after.

Joshua's behavior did make Kit wonder whether Percy was telling her the truth. Yet she knew she had no reason not to believe him; he seemed like an honest person who, like her, was concerned for Maggie. Judging by appearances, Maggie and Joshua were a couple happily in love, even though that behavior was strictly forbidden at the Harvey Restaurant. Mr. Tate seemed to be the only one in the restaurant who didn't see what was going on between Maggie and Joshua.

Mr. Tate announced that a replacement for Maggie would be joining the Holbrook family in the first week of November. With the announcement, Maggie's departure from the Harvey family was official. She would no longer be a Harvey Girl as soon as the new girl arrived. At night after dinner, Maggie was no longer shy about her dreams for the future but enthralled the girls with all the details of the life she was planning to lead as Mrs. Joshua Smith.

On nights when Maggie sat at the fireside in the parlor and bragged about her future, Kit kept to herself. She would read a novel or practice crochet in her room. Maggie no longer seemed to be the sensible girl Kit once knew when they came out West together; her head had been turned by a man and Kit could only pray that her gut instinct and Percy's warnings were wrong.

Unfortunately for Maggie, Kit was right to be concerned. It was the last day of October and the restaurant was packed with guests. The new train schedule was bringing both cattle men and businessmen to Holbrook, and they all preferred to eat at the Harvey Restaurant than at their hotels. Just before noon, the train arrived and many of the Harvey Girls and staff left the restaurant to greet the new arrivals. Kit, Emma, and Annie stood with Mr. Tate, Joshua, and Percy as the passengers stepped onto the platform.

They gave the customary greeting as they invited the guests in to have a steak and cup of coffee. A passenger standing alone on the platform caught Kit's eye. She was petite, with dark hair piled high under a striking straw hat. Her suit was cut in the latest fashion, and was a brilliant red that set off her rosy cheeks. The woman was beautiful, and Kit wondered who she was, as it was practically unheard of for a woman to travel alone with Holbrook as her destination.

Joshua smiled at Percy and joined the beautiful lady on the platform. Kit watched in horror as he gave her quick peck on the cheek and then embraced her.

Percy looked at Kit and Kit retuned his glance. "That would be Juliet," he whispered to her, as he held the door for a customer.

"Yes, it does look that way. Percy, are they married?" she said quietly so that only he could hear her question.

"I think so. I never read his letters, but they have arrived regularly once a week the whole time he has been here."

"Oh no, poor Maggie." Joshua escorted the woman from the platform to a carriage. "Where are they staying? Surely not at your house?"

"No. He has rented a cottage not far away."

Emma and Annie watched the scene play out with looks of shock on their face. Annie calmly asked, "Kit, was that Joshua?"

"It was. Now, let's get these guests served."

"Was that his sister?" asked Emma.

"I don't know. Come on ladies, we have a job to do."

Kit urged the girls into the restaurant. There would be time for news and gossip later.

It didn't take long for Emma to ask Maggie where Joshua had gone. Maggie told her she didn't know and kept serving customers. Kit watched as Maggie kept nervously checking the kitchen, her curiosity getting the better of her, until Maggie boldly asked Mr. Tate whether Joshua was ill. He answered that he had taken the afternoon off, and would be returning the following morning.

Maggie returned to her usual cheerful self, her concerns for Joshua's health soothed. That night at the house, Emma and Annie were quiet and retired to their rooms early, as did Kit. Not one of the girls asked Maggie about Joshua or her plans for the future that evening.

The next day Maggie, Kit, and the girls were tidying the dining room before the restaurant opened for business. Joshua came to work late, accompanied by a guest. The stunning young woman from the train station was at his side; Kit noticed she was even more beautiful than she had seemed at a distance.

102

"Mr. Tate, everyone, I want to introduce my wife, Mabel Worthington Smith. Annie, Hattie, Emma, Kit, Henrietta, Maggie, this is my Mabel."

There were several gasps of surprise and all eyes turned to Maggie. Kit watched all the color drain from Maggie's face, leaving her looking stricken and suddenly unwell.

"It is so good to meet all of you, especially you, Maggie. Joshua has told me all about you; you've been like a sister to him and I appreciate that. It can get so lonely on these assignments."

Maggie managed a weak, "It's nice to meet you…if you will excuse me," before she rushed out of the restaurant.

Kit's first instinct was to run after her friend, but there was a train arriving soon and she needed to be at the restaurant.

Mabel met everyone in the kitchen and charmed each man in her company before she left her husband to do his job. The tension was high among the girls and Joshua – all the waitresses felt as though Joshua had not just slighted Maggie, but had proven his character to be less than reputable. Kit considered writing a letter to Mr. Harvey, but then she thought about Mr. Harvey's rules regarding romance while the girls were employed as waitresses. It was to keep romance and all the trouble that came with it out of his restaurants – and prevent this very kind of situation.

When the girls were by themselves, all they could talk about was Maggie and Joshua. It was heartbreaking for Kit to hear, but she had tried to warn Maggie, and Maggie refused to listen. Kit said a prayer for her friend as the restaurant closed for the evening.

Maggie was missing from dinner. The mood in the parlor was subdued, and Kit thought about knocking on her friend's door to try to comfort her. When she lingered at Maggie's doorway, all she could hear was the sound of sobbing. Maggie's heart was broken and Kit could do nothing to fix it.

Maggie did not show up to work at the restaurant the following morning. Kit was not surprised Maggie didn't want to face her humiliation so publicly. But by noon, she began to worry about Maggie and asked Mr. Tate's permission to leave and check on her. Reluctantly, Mr. Tate agreed, and Maggie rushed back to the house.

She found the house empty except for Mrs. Hill in the kitchen…and Maggie still weeping behind a locked bedroom door, upstairs.

Swallowing her pride, she knocked on the door. "Maggie, please let me in. It's Kit."

"Go away, I don't want to see you."

"I know you don't. I just want to make sure you aren't sick; I was worried about you."

"I'll bet! You just came here to gloat!" came the voice from behind the door.

"Is that what you think? I came here because I care."

"I don't believe you," said Maggie. "Just go away and leave me alone."

Kit traced part of the doorframe with her finger, hesitating. "If that's what you want, alright. Goodbye, Maggie."

Kit turned to walk down the stairs. When she heard the creak of the bedroom door opening, she turned to see Maggie's tearstained face in the doorway, "Kit, I'm so sorry, please come in."

Kit wasn't sure if Maggie meant it, but as she approached her friend, Maggie began crying. "Kit, I've been such a fool. You tried to warn me and I was so mean to you. I said horrible things and I'm so sorry."

Kit held Maggie as she cried. "Maggie, you were in love and wanted to believe he loved you, too. It's not your fault. Did he tell you he loved you and wanted to marry you?"

Maggie shook her head. "No, he didn't. He kissed me and held my hand, and I foolishly believed that his intentions were honorable. I didn't know men would act that way with a girl they didn't love."

"Can you get your job back? Should we send a telegram to Mr. Harvey?"

"I don't think it will do any good; I didn't care much about how I acted lately, and I'm sure once Mr. Harvey hears that, he won't want me. Besides, I don't want to stay here and work in the same restaurant with Joshua. I can't look at him every day, I feel like such a fool."

"Maggie, my dear, what will you do?" asked Kit.

104

"Go home, I suppose. I am certain my family would love for me to return to Raleigh. I bet I can be married by Easter, if I want."

"Do you have enough money for a ticket home?"

"I do. Besides, Kit, you need to save your money. You are going to need it when you get to California."

Kit cried as she thought about her dream to go to California, "Maggie, it won't be the same without you! I wanted us to go together; who will I take now?"

Maggie wiped her eyes and answered, "It looks to me like you will have your choice of candidates, although I daresay Annie seems like a proper companion for an adventure."

"I guess you're right; Annie so reminds me of you. Maggie, please write – and promise me we will stay friends no matter how far apart we are."

"You have my word that we will always be friends and I will never let another foolish man get between us ever again."

"I have to get back to the restaurant; I will see you tonight at dinner," said Kit.

"Thank you for trying to warn me. You acted as a true friend and I was just too blind to see it. Make my apologies at the restaurant. Since I am no longer a Harvey Girl, I will buy a ticket for the next train out of town."

"See you tonight, I'll help you pack and we can have a going away party."

"Thank you, Kit."

Kit left Maggie and returned to restaurant, where she took Mr. Tate aside. Without explaining the specifics, she extended her regrets that Maggie would be leaving before the replacement arrived, due to unforeseen circumstances.

Mr. Tate was not pleased with the loss of staff, but he understood and whispered to Kit, "Poor girl, I should have warned her about Mr. Smith. Before you girls arrived I had to speak with him regarding his behavior with a saloon girl…but of course, I never told you that."

~

Maggie left the next day and Kit felt as though her own heart was breaking. Her closest friend, and the only person who had been with her since the beginning of this adventure, was gone. It was hard to believe it had only been a year since she left home, but Kit had seen and done more in those twelve months than she had her whole life in Fish Town.

The new girl arrived from Topeka to take Maggie's place. She was bright, articulate, and spoke with a slight Irish brogue. Kit worked with her and by Thanksgiving, the new girl, Colleen Connelly, was even more efficient and faster than Kit had ever dreamed of being. Despite Maggie's leaving and the tension between the cook and the girls, the restaurant was a model of efficiency.

The day after Thanksgiving, a telegram arrived at the restaurant addressed to Kit and Mr. Tate. Mr. Harvey wanted to meet with her in person, in Topeka. Mr. Tate was as shocked as she was. She read the telegram over and over, trying to derive some meaning from the blank space between the words.

"Mr. Tate, what do you think it means? Am I in trouble because of Maggie? After all, I was the acting matron."

"No Kit, I don't think he wants to discipline you. This can only be something good, something important. After all, he is paying for the train ticket."

"I didn't think of that. Thank you, Mr. Tate." She resumed her duties.

Kit would be meeting with Mr. Harvey on the following Tuesday, and staying for two nights in Topeka. The night before her trip, she packed a bag. She included her lilac dress and her two best suits. She went to the box behind the loose board in the closet, where she kept important or valuable things. She counted out a stack of cash. While she was in Topeka she was going to go shopping, and maybe even find an ice cream parlor. Kit didn't care if it was December and the weather was freezing cold.

Mrs. Hill made her a hamper of cookies, fudge, and sandwiches for the trip, and Kit carried her old worn bible. There would be plenty of time for reading while she was on the train back to Kansas.

It was early the next day when she arrived at the Topeka station, where she was surprised to be greeted by her friends Lucy Barrows and Mrs. Appleton. She cried tears of joy to be back at a place had she once called home. Lucy and Mrs. Appleton escorted her to the dormitory, and Mrs.

Appleton beamed with pride that her star pupil was home, even if it was only for two days.

Kit was permitted her own private room, and shared a bathroom with Mrs. Appleton. Some of her old friends were still in Topeka, and they fussed over her as they dressed for work. Charlotte was still her outspoken self and Anne greeted Kit like a long lost sister.

"Kit, you must come and see mother while you are in Topeka; she will want to make you a home cooked meal, I promise. I will even ask her to make you a plate of biscuits, just like we used to have back home."

"I wouldn't dream of missing an opportunity to see your mother. Can you get a message to her? We can go tonight, if that would be convenient."

"It sure would. It's so good to have you back in Topeka," Anne said as she finished pinning her white bow on her head.

The girls left for work and Kit changed out of her traveling clothes into a fresh suit. She went downstairs to the dining room and ate breakfast while trying to calm her nerves. Her meeting with Mr. Harvey was later that morning, and she was anxious despite Mr. Tate's assurance that it must be good news.

The carriage arrived at quarter past ten and Kit tried to keep her mind on the scenes of life in Topeka outside her window. It had only been half a year since she'd left the city, but it seemed like an eternity since she was in a city full of people, department stores, and churches. As the carriage made its way towards the offices of the Harvey Company, she realized just how small Holbrook was in comparison; it was such a backwater that it might as well have been in another country.

The carriage arrived at the office building and a well dressed office clerk met her at the door. She straightened her deep forest green skirt and adjusted the embroidered jacket as she waited for the clerk to announce her arrival to Mr. Harvey.

A minute later, she was shown into the office she remembered from her last visit. It was still just as imposing, but Mr. Harvey was as warm and gregarious as she recalled from the spring.

"Please, Miss Pridgeon, have a seat. I know it's been a long journey from the wilds of Holbrook."

"It has. Thank you, Mr. Harvey."

"Tea, please," he said to the clerk.

Kit was seated on the leather settee by the fireplace and Mr. Harvey sat opposite her. They exchanged pleasantries as the clerk brought in a shiny silver tea service and a tray of sandwiches and cake.

"I hope you don't mind my taking you away from your work, Miss Pridgeon, but there is a matter of some importance I would like to discuss with you."

Kit sipped the hot tea and tried to control her shaking hands as she placed the teacup on the saucer, setting it down on the marble table in front of her.

"Yes sir," she said.

"I regret that Miss Lawson chose to resign. I had hoped to include her in this announcement but I am certain there are other hard working ladies such as yourself that will value an opportunity."

"An opportunity, sir?" Kit asked, her heart racing.

"Yes, an opportunity. You've done a splendid job in Holbrook. Even in a town so small, that is one of our busiest restaurants. I have sent a casual observer to the restaurant from time to time, and each has returned with a glowing report of the food, the service, and your unique offering of tea served cold."

"Yes sir, I can explain."

"There is no need. You have taken up the mantle of matron, in addition to training the staff and leading them in the right direction. Mr. Tate has sent reports praising your skill and I want to offer you a raise."

"Thank you, sir," Kit replied with a smile.

"Your work ethic is outstanding and you have set a good example to all the girls on your staff in Holbrook. Even the Topeka staff still miss you, as I understand it. Although it has only been a few months and you have just celebrated your one-year anniversary with our company, I would like to offer you an opportunity that I mentioned to at our last meeting. Regrettably, there has been a delay in the California expansion, but I do have news that I believe you will find invigorating. I have decided to build a new restaurant in the recently incorporated Pueblo, Colorado."

"Colorado? What's in Colorado?" asked Kit as she tried to hide her disappointment regarding the news of California.

"Miss Pridgeon, what I am offering you is a better opportunity even than California. Pueblo is a city that rivals many back East for opportunity, culture, and industry. It has agriculture, and steel, and it even boasts genteel society."

Kit had to admit it sounded good. It was a chance to go somewhere new and live in a town she had never seen before. She stared at the fire and collected her thoughts. She asked, "Since this is a town of some size, might I assume there are churches?"

Mr. Harvey smiled at her and answered, "Oh yes, my dear. This is no lawless cow town like Holbrook. No, this is a thriving city that reminds me so much of Topeka. We already have a small restaurant there, but I am completing a new, larger one to serve all the travelers who are arriving in Pueblo every day, wanting to take advantage of the opportunities the city offers. Pueblo has been called the 'Chicago of the West,' and I believe that it will be the jewel in our crown one day, with the right staff. I would be pleased if you would consider the position of head waitress and matron at the new restaurant. I will increase your salary to $20 per month, and you will have your own private room and bath."

Kit considered his offer. It was generous, and a private bath would be lovely. "When were you going to open the restaurant?"

"We are projecting a spring opening; the weather in Colorado this time of year is not always conducive to construction projects. I would need you to report to your new post by the first week of April. You do not have to make a decision this morning, if you would prefer to take some time to consider it."

Kit reached for her teacup with hands that no longer shook. Sitting in his office, she thought about her dreams of California. She knew she would get there one day to see the Pacific, just not yet. The opportunity he was offering her was another chance of a lifetime. A raise and a promotion after only one year of service was a compliment, and Kit knew she didn't need any additional time to think about his offer. She already knew her answer. "Mr. Harvey, thank you for the kind and generous offer. I don't have to take time to think about it, you may rely on me. However, may I make one simple request?"

"I'm listening; what is your request?" he asked.

"This new restaurant – it's going to be bigger than the old one, is that correct?"

"It is. What were your thoughts regarding that?"

"If I am to be the head waitress, may I request certain staff members to accompany me to Pueblo, staff that I believe will be essential in the efficient running of the new restaurant?"

"Miss Pridgeon, you have shown an outstanding gift for efficiency and training. If there are members of staff that you would like to take with you to Pueblo, then I will entertain those requests."

"Thank you, Mr. Harvey. I greatly appreciate this opportunity."

"No, Miss Pridgeon. I should be thanking you, for making every restaurant you are employed at a success. If it wasn't for the hard work of decent, upstanding girls like you, my company wouldn't be what it is today."

Kit left the office and her meeting with Mr. Harvey refreshed and with a new sense of purpose. Alone in the carriage, she thought about California and realized that, like Maggie's dreams of Joshua, it was not meant to be. As the carriage carried her through the streets of Topeka, she realized that California for her was never about a specific town or place – it was always about the adventure, a new place just waiting to be explored.

She watched as small snowflakes drifted past the carriage window, just as unexpected as this opportunity to go to Colorado. She had wanted an adventure, to go somewhere she had never been, and see a place she had never known. Kit understood in that moment that it didn't matter if it wasn't California; she was on the adventure of a lifetime.

Christmas in Holbrook was quiet and subdued, although the girls and the staff at the Harvey House tried to make the most of the season. Struck by the holiday spirit, Mr. Tate gave Kit permission to organize a Christmas Eve party at the restaurant, as it was the only space in town large enough for an event where respectable people could enjoy a bit of dancing and revelry.

Invitations were sent to select members of the county and Kit was surprised by the number of people who attended. Many of the ranchers' wives brought pies and cakes to add to the delicious spread laid out by Joshua and Percy with the help of the kitchen staff. Several cowboys that Kit knew from the restaurant even dropped by, and were on their best behavior. Carols were sung, parlor games were played, and dancing made the party a success.

Kit enjoyed the party but her thoughts were never very far from the people she loved during the Christmas season. This was her second Christmas away from the place she'd once called home. The people she cared about were far away, in the state of North Carolina, all the way across the country. The desert of Arizona was very far removed from the green trees and blue waters of her home, so Kit became uncharacteristically nostalgic at Christmas, although she would not change her decision to come out West. Her life back in Fish Town had been far from idyllic, but she still missed her loved ones in that small corner of the world. During the holidays, her thoughts drifted to her family, Mrs. Cates, Letty, and Mrs. Taylor, and recently to her friend Maggie.

Maggie's decision to leave the Harvey Company had been a stinging blow to Kit. Never having been close to her own siblings, she thought of Maggie much like she did her friend Letty – as a sister – and she wished Maggie had stayed in Holbrook. In her heart, she knew that Maggie felt the same way. If only Maggie had never fallen in love with Joshua Smith, she would be still be in Holbrook, planning the adventure to Colorado with Kit.

Watching Joshua dancing with his wife, laughing as they found the mistletoe, only made Kit feel frustrated that her friend had been blinded by love for that scoundrel. Maggie's dream of adventure was over and yet Joshua was happy, and had come out of the whole unfortunate affair smelling like a rose. It was a bitter pill for Kit to swallow.

As she glared at Joshua, her gaze turned to the Christmas decorations made by the other girls and she was reminded that it was Christmas, a time for rejoicing and celebrating; not a time for anger and resentment. If Joshua was guilty of any wrongdoing, it was not up to Kit to judge him. Deciding not to let Joshua ruin her Christmas, she turned her attention to Mr. Tate, who had joined her by the refreshment table. Smiling, she accepted the invitation to dance with him.

Dancing with Mr. Tate, Kit discovered she was not the only person at the party thinking of Maggie.

Mr. Tate cleared his throat as they danced and asked, "It may be forward of me to ask, but have you heard from Maggie – I mean Miss Lawson – since she left Holbrook?"

"I have heard from her, Mr. Tate; she sent me a letter only last week. She has returned to Raleigh and misses us all. I will be sure to mention in my next letter to her that you asked about her."

"Thank you, it would be kind of you to send her my regards. I find that I cannot shake the guilt I feel over her sudden departure from a promising career. If only I had spoken to her regarding Mr. Smith, but I was intending to be gentlemanly, and did not want to share impolite or scandalous news with a lady whom I respected."

Kit understood the pain Mr. Tate felt, the frustration that he had been unable to do anything to stop Maggie from making a terrible decision. She said, "Please put your feelings of guilt away at once; there is no need for you to blame yourself. I tried to warn her too, on countless occasions – but to no avail. Even if you had spoken to her, using the plainest of words, she would not have listened. It was not in her heart to listen to anything but the sweet nothings of a scoundrel. I am sorry to use that word, but it is how I feel about the man."

Kit searched Mr. Tate's face for any sign that she had spoken too harshly about an employee who outranked her in the company. Instead, she saw the lines in Mr. Tate's brow soften.

He replied, "I'm reluctant to admit the truth, but I've been blaming myself for some time. Your words have lifted that enormous burden from my shoulders." Leaning in close, he whispered, "I agree with you; he is a scoundrel of the worst sort. I am unable to dismiss him without revealing the reason behind my decision, and that would bring Maggie's good name into question."

Kit sighed. "We wouldn't want Maggie's name to be smirched. At least we can take comfort that no real damage was done to her reputation, as no one knows of the incident except for the staff here in Holbrook."

Mr. Tate replied, "That is how I intend to keep it. I will provide her with the highest recommendation, and a reference, without hesitation."

"Mr. Tate, you are a wonderful person. We are fortunate to work for you."

Mr. Tate blushed in response to Kit's compliment, and as the music came to an end they parted ways on the dance floor. Kit felt a flutter in her chest, a pang of regret that she would be leaving behind good people here in Holbrook when she left for Colorado in the spring.

~

The week after Christmas, temperatures plummeted and Holbrook was gripped by a cold snap that surprised even the grittiest of cowboys. Water froze in the watering troughs that lined the dirt streets of the town, as frigid winds made any time spent outdoors miserable. At the restaurant, the waitresses huddled around the ovens in the kitchen and the small number of customers did not mind wearing the required jackets.

After hours at home, Kit and the other girls crowded around the fireplace in the parlor dressed in coats, gloves, and hats. Not one of them wanted to be away from the fire for even a minute, it was too cold. Everything came to a standstill in Holbrook for those few days, except the train. It still arrived on its daily schedule, but was devoid of customers during the bad weather. The restaurant was nearly deserted except for the sheriff and a few die-hard cowboys who spun stories of the sights they had seen in the frozen landscape around Holbrook.

Life was at a standstill as Kit waited for the mail to run once more, since that was also delayed. The cold was affecting everything west of the Mississippi; blizzards and terrible weather gripped every western state, according to a traveler from Kansas. Looking out the window at a world held hostage by winter's might, she believed him.

After several days of record-breaking cold temperatures, the cold snap ended – and no one was more pleased than Kit. At Christmas, she had spent several hours in her room writing letters to everyone she missed. She was hoping to hear back from her loved ones and was starved for any news. With no other form of entertainment, she looked forward to the mail with the same enthusiasm children felt for an upcoming birthday or holiday.

Two weeks went by before dependable mail service returned to Holbrook. Kit was almost bedside herself with anticipation when she heard rumors that a mail bag had been delivered to the train station. All the girls were giddy with excitement for any letters or scraps of information as it had been three weeks since a single letter had been delivered in Holbrook.

After the restaurant closed for the evening, the girls made their way home, where they were delighted to find a small bundle of mail in the foyer. Descending upon the mail like hungry wolves, they quickly sorted the envelopes, and the girls retired to their rooms in silence, all reading letters from home – all except for Annie.

Kit stood by her friend and put her hand on her shoulder. "Cheer up, Annie, you may not have any letters, but at least you won't have any bad news, either."

Annie smiled and nodded her head, "I suppose you're right. It's just hard sometimes."

"I know – it feels like we're so far away from our old life, like it's a distant memory."

Annie pointed at the small bundle of letters in Kit's hand, "Looks like you have plenty to keep you busy. Don't worry about me; go read your letters."

Kit smiled and left Annie in the foyer as she turned and rushed upstairs. Turning on the kerosene lamp, Kit sat by the bed and opened the letters one by one, savoring each word. Maggie missed her and her work as a Harvey Girl. Her father was delighted to have her back at the family store, but Maggie was already bored. Mrs. Taylor sent her love and promised to send her a leftover Christmas fruitcake. Mrs. Cates sent a postcard from Bridgeton that Kit studied with interest.

The postcard depicted main street along the docks and marina. Kit sighed. In her mind she remembered the ice cream parlor, the general store, the way she and Letty would run along the dockside, waving at the boat captains they knew. It had been a long time since she had seen Bridgeton, a place she'd sworn she would never see again when she ran away. Wiping away a tear, she opened the next letter absentmindedly and was shaken to her core by its contents.

Sister,

Letty made me promise not to write to you but it wouldn't be right not to. I am not a man for words so I will come to the point. Letty is ill and she won't be with us much longer. She misses you and wants to see you one more time before she is called to Heaven. I pray this letter finds you in time.

Thomas

114

Kit gasped as she read the words. Letty was dying? How was that possible? She hadn't said a word about it in her letter before Christmas. Frantically, Kit tried to imagine likely scenarios that may have led to dear Letty's illness. Had there been an accident? She read the letter again, trying to decipher any meaning at all from the brief message her brother had sent.

Kit knew her brother Thomas was a hardworking man but barely educated, so he must have had someone else write the letter for him – someone who didn't know what had happened to Letty. That was the only reason she could figure why he wouldn't have written anything to explain just how Letty was sick.

Her mind racing, Kit hastily threw her clothes and shoes into the trunk that sat at the end of her bed. She was so preoccupied by her preparations that she forgot all about dinner until Annie knocked on the door.

"Kit, are you unwell? You missed dinner," Annie asked from the other side of the door.

Kit opened the door and began sobbing uncontrollably. "Oh Annie, this is horrible, horrible!"

"My dearest Kit, what has happened? Are you unwell? Shall I call for the doctor?"

"No, I'm fine, but Letty, my friend from back home…she's dying, look, it says it here in this letter." Kit thrust the tearstained letter at Annie.

Annie read the letter. "Kit, come over here. Sit down," she said, as she urged Kit to sit on the bed. "Take a moment to think."

Kit moved a pile of hats out of the way and sat on the bed, her face wet with tears. Her chest was heaving as she tried to catch her breath.

"That's better. This letter is vague; it doesn't tell you what happened to her. Perhaps it's not so bad?"

"Oh Annie, I pray that you're right but you don't know Thomas, my oldest brother. He can barely read or write, so for him to send me a letter, he must expect the worst."

"My dearest Kit, I understand, I do, but you must be strong. Modern medicine has come a long way, maybe with a good doctor she'll recover from whatever misfortune has befallen her?"

"Oh, Annie, that's all I can hope for, but the place I came from its not like Boston. There was never enough money for even the simplest things – no one I knew ever had enough to pay for a fancy doctor."

"We'll see about that!" said Annie as she stood up. "Keep packing, I will be right back."

Kit closed her trunk, all packed and ready to go. She thought about the train ticket back to Fish Town and wondered how much money it was going to cost. Opening the desk drawer, she removed a small cigar box. She lifted the lid and counted the money she had managed to save. Walking to the closet, she retrieved yet another box from behind a loose board in the closet. This box contained sentimental treasures and another small stash of cash.

One of the only bright sides to living in Holbrook was not having a single department store that tempted her to squander her earnings on a new hat or waistcoat. Counting the dollars and coins, she was amazed to find that even after the trip to Topeka in November, she still had nearly one hundred dollars saved up. After the train ticket to Bridgeton and back, she would have a little money left over. Maybe enough to pay a doctor, she hoped, if she didn't stay at a hotel or buy food along the way.

As Kit contemplated ways to save money on her trip Annie returned, gripping an embroidered silk purse in her hand.

Annie closed the door and handed the purse to Kit. "Take this with you, you might need it."

Kit held the exquisitely sewn purse in her hand, puzzled why Annie would think she would need an expensive handbag in Bridgeton. But it was a lovely gesture. Kit was impressed by the purse, a relic of Annie's life as a socialite.

"Kit, open it," Annie said with a tender smile.

"Oh." Kit finally understood. She opened the purse to find a roll of money stashed inside the delicate bag. Removing the money, Kit gasped. She'd never held that much money in her hand in her life – by her estimation it was well over a thousand dollars. Shaking her head, she thrust the money back into the bag and handed it to Annie.

"Annie, that is a thoughtful gesture, but I can't take your money."

"Yes, you can. If it saves Letty's life, you can take that money and do some good with it."

"But Annie, what if you need it? I don't want to take all the money you have in the world – I don't know when I can ever pay it back."

"Trust me, that is not all the money I have in the world. My family may have disowned me, but I am not without means."

"It wouldn't be right." Unsure what to do with the purse, Kit set it on the dresser and fiddled with a stack of blouses. "I can pay you back, but it may take years."

"Look, if you don't feel right about taking all if it, just borrow a few hundred. If you need more, or a letter of credit, send me a telegram."

Kit considered Annie's words, but she was raised not to take money from others and it was hard for her to accept charity.

"Kit, listen to me; this is very important. That money is collecting dust but it may save a life and it would make me happy to know it did some good in the world." Annie reached for the purse and pulled out a small stack of cash, handing it to Kit. "I will not hear one more word about it, do you hear me? You saved my life when you convinced me that I could do anything, that I could live a life of adventure, that I could be someone I'd never imagined. This is the least I can do. Promise to send me a telegram if I can do more."

Kit knew that Annie was right, so she swallowed her pride. Vowing not to let herself get in the way of helping Letty if she could, she said, "Annie, whatever I don't spend, I will bring back to you, I promise. Thank you – this means so much to me."

"Your friendship means so much to me. I only wish I could go with you, but someone is going to have to stay here and keep these hungry cowboys and travelers fed."

Kit nodded and wiped a tear off her cheek, feeling a little better about the unexpected trip back home. She only hoped she would not be too late to save Letty, and if she couldn't do that, say goodbye.

~

Kit was moved by Annie's generosity, and pleasantly surprised that Annie was not the only one willing to help her in her time of need. After receiving Kit's urgent telegram requesting time off for a family crisis, Mr. Harvey forwarded instructions to Mr. Tate to purchase a round trip ticket for Kit and put it on the company tab. Mrs. Hill prepared a hamper of cookies for the trip, and Percy sent along her favorite chicken salad sandwiches.

Kit was nearly brought to tears when Mr. Tate handed her a small envelope that he collected from the girls and the staff at the restaurant. Inside the envelope, Kit found fifty dollars of 'traveling money,' as he called it. Her heart was full of gratitude for her adopted family in Holbrook, which made the decision to go to Colorado in the Spring even more bittersweet.

As Kit traveled eastward, back to her hometown of Bridgeton, she tried to concentrate on the view outside her window and the pages of her favorite book. The book, *Pride and Prejudice,* was a gift from Mrs. Cates to Kit before she had left for Kansas. Reading the familiar words, she found that every passage about Elizabeth's sister Jane reminded her of Letty. Thinking of Letty, she prayed that she would see her friend alive once more.

After many days on the train, she arrived at the station in Bridgeton at lunchtime. Stepping off, she was struck by how familiar her hometown was to her eyes, and yet it felt strange and alien at the same time. The pine trees, green even in winter, seemed to be bright and decadent after months spent in the red and brown dust of the desert.

As she breathed in the salt air, it seemed like a lifetime since she left home. Unsure of the reception she would receive at home in Fish Town, Kit walked into the train station and asked the station master about a carriage for hire or a cab to a hotel not too far from her home.

He called a porter and arranged for a carriage to take her to the Bridgeton Hotel, a three- story brick and timber building on Main Street. As the carriage approached the hotel, Kit had the uneasy feeling she was going to be found out at any moment, that the carriage driver would turn around and say to her, "You don't belong here, you belong in Fish Town."

Kit had not made a reservation for her stay at the hotel, and she hoped there would be a vacancy. As she entered the lobby, she was greeted by a well-dressed man who appeared to be only slightly older than herself. He greeted her as though she belonged in that part of town, the rich section. Despite her anxiety for Letty, she smiled to herself as she enjoyed being mistaken for a lady.

118

The hotel had several vacancies and Kit asked for a modest room. Within minutes, the bellhop transported her trunk up the stairs and showed her to her room. The room was opulent by Bridgeton standards, with a brass bed and a view of the marina where wealthy citizens moored their private yachts.

The bellhop showed her the private bathroom adjoining the room and the gas lighting. She tipped the young man and then left the beautiful room with its delightful view and returned to the concierge to request a carriage.

The carriage driver asked for an address and looked puzzled when she said Fish Town. She repeated the address, and he replied, "Ma'am are you aware that part of town is not safe for you?"

Kit smiled. "I am, Sir, thank you. You do not need to go all the way to Fish Town. If you prefer, you may take me as far as 5th Street."

"I will deliver you to the address you requested, if that is your wish, Miss."

"It is, thank you."

The carriage made its way through the rich section of Bridgeton and Kit prayed that she was not too late, that the letter had not been too delayed. The houses outside the carriage window became storefronts and churches, then modest middle-class homes crowded her view as the scenery changed. Kit would have enjoyed this view of her hometown, but her thoughts were consumed by her friend's welfare.

Small, ramshackle houses crowded together in rows, many with broken porches and slanting rooves. Scrawny children dressed in ragged coats, without shoes even in winter, rushed to do their chores as the carriage slowly passed by. People stopped and stared at the sight of a carriage in Fish Town, just as she would have done not too long ago. Anyone wealthy enough to afford a carriage ride had no business in this part of Bridgeton.

Finally, the driver stopped the carriage in front of Letty's house, and climbing down, he knocked on the carriage door. As Kit opened it, he said, "Ma'am are you certain this is the correct address? Would you like for me to wait for you? This is no place for a lady."

"Thank you for your concern, but I will be fine. There is no need to wait," she said. She paid him and stepped out of the carriage.

After it drove away, she looked at the front porch of Letty's house. Her lip quivering, she tried to be brave and face the possibility of her friend's death. Walking through the gate and up the front steps, she realized that she had never used the front steps or knocked on the front door. All her life, she'd used the kitchen door. As she knocked with a gloved hand, she realized that she no longer felt at home here in Fish Town.

~

The door of Letty's home was opened by Mrs. Harper, who looked thinner than Kit remembered. The woman didn't recognize Kit as she asked, "Ma'am, what is your business here?"

Kit smiled warmly, "Mrs. Harper, it's me, Kit," she said, hesitating to finish the sentence. "I've come to see Letty."

Mrs. Harper exclaimed and burst into tears, and Kit stepped in and put her arms around the woman. "I'm so sorry Mrs. Harper, I got here as fast as I could, you see there was a delay in the mail..."

"Letty is upstairs. She'll be happy to see you, Kit, if she recognizes you."

Kit's heart burst with happiness. Letty was still alive. She wasn't too late after all!

"Can I go up and see her?"

Mrs. Harper shook her head and wiped her eyes with her apron. "You know you can. Please go on up, I'll be up directly with some tea for you and broth for my girl."

Kit lifted the hem of her skirt, trying not to trip on the steep stairs that led to the second floor. Racing up the wooden steps and down the hall to Letty's room, she felt like a kid again.

The door was open and Kit saw Letty's small frame under a mountain of quilts. An older woman, Mrs. Quidley, sat at her bedside with a bible in her lap. Kit knocked on the open door and stepped into the room, not wanting to disturb Letty if she was asleep.

Mrs. Quidley turned to look at Kit, a glimmer of surprise on her face as she spoke in a whisper, "Kit Pridgeon, I thought you were dead or run off, what brings you back to Fish Town?"

Mrs. Quidley was nearly eighty years old, and had been nursing sick folks and midwifing for the people of Fish Town since she was a girl. Kit felt good to be recognized by her, as Mrs. Quidley was a respected member of the community and a woman Kit had always looked up to.

"Mrs. Quidley, I feel better knowing you are sitting with her. Is she asleep?"

"She is. She goes in and out of sleep more and more these days."

"What happened to her? Can she be cured?"

Mrs. Quidley slowly stood and motioned for Kit to follow her into the hallway. Closing the door to Letty's bedroom, Mrs. Quidley told Kit about Letty's condition.

"My dear, it is a blessing you are here. When I heard you left to go out west, I knew you were going to be fine, going to do something with your life. You're smart and quick, and you got here just in time."

"Just in time? What do you mean – is she bad off?"

"She is, make no mistake about it, but her ma and pa won't listen to me when I tell them she needs a doctor. I have done all I can do for the poor lamb, but what she has wrong with her, no amount of my nursing is going to fix. There ain't a tea, a tincture, or a compress that will bring her back to health."

"Have they called a doctor to come see her?"

"No, they haven't." Mrs. Quidley lowered her voice and leaned in close to Kit, holding onto her arm to keep steady on her feet. "Jacob and his father were caught out in a squall back in November – a terrible one it was, and their boat ran aground. They survived, but it took every last dime of the family's money to fix their boat so the family wouldn't starve. I don't think they got two pennies to rub together, but you know how the Harpers can be. Their pride won't let them ask a soul for help."

"So they haven't called the doctor because they don't have any money to pay one." Kit's heart lifted.

"That's what I think but it's not all. It don't help none that her father believes that if God meant for her to be healed, He would heal her. Old-fashioned notion in this day and age, but he won't be budged."

121

Kit frowned thoughtfully. "Mrs. Quidley, I believe you're right. I came home just in time."

"I've been praying for a miracle. It's just like the good book says, the Lord works in mysterious ways. Maybe he sent you to be that miracle."

"Don't say that, not yet. What do you think is wrong with her?"

"I can't say for certain. All I know is she won't eat a bite of food. Her fever won't budge an inch no matter how many cold compresses I put on her, and she screams in pain if she is moved."

Kit leaned against the door for support. "My poor Letty. You are right, Mrs. Quidley, she does need a doctor. Do you know a good one here in town?"

"I do, but I don't have any money to pay him."

"Don't you worry about that, I have some money. Where can I find him?"

"If you will stay here with Letty, I'll send my grandson to go get the doctor. He can get there a whole lot faster than me or you can."

"Yes ma'am, I will stay right here."

Kit walked into Letty's room and picked up Mrs. Quidley's bible from the chair by Letty's bed. The leather was faded and the pages crinkled in a soft and reassuring way as she opened the book. Letty was sleeping, or at least she looked as though she was. Kit reached out and put her hand on her friend's forehead.

Mrs. Quidley was right – Letty's skin was burning with fever. Placing the bible on the nightstand, Kit walked to the washstand and poured water into the basin. Soaking a towel in the cold water, she folded it into a compress and placed it gently on Letty's forehead.

Letty murmured incoherently in her sleep as Kit sat down at her side. Seeing Letty like this was almost more than Kit could stand. The Letty she knew was funny and full of energy, with a rosy complexion. This ashen, shriveled woman who lay in bed was a pale shadow of that girl. To Kit, she looked as though she was not far from the grave.

Kit's eyes filled with tears as she stared at her friend. It was impossible that Letty was dying – she just would not accept it. She lowered her head in prayer as Mrs. Harper brought up a pot of tea, a bowl of broth, and a plate of toast and butter. Kit looked at the plate and thought about what Mrs. Quidley said about the family not having any money. She saw the gesture for what it was worth, and felt guilty for accepting it, but if she said no, it would be an insult.

"Mrs. Harper, how kind of you to bring tea and toast. I'm starved and haven't eaten a bite since dinner last night."

"I doubt you been fed right since you left home. You look peckish."

"Yes, ma'am."

"I know my Letty is glad to have you home, have you seen your pa and ma?"

Kit bit her lip at the mention of her family. She had not spoken to them or told them she was coming home, so she answered, "No ma'am, I came straight here."

"You didn't bring a bag with you, did you? I didn't see one when you come in the house."

"No ma'am, it's back at the hotel."

Mrs. Harper's eyes opened wide in surprise that someone she knew was staying uptown at the hotel. "The hotel? You staying there? What in the world for?"

"Ma'am, I don't mean to speak ill, but my folks and I aren't on the best of terms."

Mrs. Harper flapped her hand tiredly. "I'm sorry, I didn't mean to meddle and pry. It's none of my business. You can stay here with us if you like – there's always room. I could you put you up in Rosie's room, she won't mind. Reckon she'd like the company."

"Mrs. Harper I don't want to be any trouble. You have your hands full enough as it is without me being in the way."

"Stuff and nonsense, you wouldn't be no trouble. I'm thankful you're here with my girl. If anyone can lift her spirits, it's you. She's missed you something terrible."

123

Kit felt guilty that she had left Letty all alone in Fish Town, but she knew her friend. Letty would never have been happy out west and Kit would never be content to live her life stuck in a small town, always defined as a Fish Town girl.

"Mrs. Harper, I appreciate the invitation, but I already paid for a room at the hotel for tonight."

"I know it's not much, but I would appreciate it if you would stay here."

"Yes, ma'am."

"I'd better see about supper. Holler if you need me."

Mrs. Harper walked out of the room, leaving Kit alone with her best friend. Kit wiped her face and poured a cup of tea. Opening the sugar bowl, she was surprised to see a small amount of white sugar in the bottom of the dish. Mrs. Harper was treating her like an honored guest, and it nearly broke her heart.

In so many ways she felt like the same girl who used to run barefoot down the streets here in this poor neighborhood, but a glance at her clothes, her stylish shoes and purse quickly reminded her that she was different than she used to be. She was no longer the poor daughter of a fisherman, she was a Harvey Girl – something that these people she'd once called family would never understand.

Kit was beginning to wonder if the doctor was ever coming. Mrs. Quidley was the oldest woman she knew; was it possible she was not as sharp as she seemed? Had she somehow forgotten? As the afternoon began to fade, Kit began to feel frustrated and worried. Sitting beside Letty's bed, she watched her friend breathe, hoping that each one would not be her last.

The quiet rhythm of Letty's breathing and the familiar sounds of the Harper household soon lulled Kit into a deep sleep that came from the physical exhaustion of the trip and the mental exhaustion of the fear and anxiety that Letty would die at any moment.

And so she was unaware that she was being watched from the doorway until a gentle masculine voice spoke to her.

124

"Kit. Kit, wake up. It's Jacob."

Kit's eyes fluttered open and she was pleasantly surprised to see Jacob's familiar face. Letty's older brother was standing at her side.

Kit jumped up and threw her arms around him in an unmannerly expression of joy. "Jacob! It is so good to see you!"

Jacob wrapped his arms around her in a bear hug. "Kit, y'are a sight! I was right. Y'are a fine woman."

Kit drew back from him, realizing that her behavior was too forward. "I am sorry Jacob, I didn't mean to do that. Forgive me."

"There's nothing to forgive, Kit. It's good to have you home. Letty will be happy to see you."

Kit wondered if Letty would ever wake up again; she had slept all day and never even batted an eyelash. To Kit, it looked like Letty was slipping away.

"Jacob, I fear she may not wake up, that I missed saying good bye to her."

Sorrow deepened the lines on his face. "It doesn't matter. She knows yer here, that you came all this way. That's what's important."

Kit and Jacob talked about Letty and Jacob's wife Emily, Kit's younger sister. They spoke as old friends, which was exactly what Kit needed that afternoon as she waited for the doctor.

Shadows began to creep across the room as Kit turned on the kerosene lamp by Letty's bed. Sighing, she was beginning to believe that help was never coming. Jacob sat at her side and together they both watched Letty sleep. The silence was broken by the return of Mrs. Quidley. who was accompanied by a well-dressed young man, whom she introduced as the doctor.

"Jacob, Kit, Letty, this here is Doctor Kellerman."

Kit was the first to speak to the doctor. "Doctor Kellerman, I am Kit, Kit Pridgeon. I am so glad you are here. Thank you for coming."

125

The doctor smiled at Kit and said in a soothing voice, "It was no trouble, none at all. Who is this young woman's next of kin? I must have permission before I examine her."

Mr. Harper wasn't home, so Kit and Mrs. Quidley both looked at Jacob. Kit hoped Jacob didn't share his father's views on faith, healing, and medicine. Holding her breath she waited for him to answer. "I'm her older brother. You have my permission to do whatever you have to do to save my sister, but Doctor, I'm ashamed to say, I can't pay. I can pay a little over time but I don't have money to pay you tonight."

Doctor Kellerman put his hand on Jacob's broad shoulder and said, "Mr. Harper, I'm not worried about payment. Let's see how this goes – if it goes well, maybe we can work out an arrangement. I don't get enough fresh fish to eat, and I understand you are in the fishing business."

Jacob's face lit up at the suggestion that he could repay the man in trade. "Much obliged, doctor."

Doctor Kellerman turned to the ladies in the room and said, "If I can have one of you ladies stay in here with me while I examine Miss Harper, I would appreciate it."

Mrs. Quidley spoke up. "Kit, why don't you stay in here. Jacob and I will wait in the hall."

After Jacob and Mrs. Quidley left, Kit found herself alone in Letty's bedroom with the handsome young doctor. He was slightly taller than she was, with dark hair and a trim beard. His frame was slim and his shoulders not much wider than her own, but Kit found that she liked this man immediately.

"Miss Pridgeon, can I get you to hold that lamp while I examine your friend?"

Taking the lamp, Kit whispered, "Doctor, it was nice of you to tell Jacob he could pay you in fish, but I have money to pay you with, if you need it. If it will help."

"That won't be necessary. My wealthy patients pay me enough that I don't have to charge everyone who needs my help."

His generosity warmed Kit's heart as she held the lamp. In the light of the kerosene lamp, Kit watched as Doctor Kellerman carefully, tenderly touched

Letty's forehead, checked her pulse and carefully moved to her abdomen. At the slightest touch, she moaned in her sleep and stirred, as though trying to avoid his touch.

He turned to Kit and asked, "How long has she been like this?"

"I don't know for sure. I only just here, Mrs. Quidley knows, I will call for her."

Mrs. Quidley came in the room and Doctor Kellerman conferred with the older woman as though she was a colleague. After speaking with her, he made a diagnosis that was hopeful and terrifying.

"Letty is suffering from an inflamed appendix. It has not ruptured, but it may any time. Her condition is most dire. She must have surgery or she will die."

"But...isn't surgery dangerous?"

"It is, but if we do nothing, she will die. The nearest hospital is in New Bern. They can perform the procedure, but her chances of rupturing the organ on the rocky roads to town are too great to risk it, and there is not a moment to lose."

"What are you saying, Doctor, that there is no hope?" Jacob asked in a stern voice.

"The chances are small, but I may be able to perform the procedure here. I will need more light and a clean place to do it. I don't have any ether, but she is unconscious already, which may be a mercy."

Kit suddenly felt faint as she realized what the doctor was suggesting. "You want to operate here, at her house, tonight?"

"Yes, tonight."

"Doctor, I can assist you," said Mrs. Quidley.

"Good, with your experience, I am certain she will have the best chance we can give her."

Jacob sat in the chair and said, "Doctor, my pa and ma will never let this happen without good reason. Can you give me a moment to talk to them?"

"Do what you must to convince them. Truthfully, this is the only way to save her life."

Jacob nodded his head and turned to leave, Mrs. Quidley watched him and said. "I am going too. If he can't talk some sense into the Harpers, I sure as heck will!"

Kit thought about Letty's feelings for her brother and his heartfelt letter. She knew he would want to be there for this. She walked out of the room and down the stairs, where she found Letty's younger brother, Edward, listening at the parlor door.

"Edward, would you like to make a dollar?"

The teenager's eyes opened wide at the mention of money. "I sure would!"

"I will give you a whole dollar if you run and fetch my brother, Thomas. Tell him it's urgent and that it has to do with Letty."

The young man looked at her, quizzically. "I sure will. But wait – who are you, and where do you live?"

She swatted his arm. "Edward, you know full well who I am. It's me, Kit Pridgeon! Now hurry! If you rush I will throw in an extra quarter!"

"Yes, ma'am!" he said as he raced out the front door.

From the sound of the voices in the parlor, there was a heated discussion going on. Kit hoped Jacob and Mrs. Quidley could convince the Harpers that God sometimes needed a little help. If that didn't work, then she hadn't come all this way to save Letty's life.

She had come all this way for a funeral.

CHAPTER 8

Edward returned, out of breath, twenty minutes later, with Thomas right behind him. Kit hugged her oldest brother and paid Edward $1.25 for his effort. The young man beamed as he ran upstairs with his new-found wealth. Thomas looked at his sister and shook his head as the discussion in the parlor turned into an argument.

"Kit, I see my letter found you. What the devil is happening? Is Letty still alive?"

"She is, but she needs surgery tonight or she won't be much longer. Jacob and Mrs. Quidley are trying their best to convince old Mr. Harper to let the doctor do what has to be done."

"Surgery? Sounds mighty dangerous."

"It is, but Thomas, are you ready to lose her? Don't you want to marry her and have a house full of children?" asked Kit as she brushed a strand of blonde hair out of her eyes.

Thomas leaned against the door of the parlor, from where the sound of Mr. Harper's voice was now booming through the house. He looked at Kit, and then to her surprise, he threw open the door.

Kit stood in the hallway and witnessed what happened next. Her brother walked into the room and immediately commanded the attention of everyone there as he said, "Mr. Harper, do you claim it's God's will for daughter to die? Is that true?"

"It is, son. It's Letty's time to be called to Heaven. It's God's will."

"I disagree with you, and I have the right to demand that you allow this surgery to take place. I intend on marrying your daughter, so you are not only deciding for her – but now you are speaking for me, her future husband. I say that God has sent us this doctor and that if we keep him from doing all he can to save her life, then we are guilty of questioning God. I don't want to be guilty of that, do you?"

Kit watched as Mr. Harper looked down at the hardwood floor, a look of confusion spread across his face. Finally, he looked up at Thomas and said, "Thomas Pridgeon, I have known your family for many years. I respected your grandfather and your father, and I can't fault ya for saying what yer saying but I don't trust it. It's not right for man to be playing at being God."

Thomas listened, and nodded. "Mr. Harper, you've said your piece, now let me be plain. You can agree to let her have the surgery here in this house, or make no mistake – I will carry her out of here and the doctor can do what he has to do at my house. If we leave here like that, I promise you and your family will be dead to me and my kin – as dead as Letty if you let her die."

Kit stood in silence watching the drama unfold. She'd never heard her brother speak to anyone like that, and she was even more amazed when Jacob stood up beside him. "Pa, I respect you but I got to stand with Thomas on this. If you let Letty die, you might as well bury me right along with her because I won't be a Harper no more."

Mr. Harper's shoulders slumped in defeat, and he growled, "I can't fight all of ya. If she dies because of this foolhardy new-fangled medicine, I want ya to know that I believe both of you will burn in hell!"

He stormed out of the room, glaring at Kit as he passed her in the hall.

"Kit, go tell the Doctor he can get started!"

Kit ran up the stairs. The Doctor was monitoring Letty's pulse and said to Kit, "Her pulse is weak. I fear she may not have much longer to live, even with the surgery."

"Doctor, do what you have to do. If there is any chance at all that she will live, you have to try to save her."

"I will do everything I can, Miss Pridgeon. You have my word."

Mrs. Quidley, Thomas, Jacob, and Mrs. Harper joined Kit as they scrambled to gather every lamp and candle they could. It was decided that the parlor was the cleanest room of the house, with its sparse furnishings and wood floors. A roaring fire was lit in the fireplace and Mrs. Harper's kitchen table was brought in to be used for the operation. Kit boiled water and gathered rags as the doctor washed his hands with the strongest lye soup Mrs. Harper had at her disposal.

Mrs. Quidley asked Kit to help in the operating room as Mrs. Harper was nearly faint, and it would be indelicate for the men to see Letty in a state of undress. Praying for strength, Kit pulled Mrs. Quidley aside as the doctor rushed to prepare for the operation.

"Mrs. Quidley, I'm scared to death. I've never seen anything like this. I faint at the sight of blood, what am I going to do?"

Mrs. Quidley held her hand and looked into Kit's eyes and said calmly, "My dear girl, you are stronger and braver than you know. You live out west with them cowboys and Indians and you're worried about a little blood? Stuff and nonsense – there ain't nothing to it. Letty is your friend – heck, if your brother has his way she'll be your sister before too long. Think of her, of how much you want her to live, and pray that God gives you courage and strength."

Kit nodded her head at Mrs. Quidley's words. As Jacob carefully brought Letty downstairs, Kit prayed to God for strength and a miracle. Letty was going to need one. Jacob lay his sister on the table and kissed her forehead before walking out of the room. Kit walked over to her friend and held her hand. Speaking to Letty as she lay unconscious on the table, she said, "Letty, we promise we aren't going to let you down. We are going to be strong for you, but you have to promise me that you are going to fight. You have to fight with everything you have to live. You can't give up! Thomas promised to marry you if you lived so if you don't survive for me, do it for Thomas."

Doctor Kellerman quietly spoke to Kit. "Miss Pridgeon, it's time. Don't worry, we are all going to take good care of her. If all goes well, I expect you to take me to the wedding as your guest."

Kit smiled at Doctor Kellerman and picked up the kerosene lamp. She felt confident that if anyone could save Letty's life, it was this man. Trying not to faint, she turned away as he made the first incision.

It was after midnight when Doctor Kellerman made the final stitches in the incision. Kit's arms were tired and cramping from holding the lamp, but it had all been worth it – Letty was still alive and her appendix had been removed before it burst. Despite the late hour, the parlor being covered in blood-soaked rags, and Kit's exhaustion, it had all been worth it.

"Ladies, we've done all we can for her. The rest is up to Letty and God."

"Doctor, I want to thank you for all you did," said Mrs. Quidley as she sat down on a plain wooden chair by the wall. Poor Mrs. Quidley was as tired as Kit was; it had been a long day and they could both use some rest.

"Mrs. Quidley, why don't you go on home. I will stay with Letty while you get some rest," said Kit.

Doctor Kellerman spoke to them both. "Ladies, you both need some rest. She will need round-the-clock care for many days and I trust you both. Go home, and I will stay with her for the first watch."

Kit didn't argue with him. She was so tired she could barely stand. She stretched, thinking about the long walk back to the hotel, but before she could even ask, Doctor Kellerman offered her and Mrs. Quidley the use of his carriage. "I will see if Thomas or Jacob can drive you both home. It is too late to walk."

Kit and Mrs. Quidley offered to help clean up the parlor, but he would hear none of it. Wishing them both good night, he saw them to the door.

Kit could barely remember the carriage ride back to the hotel. Jacob had driven her all the way across town in the dead of night – scandalous behavior for Fish Town – but luckily there was no one awake at that hour to witness it.

She said goodnight to Jacob and dragged herself upstairs to her room. Falling onto the bed, her last thoughts were of her best friend, as she prayed that Letty would survive the night. Under Doctor Kellerman's watchful eye, she knew Letty stood a good chance of surviving. Hoping that her confidence in the young doctor was well founded, she closed her eyes and lay down. The moment her head touched the pillow of the shiny brass bed, she was fast asleep.

The next morning, Kit woke still fully dressed from the night before. The morning light came pouring in the window, much too bright for dawn. Sitting up, she realized that she had slept late. It had not been her intention to sleep the day away, knowing that she and Mrs. Quidley had agreed to take the next watch.

Dressing quickly, she braided her hair and wore it in a simple bun. There was no need of a fancy pompadour if she was going to be a nurse today. She rushed downstairs and requested a carriage. The manager was happy to assist her and in only a few minutes the same driver from the day before met her outside the hotel.

"Same address in Fish Town?"

"Yes sir, same address."

"Very good, Ma'am."

Kit sat back in the carriage and tried to ignore her growling stomach. There had not been time for coffee, tea, or breakfast that morning and she hoped Mrs. Harper would be kind and offer her a few pieces of toast with butter when she arrived. Her heart raced as she thought about Letty. Doctor Kellerman had warned her that in Letty's weakened state, she may still die. Kit prayed that Letty was stronger than he thought, that she would refuse to die.

The carriage arrived at the Harper house and the driver asked once again if he should wait, but Kit paid him a generous amount and sent him back to the hotel. Taking a deep breath, she walked to the house and knocked on the door. She was greeted by Jacob, who should have been fishing. Fearing the worst, she was afraid to ask about Letty. "Jacob, what are you doing home?"

"I couldn't leave you and Mrs. Quidley to deal with this alone, could I? There was too much to be done – the parlor needed cleaning, and all those rags had to be burned. You were so brave last night, I couldn't let you do all the work. Emily came over and she and Ma are in the kitchen cooking up some fish stew for you and Mrs. Quidley, seeing how neither of you have had hardly anything to eat, or any rest."

"Emily is here?" Kit's heart skipped a beat.

"Yes, she is. Kit, you were brave last night – braver than I could've been. I don't care what your family or anyone thinks about your decision to leave

133

town. You have my respect, and I know your sister and brother feel the same way."

"Kit, is that you?" said Emily from the hallway.

Kit barely recognized her own sister. Emily had grown taller and put on a few pounds, which made her look less like Kit's younger sister and more like a grown woman. Kit ran to her, and they embraced.

"Kit, I have been so worried about you! It's good to have you home."

"I am glad to be here, congratulations on your wedding."

"Thank you, and thank you for telling Jacob about me. We are so happy."

"You two make a good couple. I have to go check on Letty, can you sneak me some food? I'm so hungry – a crust of bread, anything!"

"Right away."

Kit climbed the stairs and opened the door to Letty's room. She was expecting to find Doctor Kellerman, but was surprised that Mrs. Quidley was sitting there instead.

"Kit, you're back. Good to see you."

"Mrs. Quidley, where is Doctor Kellerman?"

"That poor dear. He's gone home to get some rest. He said he would be back later."

"And Letty, how is she doing?"

"Her fever has already gone down some and her color is looking better, but she still hasn't woken up yet."

Kit looked at Mrs. Quidley and could see the older woman was exhausted, although she did not complain.

Kit asked, "Do you want me to stay with her for a while, so you can get some rest?"

"Would you? I just need to go home for a few hours and then I'll be right as rain."

"Is there anything I should do?"

"Not a thing to worry about. If you need me, I'll be at the house."

Kit sat beside Letty for the remainder of the morning, though Letty did not move except to breathe. Every moment that Letty was alive, Kit considered a victory as she talked about her memories of childhood and how much she missed her. She didn't know if Letty heard her or not, but she had a feeling that maybe she did.

After lunch, Mrs. Harper came upstairs and took a turn sitting with her daughter. Kit didn't want to return to the hotel, so she decided to walk over to her to see her family. Even if they didn't approve of her or her decision, she wanted to see her mother.

Knocking at the back door, Kit waited with her heart in her throat as she heard footsteps growing closer. The door opened and Kit saw her mother for the first time in year and half. The older woman stood at the door for a long time, staring at her eldest daughter before inviting her in.

"Kit, is that really you? You've changed so much. Have you come back to us?"

"Not to stay, mother. Letty is ill; I came back because of her."

"It's good to see you. Your father and brother are on the boat, but I know your father would want to see you."

Kit's mother was treating her like a stranger, and it nearly broke Kit's heart. She tried to appeal to her mother as a woman. "Ma, please forgive for me leaving like I did. I wanted to go and explore the world, to be something more than just a fish girl, and I didn't think Pa would let me if I asked him."

"No, he wouldn't have let you and neither would I. It was a foolish thing to do, to go gallivanting off out west somewhere. No God-fearing woman would have chosen a way of life in a lawless world full of Indians and saloons."

Feeling cold all the way to her core, Kit turned to leave. "Ma, it's not like that. I work for a respectable company and I go to church. Maybe one day you will be proud of me. I love you and I wanted you to know that."

Kit opened the door and left the kitchen she'd spent so much time in as a child, learning how to cook and bake. Her suspicions had been confirmed –

she had made the right choice to run away from home. Now, she no longer had any doubts about it. Her mother and father would never have allowed her to be anything but a worker in a cannery, or a married to a fisherman.

Thinking of the love and generosity she had received from her new friends at the Harvey Company, she knew in her heart that she had made the right decision. Walking back to the Harpers', she could smell the delectable aroma of fish stew, a smell she had not experienced for far too long. Her mouth watered as she walked into Letty's house.

Emily met her at the door and with only a little coaxing, convinced her to sit down at the kitchen table for a bowl of stew with a plate of fresh cornbread. The stew was heavenly and the cornbread melted in her mouth. The food made with love by her own sister took away some of the sting she felt from her own mother's rejection.

"Kit, I am so proud of you, and so are Thomas and Jacob, but you must know, Letty was the one that helped all of us to see you like that. She believed in you more than anyone. I know she's going to get better, because she knows you are home now."

Bolstered by her sister's words and a generous helping of fish stew, Kit thanked Emily and returned to Letty's room. From the staircase, she could hear the unmistakable sound of a woman weeping. Thinking of Mrs. Harper, she felt her pulse race as she opened the door to Letty's bedroom. Praying that Letty had not passed away while she was gone, she rushed in to find Mrs. Harper lying half on the bed and half on the floor, crying.

"Mrs. Harper, what has happened?" Kit asked as she tried to make sense of what she was seeing. To her astonishment, she was greeted by Letty's soft smile. Letty, who was not only alive, but awake.

Kit rushed to her bedside, joining Mrs. Harper as she was overcome with happiness.

In a quiet voice, barely audible, Kit heard Letty say her name. "Kit? Kit is that you?"

It was the sweetest sound Kit had ever heard. Letty was alive. Her closet friend was weak, but she was still alive. Kit smiled at Letty and said, Dearest Letty, thank you, my wonderful Letty, you have given me the best gift – you are alive."

"No, Kit, you are the gift. Welcome home." Letty said, and Kit wept with joy.

In that cramped bedroom in Fish Town, Kit felt as though she *was* home. It wasn't an address or a place, it was people who made home for Kit. Letty, like Maggie and Annie, accepted her and loved her for who she was. She was the ragged girl from Fish Town, and she was a stylish Harvey Girl. She was both at the same time, and where her friends were, that was where she belonged. That was home.

CHAPTER 9

With every passing day, Letty slowly regained her strength. Although still sore from the surgery, she was becoming bored by the enforced bed rest that Doctor Kellerman insisted was a necessary part of her recovery. She still had two more weeks of rest before the doctor would even consider letting her walk down the stairs.

Kit tried, without much success, to explain the necessity of resting to a headstrong Letty. "You have to be patient – you almost died," said Kit as she was faced with a best friend who was pouting and staring out the window.

"It's not fair. I just want to go outside. I know it's winter, but I want to feel the sunshine – not just see it!"

"You have to obey the doctor's orders; those stitches have to heal and you don't want to get an infection. If you don't rest, you could undo all the hard work that Doctor Kellerman did, and I am in no mood to attend a funeral."

Letty pouted. "I know you're right, but that doesn't make it any easier."

"You're being stubborn and mule-headed."

"It's good to have you home, Kit. We haven't argued like this in a long time."

Kit smiled. "No, we haven't. Think about it, if you rest like you're supposed to, and get better, we can plan your wedding. Isn't that worth the time you are stuck in that bed?"

"Thomas is really going to marry me, isn't he? Ma told me how he stood up to Pa the night I had my surgery. You were there; is it true?"

"It sure is. He must love you something fierce, the way he stood up to your Pa."

Letty touched Kit's hand on the blanket. "I know you aren't here to stay, but can you stay until I get a little better?"

"I can stay a while longer, but I have to get back to Holbrook."

"Tell me again about your adventures. Is it true you know real cowboys, and have you met any outlaws?"

"I'm sure I have met a few lawless men, and I do know a few cowboys."

"I sure am going to miss you when you leave. The other ladies that sit with me just read bible stories to me, and I know all of them by heart."

"I guess you want me to tell you some new stories. Let me see what I can do."

As Kit recounted her adventures and told Letty about the girls she worked with, and the interesting people she knew from the restaurant, her thoughts turned to Maggie. Maggie was in Raleigh, just a short train ride away. A plan began to form in Kit's head, but it would have to wait. At this moment, her attention was focused entirely on seeing that Letty recovered and was well enough to walk down the aisle in the spring.

Kit was just finishing the tale of the runaway Boston socialite when a knock at the door preceded the appearance of a familiar face.

"Miss Pridgeon, Miss Harper, how are my favorite nurse and favorite patient doing?"

Kit impulsively smoothed a stray hair from her face as she smiled warmly at Doctor Kellerman.

Letty greeted the doctor with a frown, "Doctor, when are you going to let me get out of here? I feel better, I do."

"Well, Miss Harper, you just stay where you are for two more weeks and then we will see. You don't want to jeopardize your recovery."

"No, Doctor. But I'm going crazy – if it wasn't for Kit, I'd be dead of boredom."

Doctor Kellerman smiled. "Boredom! Wonderful. That is irrefutable medical proof that you're getting better. I'd be worried about you if you weren't being spirited, as I am to understand that is a quintessential part of your nature, Miss Harper."

Letty looked at the doctor, and then to Kit and said, "Kit, you'll have to tell me what all those fancy words meant that he just said. He talks like you do."

Kit tried not to laugh, but it was impossible not to smile. "Letty, don't you play dumb; I know you're being silly. You'll have the doctor believing you are a simpleton."

"I highly doubt you have that to worry about, Miss Pridgeon, I don't consider either of you ladies to be simpletons. On the contrary, your conversation is far more entertaining than any other address in Bridgeton," the doctor said, looking at Kit.

Kit could feel color rising to her cheeks as she met his gaze. The doctor's dark brown eyes were kind and gentle, much like his personality. The moment was only broken by the arrival of Mrs. Harper.

Mrs. Harper was emphatic, insisting that the doctor speak to Letty. "Doctor, thank heavens you have come. Maybe you can talk some sense into my girl – I caught her trying to sneak out of her room last night."

Doctor Kellerman turned to Letty. "Miss Harper, you'd better behave or else we will have to take measures. We don't want to treat you like a prisoner. Do I have your word that you'll be good, and do as I ask? Stop giving these ladies so much trouble?"

Letty sighed and answered, "Yes, Doctor, I promise I will be good."

"That's better. I understand you like ice cream and sweets. If you promise to be a model patient, I will take you to get ice cream when you can go out."

Letty's face brightened up. "Doctor, would you?"

"Yes, I would. Now, as much as I am enjoying our little chat, I must examine you and see how those stiches are coming along."

Kit stepped out into the hallway as the doctor examined Letty under Mrs. Harper's watchful eye.

After the examination, he left a small bottle of medicine for pain, and gave Mrs. Harper and Kit strict instructions to use it sparingly. Kit promised to comply, as Doctor Kellerman wished the Harper ladies a pleasant afternoon.

Turning to Kit, he said, "Miss Pridgeon, may I have a word with you before I leave?"

"Yes, Doctor, anything you ask."

Kit followed the doctor downstairs to the front door. He hesitated, looking down at his feet. "Miss Pridgeon, I hope you don't think of this as forward, but I have a request to ask of you."

Kit answered sincerely. "Doctor, you saved my best friend's life. If you asked me for the moon I would try to find a way to get it for you."

The doctor looked into her eyes and said, "I'm not very good at this, and it may seem inappropriate to ask, but would you do me the honor of having dinner with me tomorrow evening?"

Kit was astonished that an educated man was interested in having dinner with a poor girl from Fish Town. Without hesitation, she answered, "Doctor Kellerman, you flatter me with your request. Yes, I would be delighted to have dinner with you."

As Kit watched the doctor walk to his carriage, she wanted to squeal in delight like a schoolgirl, but she chose to stand at the door and wave goodbye, behaving like the Harvey Girl she was.

Kit was annoyed. She'd left Holbrook in such a rush, never thinking to pack her prettiest evening dress – never imagining she'd need it. Considering her options, she chose the nicest dress she had, a simple blue gown with embroidered flowers on the bodice and puff sleeves. It was more suited for church, but the color complemented her rosy complexion and fair hair.

For an occasion such as this, Kit wanted to be fashionable. She arranged her hair in a pompadour and selected the best earrings she had, a small pair of pearls that were a gift from Annie at Christmas. After two hours of fussing with her hair and her outfit, she looked in the mirror one final time before leaving the safety of her hotel room.

Walking down the staircase of the hotel, she was desperate to quell her nerves. She was not prone to fits of nervousness, but she was terrified of saying something dreadfully ignorant – or using the wrong fork. Realizing she was being silly, she calmed down. The doctor knew where she was from, and she worked in a restaurant, so she laughed off her own fears as being ridiculous as she stepped into the lobby of the hotel.

Doctor Kellerman cut a fine figure in his suit and hat. He was dressed fashionably and looked as though he would be at home in city such as Topeka or Raleigh, rather than a small town like Bridgeton.

He removed his hat and bowed as he greeted Kit. "Miss Pridgeon, you honor me with your presence."

"Doctor Kellerman," she said with a nod, her blond pompadoured hairstyle staying perfectly in place.

He offered his arm. "If you will accompany me to the dining room, I have found the food here at the hotel to be the best in Bridgeton."

"Lead the way, sir." They walked from the lobby to the main dining room, which overlooked the water. From the table, Kit could see the lantern lights of boats and lamp lights along the boardwalk.

"That is beautiful. I've never seen this view before," she said, captivated by the lights on the water.

"I find that astonishing. Have you never dined at the hotel before this evening?"

"Regrettably, I have never dined here. As a matter of fact, this is my first time staying here, at the hotel, I mean," she answered, turning to the handsome doctor.

"If I may ask, you're friends with Miss Harper and her family – that is splendid, that you find their company amicable. I was wondering how you came to know them?"

143

From the doctor's question, Kit realized that he didn't know she'd been a resident of Fish Town. She could easily have lied, but she chose to tell him the truth despite what he might think of her. "I came to know the Harpers as a small child. That's where I'm from, Fish Town. My family's house is only a short distance from Letty's."

Kit waited for the doctor to withdraw, maybe even to tell her that he had made mistake asking her to dinner, but he didn't react that way at all.

"My dear Miss Pridgeon, please accept my sincerest apologies. I did not mean to offend you or offer you insult."

"I know you didn't mean any harm, Doctor. You have been so gracious and treated Letty and her family with respect and dignity. People like us aren't used to that, I can only offer you my deepest gratitude."

"I must say in my defense that you do not appear to be a native of Fish Town."

"I doubt I ever did. It's true I was born and raised there, but not once did I think of myself as a native. To be truthful, I never fit in. I read too many books and dreamed of going out in the world – something women in that part of Bridgeton don't make a habit of doing."

"You are staying at the hotel, so I assumed you were from a city like Savannah or Charleston."

"How kind of you to say that, but no. I'm from this little town right here. I ran away and left home in a mail car. I went out West and became a Harvey Girl."

He laughed. "A mail car? Really? You must be brave and determined. Miss Pridgeon, may I call you Kit? Please call me by my first name; it's Levi," he said with a dazzling smile.

"Yes, Levi, you may call me Kit. And I did really leave here in a mail car. You should have seen the porter's face when I climbed inside and sat on a bag of mail!"

A waiter arrived with menus. The doctor ordered a bottle of wine and a steak with all the trimmings, and Kit ordered roast chicken with braised vegetables.

After the waiter left to bring the drink order, she mused, "I am not used to being served in a restaurant; I always do the serving. I will try to resist the urge to jump up and run to the kitchen to retrieve our orders."

Levi laughed as he said, "I can't believe my luck. I'm having dinner with an actual Harvey Girl. I may have to ask for an autograph. I have seen pictures of your coworkers in the paper and always thought that if I traveled out west I would have to give a Harvey restaurant a try."

At the mention of the Harvey restaurants, Kit was reminded that her stay in Bridgeton was brief. Dinner with the handsome doctor was unexpected, and an unplanned part of her stay. She'd never suspected she would find a reason to stay in Bridgeton, especially a reason as handsome and charming as Doctor Levi Kellerman.

"Come to think of it, this is the first time I have been asked to dine. Isn't that funny, that it happened here at home."

"I don't believe that – as intelligent and beautiful as you are, Kit, I find it impossible to believe that you are not engaged."

"Oh no, we aren't allowed to court, not while we are employed as Harvey Girls. It's strictly against the rules."

Levi looked around the restaurant and then quietly said, "I feel privileged that you are breaking the rules just to dine with me. I must have said or done something you found worthwhile for you to take a risk like the one you are taking now."

Kit whispered, "I don't think I'm in any danger of being found out; I doubt anyone in this hotel, or in this part of town, knows who I am."

The waiter brought the soup course and served the wine. Kit had never tasted wine before; it was an evening of many firsts for her.

"Kit, at the risk of seeming patronizing, I must admit I have never met a woman like you before. You are smart, ambitious, and brave. There are not many men I know who would have run away and headed out west like you did."

"Call it brave if you like; I still can't believe I had the courage to do that. Honestly, I didn't have very much money and I had no ticket back home. I didn't have a choice – I had to succeed."

145

"A career woman, you are quite amazing. I suppose when I saw you at the Harpers', it never occurred to me that you lived so far away."

"It's not so far away by train, it only seems so when you look at a map. The country is getting smaller every day. You should see the cities out west; they rival Raleigh."

The waiter cleared away the soup course and brought out the main entrees. Kit was feeling self-conscious that they had talked about her all evening; she'd never expected that a man would find her life so fascinating.

"Levi, you haven't said a word about yourself. I don't remember ever seeing you before this trip; are your people from Bridgeton, or nearby?"

"I must admit, when you referred to Raleigh as a city I found that delightful. Where I am from, Raleigh seems quite small."

"Let me see…you don't talk like you're from these parts, and I have never met anyone with your last name. I would have to guess you are from up north."

"Very good. I am from New York."

"New York? How did you find this little town, and why did you come here?" she asked as she leaned closer to him.

"Like you, I wanted to go somewhere I had never been before."

"I understand that, but how did you pick Bridgeton?"

"By chance, really. Doctor Greenbaum, one of my mentors at the hospital I worked at in New York, would take a month off every summer to come down south to the coast and fish. He visited fishing lodges, islands, and chartered boats. He spoke of this town many times, and said it was one of his favorite places to visit and to fish."

"If you like to fish, you have found the right place," said Kit.

"The funny thing is, I've never fished before in my life and here I sit in a town that is so involved in fishing that it has a cannery and a neighborhood called Fish Town."

Kit laughed. "Don't remind me! I've been trying to forget about fish ever since I left."

146

After dinner, Levi and Kit sat at the table, drinking coffee and conversing like old friends. Kit forgot about being nervous around the doctor, instead, she was laughing and joking with him like she'd known him for many years. She did not want the evening to end, but the hour grew late and the restaurant was soon empty of other guests.

Levi paid the bill and said to Kit, "I've enjoyed having dinner with you, may I assume from your smile that you did too?"

"I had a marvelous time."

"If I may be presumptuous, I would like to see you again. I know you have to return to your job but I want to see you as much as I can before you have to leave. You may say no. I don't want you to feel any obligation to me, and I will understand if you would rather not."

"I am obligated to you – you saved Letty's life – but that isn't why I came tonight, and that is not why I want to see you again."

"What about luncheon tomorrow? I can call for you at the Harpers if you plan to be there."

"I look forward to it. Thank you for dinner; you have made this night so magical I don't want it to end."

"Neither do I, Kit." Levi reached for her hand.

CHAPTER 10

Kit was just about to open the door to Letty's room when she heard her best friend's voice call out, "Come on in, Kit, I know it's you."

Kit opened the door. Letty and Mrs. Quidley were smiling at her, and from their expressions, she knew why. "Good morning, Mrs. Quidley, Letty."

Letty winced as she rolled over on her side and said, "Kit, you have to tell me everything. Every detail, every word. I must know."

Mrs. Quidley slowly stood. She patted Kit on the arm and said, "Letty tells me that you and Doctor Kellerman are sweet on each other. I'm glad to hear it. He is a good man, and he will make some lucky girl a fine husband, mark my words."

"Mrs. Quidley, I barely know him."

"Stuff and nonsense. I knew it right away that you two were sweet on each other. When you get my age you don't miss a trick."

"Mrs. Quidley, I don't know what to say, I don't think I'm right for him; he may realize that too. He's a doctor – what am I?" Kit bit her tongue as she almost finished the sentence by saying a just a girl from Fish Town, but she was sure that Mrs. Quidley and Letty did not feel the same way about their part of town as she did.

Mrs. Quidley pulled Kit closer and said, "Kit, you are a strong, fine young woman, and a darn pretty girl. Any man would be a fool not to want you for a wife, and bedsides, you've had your adventure. Time to start thinking about finding a husband and settling down."

"What about my job?" Kit asked the older woman.

"What about it? Time to get to work raising a family. That doctor is a handsome man and he won't be eligible for long – not when those rich young ladies come to town for the summer."

"Yes, ma'am."

"Don't you 'yes ma'am' me, young lady – you listen to what I'm telling you. Marry that doctor the moment he asks, and come home."

Kit smiled and helped Mrs. Quidley down the stairs. Her heart fluttered to think that Mrs. Quidley thought she and the doctor were sweet on each other. Closing the front door, she raced upstairs to an impatient Letty.

Letty complimented her friend as she returned to the bedroom. "Kit, you look nice today, and you fixed your hair. I hope you didn't go through all that trouble for me."

"I'm supposed to have lunch with Levi."

"Levi? You mean Doctor Kellerman? He must be falling madly in love with you if he already asked you to lunch."

"Maybe. I think he just wants to talk with me and be friends. He knows I have to return to Arizona soon."

"Don't even say it! I may have to get sick again just to keep you here."

"Letty, I miss you too. I wish you could go with me to see it all for yourself, but I think you have a wedding to plan."

"Maybe you do, too. Sit down and tell me all about last night. What did you wear, what did he say – everything."

Kit told her friend nearly every detail, leaving out the parts about Fish Town. As she talked about her evening with the doctor, she was struck by how much she had enjoyed being with him, even for just a few hours. Once again, her thoughts turned to her departure from Bridgeton, which from Letty's quick recovery, would be in a only few days' time.

"Kit, I can tell by the way he looks at you, he's sweet on you. He's smitten. You may not be going back to Arizona."

"I'm trying not to get attached – I have to go back. Everyone back there helped me get home to see you, and Mr. Harvey paid for my train ticket. I owe them so much."

"Sounds to me like you have a decision to make."

"No, I don't. You and Mrs. Quidley have it wrong; the doctor is just being a gentleman. He knows I traveled a great distance to come home and he is just being a good friend." Kit stood and walked to the window. It was a warm day for that time of year, and she watched as robins flitted from tree to tree in the backyard. Spring was coming, and with the spring she had a new position waiting for her in Pueblo, Colorado.

"Kit, you must be blind as a bat not to see it – that handsome doctor is going to ask you to marry him, I just know it. I can tell. I have an eye for these things."

"Letty, you wouldn't know which way is up. You just survived surgery and have been stuck here for days, so you're liable to imagine anything."

"Am I? Mark my words, Kit Pridgeon, just because you have gone out west and taken to putting on airs, don't mean you know a thing about men!"

"You take that back Letty Harper – you take that back this instant! When I have ever put on airs?"

"Oh, I don't know. I'd say since first grade when you won that spelling bee at school. Ever since then you won't listen to no one!"

"Girls, you two both behave!" Mrs. Harper came rushing into the bedroom with a lunch tray for Letty. "Kit, I can fix you some bread and broth if you like," she said as she laid the tray down.

"No, thank you, Mrs. Harper, I'm all set," answered Kit as she returned to her seat at Letty's bedside.

"Suit yourself. If you get hungry, you know your way to the kitchen. There is some leftover pie I made with the last of the blackberry preserves

151

from summer. If you want a piece, I suggest you go ahead and have a slice before Edward gets home, won't be none left after he gets finished with it."

"Blackberry preserves, I haven't had any blackberry preserves in so long."

"No, I reckon you ain't, out there gallivanting around the country. Kit, I must tell you I sure do wish you would come home. It does my heart good to hear you and Letty fighting like a couple of fussy old hens."

Mrs. Harper left the two girls together. Letty wiped a tear from her eye and said, "Ma's right. I wish you would come home. Nothing has been the same without you."

"Letty, you know I was never happy here. Cheer up, soon you and my brother are going to be married and you will have a house full of young'uns to chase after. My brother always said he wanted a big family. He'll be expecting girls to help around the house and boys to go fishing with him."

"I know. I just wanted us to be neighbors one day – you married to my brother and me married to Thomas. I wanted us to be old gossips together. I just never thought you would take off on one of your fool notions and run away."

"Letty." Kit kneeled by the bed and held her best friend's hand in hers. "You may call it a fool notion if you like, but I know for a fact that it was you who helped Jacob, Thomas, and Emily to understand why I left the way I did and what I was doing. I have you to thank for my brother and my sister. And Letty, you never abandoned me or disowned me."

"No, I didn't. How could I? I would never get the chance to play high and mighty when you came home, and tease you about it until we were older than Methuselah."

Kit could hear Levi's footsteps as he came upstairs. Letty looked at her and winked as he came in the bedroom.

"Miss Pridgeon, is our patient behaving so terribly that you are compelled to parry at her bedside?" he teased.

"No, Doctor Kellerman, not me. I was just trying to make my closest friend in the world stay in Bridgeton. I did almost die and that seemed to work, to bring her home. Maybe I have to get sick to keep her here?" asked Letty.

"Let's hope not, Miss Harper. Once you recover, I don't want to hear from you again until after you are married."

"You mean when I start having young'uns?" asked Letty.

Kit blushed and looked away as Levi answered. "I would have put it more delicately, but yes, until you start a family."

"I see you have your lunch waiting, Miss Harper. May I examine you when I return?"

"Yes, as I don't plan on going anywhere. You do have me stuck in this bed," Letty said petulantly.

"May I steal your nurse from you for an hour? I promise to bring her back."

"You may steal her, but I will be cross if you don't return her to me, since she is going to leave soon and I hate sharing. After all, I am the patient."

"I'll be back real soon, I promise. I'll send your mother to sit with you," Kit said, as she stood and joined Levi in the doorway.

"Ask her to send up a slice of that pie."

Levi was prepared to take advantage of the unseasonably warm weather; he'd brought a picnic basket and a blanket and suggested lunch in the park. Kit was delighted to be outside on such a beautiful late winter afternoon. The last time she'd been in the park, she had gone walking with Jacob. That was a memory that felt as though it had happened in a different lifetime.

Kit was reluctant to admit she was falling in love with the doctor, although she could think of no other description for the flood of emotions she felt for him. Every time her hand brushed against his or she gazed into his dark brown eyes, she could feel her pulse quicken.

He spread out the blanket on a patch of lawn that was not shaded by the lush green pine trees. The warmth of the sun on Kit's face reminded her what it felt like to be a girl running through the park, barefoot with Letty.

"You look dazzling in the sunlight; it makes your hair sparkle like gold," Levi said as he gazed at his companion.

Kit felt her heart flutter. His voice, the words he said – she had never known what it was like to lose her heart to a man. Now, she was all too aware that she was in danger of falling madly in love with this man, this man who would soon be over a thousand miles away.

"Levi, thank you, I don't know what to say. No one has ever said such things to me before."

"They may not have said them, but they thought them. I could tell you how beautiful and dazzling you are every day, but I want you to know it's more than that. You are more than that to me," he said as he held her hand.

"I know I'm not supposed to say this, but I feel the same way about you. It's not proper to tell you so, but I am not very proper and I never have been."

"You feel it too, don't you? I can't describe what's happening to me, Kit. You must understand that I've dedicated my life to my work, and I always thought romance and love were best suited for men who were not in my profession. That was how I felt until I saw you that day in Letty's room. It wasn't just your pretty face or your nice clothes, it was you – the woman at her friend's bedside offering to pay my fee. Your loyalty, the determination I saw in your eyes that day, I will never forget it." Levi brought her hand to his lips.

Kit closed her eyes, letting his words wash over her while his lips gently touched her gloved hand. "Oh, Levi, I didn't count on you. I never thought I would have a reason to stay in Bridgeton."

"Have I given you reason to stay? Dare I hope that I have made a strong enough impression on you, that you would consider staying in a town you were so desperate to leave?"

Kit withdrew her hand and looked at the doctor, a serious expression on her face. She remembered her friend Maggie and the promises she had believed, promises that led her to ruin her career.

"Levi, I must ask you a question, a very serious question, but one that I find necessary. You see, my friend Maggie lost her heart to man in Holbrook, a man she believed wanted to be with her, to love her. She left the company, only to find out he was married. Tell me, are you married to a girl back in New York? Are you engaged?"

"I am sorry that a man took advantage of your friend. It must be difficult being a girl on your own, never knowing who to trust. I understand why you ask, and no, I do not have a wife or a fiancée in New York, in Bridgeton, or anywhere else in the world. You have my word."

"Thank you. I hope I didn't upset you by asking, but a girl can't be too careful when it comes to her heart."

"You did not upset me; on the contrary, I'm glad you are thinking about me as more than Letty's doctor, but also as a man. A man who, like you, is trying to find his own way in this world. Kit, I know we've only just met, but what are your plans for the future? Somehow, I never pictured myself asking a woman a question like that, but you are the most modern woman I have ever met."

"I suppose you're right; I am modern, though I'd never thought of myself as a modern woman before this moment. As for what my plans are, Levi, I don't know. I thought I was sure of what I wanted. When I became a Harvey Girl, I was wild with ambition and excited about seeing the West. I suppose I still am. Mr. Harvey has been good to me and the girls I work with, he has given us a chance to prove ourselves, to earn a decent wage. He treats us with respect."

"Kit, it sounds to me like you love your work, as I do."

Levi reached into the picnic basket, bringing out cold chicken sandwiches, slices of cake, and two bottles of lemonade. He served Kit as she thought of a response. "Levi, would you consider coming out west?"

Levi chewed a bite of his sandwich, slowly. "I've never really thought of it before. Tell me, Kit, would you ever consider returning home?"

Kit had been afraid he would ask that question. "I never thought of that, before meeting you."

They ate quietly, both lost in thoughts and words they dared not say. Kit broke the silence by complimenting the food. "For a gentleman, you sure can cook," she said in jest.

"I am a doctor, and I don't flatter myself to think I am anything more than that. This lunch was made by my cook, Mrs. Campbell. Come to think of it, she was overjoyed that I needed a picnic lunch. It seems she thinks I ought to settle down."

155

"That does seem to be the opinion of Mrs. Quidley as well."

Levi sighed, and patted her knee. After a moment, he said, "Let's promise not to speak anymore about you leaving for the remainder of our luncheon, and as long as you remain in Bridgeton. I only want to enjoy the time I have with you, that Letty will graciously allow me to steal."

Kit smiled. "Yes, that is best. Let's not worry about that for right now. As my grandmother used to say, it's like putting the horse in front of the carriage."

"A wise woman. Let's speak only of funny stories, books we've read, and happy moments."

"Levi, you must tell me about New York. I have never been, but I work with some girls from your fair city and let me tell you, they are tough as nails."

"They can be. Wait until you meet my mother – she's the sweetest woman you ever will meet, until you make her angry. I think she could singlehandedly make an army of fighting men cower."

Levi went on to talk about his city with such love and in such detail that Kit could almost close her eyes and imagine every street, every store, and every building he described. She could imagine the snow nearly waist high after a blizzard, and hear the unending sound of buildings being constructed. He described the people from all over the world coming into the city, and how many languages he heard in the hospital. The sound of his voice was hypnotic and Kit realized that despite her promise not to speak of her journey back to Arizona, it was all she could think about.

The week after Letty's surgery passed with frightening speed. Letty was becoming more energetic and was ready to run downstairs, throw open the door, and run wild in the streets. At least that was what Kit accused her of, as she tried to convince her convalescing friend that she must follow the doctor's orders.

With Letty safely out of danger, Kit could not postpone her journey back to Holbrook much longer. In the whirlwind of nursing Letty back to health and seeing Levi every free minute she had, Kit realized there was one person she had yet to visit on this trip, a very important person. Mrs. Cates.

One morning, just after breakfast, Kit walked to the library. The air was crisp and the walk did her good. Fresh air always seemed to help her clear her thoughts, and this morning was no exception.

She had only known Levi for a short time, and yet he filled her thoughts when she was awake and her dreams when she slept. Passing by the ice cream parlor, she thought of Levi's promise to Letty, his sense of humor and his compassion. There was no doubt that he was a good and decent man, but was he the man she would give up her career for?

Kit opened the door of the library. The big oak door creaked on its hinges as it closed behind her. Returning to the Bridgeton library had special meaning for Kit, because it had been her refuge growing up. The books transported her to worlds far away from the hard life she knew in Fish Town, and Mrs. Cates had encouraged her dreams, and always knew which book to recommend to suit Kit's moods and whims.

She closed her eyes and breathed the familiar scent of polished wood, old books, and lavender. The smell of lavender could only mean one thing: Mrs. Cates was nearby. Tiptoeing to the front desk, she rang the bell and waited patiently.

Mrs. Cates appeared from the stacks. "May I help you, Miss?"

"You sure can, do you have the latest newspaper from Raleigh?" asked Kit.

Mrs. Cates looked at her, and then in an uncharacteristically loud voice, exclaimed, "My word, Kit Pridgeon, I hardly recognized you!"

"Mrs. Cates, how are you?"

Mrs. Cates gave Kit a hug. "I am well, thank you. There isn't a soul here this early in the morning, so we can catch up on all the news."

"Oh, Mrs. Cates – there is so much news to tell you! But please, you first. What have I missed since I left Bridgeton?"

Mrs. Cates filled Kit in on the latest news of the city and its inhabitants. She also mentioned the new doctor. Kit was quick to say that she'd had the pleasure of making his acquaintance. Recounting the harrowing events of her arrival, Kit confided in Mrs. Cates that she was falling in love with the doctor, an admission that Mrs. Cates applauded.

"Kit, will you honestly have me believe that you traveled all over the West and never met a man of interest? You wind up back home because of your friend Letty and meet the good doctor? That is a stroke of luck so fortuitous I would have to believe it is providential."

"I know it is. I feel the same way about him that he does about me, but what should I do? I've only just met him and we have no plans to marry, but yet I feel drawn to him, almost as though I could believe every word he tells me."

"My dear, you have managed to bewitch the most eligible young man in Bridgeton and you tell me you don't know what to do?"

"I don't know; I honestly don't. Everyone tells me to marry him, but what of my career? I've worked hard to get to where I am, and I'm about to be promoted and move to Colorado. All though the years, you gave me advice and counsel. I depended on your words of wisdom. What should I do?"

Mrs. Cates' pursed her lips. "This is not easy, and I wish I knew what to tell you. I chose a career and never married; would I change it as I look back?"

"Would you? Should I choose husband or career?"

"For me, the choice at the time was simple, but now I do sometimes wish I had done differently. Sunsets are the hardest. Not having anyone to share their beauty is difficult for me."

"So you think I should marry him?"

"No, I'm recommending you wait until he asks for your hand, and then follow your heart. If he doesn't ask you to marry him, than you have not ruined your career for a man."

"What if he does ask me, then what do I do?"

"I would say it's entirely possible that he will propose marriage, and when he does, do whatever you feel in your heart – and not what you think with your mind. That will be the right answer for you. Don't overthink it."

Mrs. Cates, that is just the problem. I've been thinking about him since I met him; I must be overthinking it."

Mrs. Cates laughed softly. "Kit, I know you. You are a smart girl, but you are going to have to *stop* using your head. You're in the unique position to

158

have to make the choice of career or marriage. Not many women find themselves in your position, so it's no wonder you are confused."

A middle-aged man came in carrying a stack of books, and Mrs. Cates went to greet him. As Kit watched Mrs. Cates help the man, she thought about the doctor. What would her reaction be if he asked her to marry him? If he came in the door of the public library, what would she do?

The man at the counter was soon joined by a woman with a small child and two elderly women. Kit said her goodbyes to Mrs. Cates, promising to drop by before she left town. The advice Mrs. Cates had given her was just what she need to hear – now, she had to learn how to trust her heart.

CHAPTER 11

Kit held the train ticket in her hand. Her unplanned visit back home to Bridgeton was quickly coming to an end, and the weight of the Southern Coastal ticket was a weight around her heart. As she sat in the hotel room, she could not escape the truth.

When she'd left Bridgeton a year and half ago, she was a different person. She'd been fed up with being the daughter of a poor fisherman, and she'd wanted to see the world. Now, she wanted to stay right where she was, to find out if she had any future with Levi.

The date on the ticket for her departure was tomorrow. She still had time to see Letty, Thomas and Emily, and Mrs. Cates, and she would spend as much time as she could with Levi. Kit had followed Levi's instructions not to speak of her imminent trip back to Arizona, but now that conversation could no longer be avoided.

Kit folded the ticket and placed it carefully in her purse. She packed her clothes, shoes, and hats into her trunk, leaving her traveling suit hanging on the door of her room. Placing all her belongings back into that heavy trunk should have been a joyous occasion for her. Letty hadn't died, and she was once again leaving this tiny town, a mere dot on the map of North Carolina. She tried to take comfort in knowing that soon she would be back with her friends out west, friends who had scraped together a large sum of money for this trip.

Today, on this last day she would be in Bridgeton, she made sure her hair was styled in a perfect pompadour. Her black skirt was offset by a pale blue waistcoat and a blue jacket, and a blue striped ribbon adorned her hair. The reflection in the mirror showed a young woman, poised and polished, dressed in the latest fashion – but inside, Kit was a poor girl from Fish Town who was trying not to cry.

Opening her purse, she counted her money. She'd barely touched the generous sum from Annie and she had still most of her own money, plus the traveling money provided by her friends in Holbrook. She wanted to return the money to Annie, and pay back Mrs. Cates. Mrs. Cates had never asked her for a dime of the money she had given her so long ago, but Kit hadn't forgotten. After paying her hotel bill and Mrs. Cates, she knew she would still have a tidy sum left and she knew just how she wanted to spend it.

The carriage ride to the Harper residence was the last she would take. The driver, the same gentlemen who had carried her back and forth from Fish Town each time, had been kind and reliable. Kit tipped him generously before he left her at Letty's house. Walking up the front steps, Kit turned to look in the direction of her own family's house. She wished it had ended differently with her parents, but she realized not every story had a happy ending.

Mrs. Harper welcomed her inside on that cold winter morning and Kit realized that was good enough for her, to be welcome at one home in Fish Town.

"My, don't you look stylish?"

"Thanks Mrs. Harper, I've come to say goodbye to Letty."

"I want to thank you, Kit, for all that you done for my girl. If it wasn't for you, Mrs. Quidley, and that handsome doctor of yours, I dread to think what would have happened."

"What would we do without our Letty?" asked Kit.

"Kit Pridgeon!" said Letty from the top of the stairs.

Kit turned her attention to her best friend. Letty was thin and small after her illness, but she was standing, her cheeks were rosy, and her spirit was as lively as ever.

Holding her skirt, Kit bounded up the stairs the way she had when she and Letty were children.

"What are you doing out of bed?" Kit asked Letty.

"Tomorrow is the day the doctor said I can walk down those stairs if I take it slow and careful, finally!"

"Oh Letty, just one more day. Now get back to bed! You've been good this long, try to be good a little longer."

"Why should I? What's one more day?" asked Letty.

"If you promise to behave I have a surprise for you. Come, back to bed with you," Kit said as she put her arm around Letty's small frame.

"A surprise? I will behave," answered Letty, as she let Kit lead her back to bed.

Kit tucked in the patient. Her bedroom was warm and cozy as a cold wind howled outside the window; winter had returned. Kit found it fitting that the chilly, frigid air and the mournful sound of wind blowing in the trees echoed her melancholy mood.

Letty sat in bed, propped on several feather pillows. Her face, though thinner than it once was, still looked as pouty and petulant as before. Kit hid all trace of her own distress at leaving her friend and the man she was falling in love with as she smiled. "Close your eyes and hold out your hand."

Letty frowned. "You aren't going to put a snake in my hand, or a great big spider, are you?"

"No, not this time, now close your eyes," said Kit.

Letty closed her eyes and reached out her hand. Kit dug into her purse and pulled out a roll of money tied with a ribbon, which she carefully placed in her friend's hand. Gently she closed Letty's fingers around the gift.

"Before you open your eyes, you have to swear that what I gave you stays a secret. You can tell my brother but no one else, you hear? You can open your eyes now."

"I promise," said Letty as she opened her eyes and opened her hand, dropping the roll of currency on the handmade quilt. "Kit, is that money?"

"It is. It's a wedding gift. I want to make sure you have enough money to buy a pretty dress, or get set up in a house, or buy whatever you need to."

"Oh Kit, I can't take this. It wouldn't be right."

"Yes, you can, and I insist. I shouldn't have left town without telling you – you've done so much for me. Because of you I have my brother and sister back in my life. I know you would do the same for me."

"I won't lie to you, it would be good to have a little money to spend on a new hat for my wedding. Thank you, Kit, thank you. I won't tell anyone but Thomas, I promise. But Kit, you are going to be at my wedding, aren't you?"

"I wouldn't miss it for the world."

Letty and Kit laughed and talked of the future. Letty's path was clear, and Kit's was not. As the hours ticked by, much faster now than they had before, Kit felt a tugging at her heart. She would miss Letty. Her only consolation was that she would be back for her best friend's wedding.

Levi arrived late in the day, greeting his patient. "Miss Harper, this is our last visit together, how do you feel?"

"Doctor Kellerman, I am ready to run down the stairs!" Letty beamed.

Levi examined Letty and said, "Looks to me like you are almost healed. Tomorrow you can leave your bed and walk slowly down the stairs, but no running, skipping, or jumping for another two weeks, do you hear me?"

"I can go downstairs and walk wherever I like, no running, but walking is allowed?"

"Yes ma'am. Take it really slow and be careful, and I don't see why you have to stay in bed any longer."

"What about work? Can I go back to work at the cannery?"

"Give that another two weeks. I don't want you standing on your feet more than you have to."

Letty turned to Kit, and winked. "Good thing you gave me that present. It looks like it will come in handy."

Levi touched Kit's elbow. "Are you ready?"

164

"I am. Give me just a minute,"

Levi left the room and walked downstairs,

"Letty, I will write to you. Promise you will write back."

"Oh, Kit. I don't want you to go, but I understand. You always were one for adventures. Maybe you can come back for good one day."

"Maybe so, but I will see you this spring. Write to me, and let me know if there is anything you need for your wedding, anything at all."

"I will. Will you promise me something? Say yes to that man, when he asks you to marry him, you hear?"

Kit leaned down and hugged her best friend. "I will, I promise you."

"Good, then our kids can grow up together and be best friends."

"Goodbye, Letty. Take care of yourself. Give my love to Jacob."

Kit wiped away a tear as she walked out of Letty's room and down the stairs. Levi was talking quietly with Mrs. Harper and turned to Kit with a warm smile as she joined him at the door.

"My carriage is waiting outside," he said quietly.

Kit said goodbye to Mrs. Harper, and she and Levi walked down the steps and to his carriage. As the carriage made its way slowly through the streets of Fish Town, Kit silently said her goodbyes to her family, hoping that one day they would understand why she'd left.

"Levi, can we stop at the library? I want to see Mrs. Cates before I leave."

"We can do anything you like, anything at all." Levi turned the carriage towards the library.

The silence between Kit and Levi was heavy and seemed impenetrable. Kit was lost in her own thoughts. The time slipping by far too quickly. Gazing at Levi, she saw that his brow was furrowed, and she knew that he felt it too – that they had run out of time.

"I'll wait here for you." Levi stopped the carriage in front of the library. He offered his hand to her as she stepped out onto the sidewalk. Kit felt the undeniable electricity that his touch always brought, and she did not want to leave him, not even for a second.

"I won't be long," she said.

"Take your time. I'm not going anywhere," he answered, words that Kit hoped he meant regarding more than waiting for her to say goodbye to an old friend.

The library was filled with students and their mothers selecting books and waiting to be checked out, but Mrs. Cates found a few minutes for Kit. Kit gave Mrs. Cates a small white envelope with the letterhead of the hotel engraved in gold on the outside. She thanked her for all her help, and promised to see her in the spring. As Mrs. Cates said goodbye, she reminded Kit to trust her heart, and Kit promised that she would.

It was a tearful day for Kit, saying goodbye to the people who had loved her and supported all the years when her own family would not. As painful as it was to say goodbye to the people she had grown up with, the most painful goodbye was yet to come.

Levi helped Kit back into the carriage, reached for her hand, and kissed it once more.

"Kit, my darling, will you not be happy? We have tonight," he said.

"I want to be happy, but saying goodbye is so hard – much harder than I thought it would be."

"I know it is, but you must not think on it right now. I have made reservations for a private dining room at the hotel. I wanted to make this last night memorable."

"Thank you, Levi, but you have already made this trip memorable,"

As the sun was setting, Levi put his arm around Kit. The temperature was dropping and Kit snuggled against him for warmth. She felt safe and secure beside him, with his arm around her. It was a display of affection not normally seen in Bridgeton, but Kit didn't care about how unseemly it may have looked. She just wanted to be close to him, to feel his warmth and smell his clean masculine scent before she had to leave him and travel to the other side of the country.

Arriving back at the hotel, Kit and the doctor were shown into a small but richly appointed dining room, where a fire blazed in the fireplace. A wall of windows framed the view of the water and the docks in a breathtaking picture, and the lanterns from the ships twinkled in the fading light of the day.

Kit stood by the windows, her eyes turned to the water, trying to compose herself – to do as Levi had asked – to be happy in their last moments together. Levi stood behind her and said, "I have arranged a special dinner for our last night together. I hope you don't mind."

"No, not at all, Levi," she said as she turned to face him. "I know you asked me to be happy, and I am happy – I am happy that I met you and that we have had this time together – but I can't lie to you. I am desperately unhappy."

Levi leaned close to her, his face only inches away from hers. "Kit, I am unhappy too. I have tried to smile and to be brave but I confess, I cannot be happy tonight. If I cannot be happy, perhaps I can give you a memory to take back to Arizona – a memory that I hope you will return to time and again when you think of me."

"What memory is that? You have given me so many wonderful memories."

"I want you to remember this," he said as he embraced Kit in his arms and kissed her, pressing his lips to hers in a passionate expression of his true feelings.

Kit closed her eyes. The feeling of his lips touching hers, and his arms around her, made everything else disappear – the breathtaking view, the dining room, everything melted away as she was swept away by his kiss.

He whispered into her ear, "Kit, I love you."

"Levi, you must know that I love you, that I think of you, and only you, every waking moment," she said as she stared into his dark brown eyes.

Levi spoke quietly, carefully. "Kit it is because I love you that I can't ask you to marry me."

Kit's moment of happiness was shattered so quickly that she felt faint. She leaned against the windowsill to steady herself, her world spinning out of control. She was reeling from the overwhelming and conflicting emotions that consumer her. His kiss promised her love, his words spoke of the emotion they both felt, yet he could not marry her.

"Levi, how can that be? You love me.?"

"Yes, my darling, that is the reason I cannot force you to give up your dreams, your career, to be the wife of a doctor."

"Isn't that for me to decide?" she asked as she looked into his eyes.

"It is, but it would be wrong of me to ask that of you – so wrong. Can you not see that I am doing this for you?"

Just as Mrs. Cates had said she should do, Kit answered with her heart, "Levi, I would do anything for you. I would give up my career, my world out west – all of it. I would gladly give up everything."

Levi held her hand and gently said, "I know you would, but I can't say the same thing. my patients need me and I can't leave them. I have no right to ask you to change your life for me."

"But Levi, you are a doctor. Your work is far more important."

"Is it? Kit, don't you see? You are far more than a waitress. Wherever you go, you bring culture, a reminder of the pleasant, good things of life. You are creating history, even if you don't know that."

"Let some other girl create history, Levi. I want to be with you."

"And I want to be with you. But Kit, I can't ask you to marry me, not just yet."

Kit searched Levi's face for any hint of what he meant. "Not yet? What do you mean?"

Levi gazed into her eyes. Slowly, he wiped a tear away from her cheek and said, "Kit, you still have a part to play in the story of the west. You have a promotion coming, and people who are counting on you – it would be a crime to ask you to leave that behind. Please understand me – I want nothing more than to marry you, but to ask you this very night – I can't."

"What if I resigned? What if I chose to stay here – then what would you do?' she asked.

"Don't do that, not yet. You owe it to yourself to find out what you could have been, to see this adventure through to the end. When I ask you to marry me, I don't want you to have to choose. I don't want you to ever regret leaving that behind to marry me, not for a single moment."

"Levi, I would not regret it. I promise you I wouldn't."

"Not now, but one day you might. My darling, I am not saying goodbye to you –I will be here in Bridgeton. I am not going anywhere."

"Oh Levi, why does this feel like the end?"

"It isn't the end, Kit. I promise you – *this is not the end.*" He drew her to him once more and kissed her. His kiss was full of passion and promise, a promise Kit hoped he would not break.

CHAPTER 12

The last time Kit left Bridgeton she'd been riding in the mail car, seated on a sack of correspondence, and bound for Raleigh. Dressed in her Sunday best and carrying just enough money to get to the capital, she'd been determined to see the world and making something of her life.

This time, she was seated in a comfortable, upholstered chair, with a hamper of treats sent by Mrs. Cates at her side. Her traveling suit was the latest fashion, and she no longer resembled that girl from mail car. But staring at her reflection in the window, Kit didn't feel confident and sure of herself – not any more. She felt nervous, uncertain about the future, and that was because of Doctor Levi Kellerman.

The note he'd sent to the hotel was folded neatly in her purse. He regretted that he was unable to see her to the station because of a sudden, urgent call to the bedside of a patient who was delivering twins. Kit would have liked to have seen him once more, to kiss his lips again before she boarded the train headed for Holbrook, Arizona, but that was not to be. His duty called and Kit understood that as a doctor, his work would always come first.

Watching the dull brown dirt of unplowed fields drift past her window, she tried not to break down and cry as a porter walked by on his way to another car. She didn't know why she was crying, not exactly. Levi had confessed his love for her. He'd said he did not want to marry anyone else, but he couldn't marry her – at least, not yet. His words had stung her and cut

171

her to her heart, because her position as a Harvey Girl had been the reason she was able to dress in clothes that gave her the appearance of being socially his equal in the first place. It was strange to think that her wages as a Harvey Girl helped her catch his attention, and yet the job was the reason he could not ask her to be his wife. It was a puzzle, and she felt as though she would never solve it.

She tried to cheer herself up by remembering that he had promised to ask her to marry him in the future, but Kit didn't know when that would be. Should she pin her hopes on a promise? She hoped it was not an empty one, like the promises made by that scoundrel head cook to her friend Maggie.

Maggie. Kit had an evening free in Raleigh and she hoped to see Mrs. Taylor at the boarding house, and her closest friend Maggie Lawson. Maggie was not expecting her, and the thought of surprising her old friend brought a smile to Kit's tearstained face.

Reaching into the hamper, Kit was astonished to find a book tucked in beside the tins of fudge and cookies. Pulling the book out of the hamper, she was pleased to see that it was a copy of *Jane Eyre*, a book Kit had loved as a girl. She opened the book and read the date of her departure written in Mrs. Cates careful hand across the top, with a message.

Just like Jane, you have transformed into a proper lady. I am sending you my hopes and prayers.

Adelaide Cates

Kit thought about the tumultuous road to happily-ever-after for the main character in the book, and wondered if perhaps that was why Mrs. Cates had selected it for her journey. Also, the book was enormous, providing her with hours of entertainment as she traveled across the country. Trying to take her mind of Levi, Kit began reading the first chapter as she nibbled on a cookie.

Late in the afternoon, the train arrived at the station in Raleigh. A porter arranged for Kit and her trunk to be delivered at Mrs. Taylor's boarding house only two blocks from the station. Hoping Mrs. Taylor had a vacancy, Kit rang the doorbell and was greeted by an older woman who grinned from ear to ear at the sight of her.

"My word, Kit! You have come home safe and sound! Come in, come in."

"Mrs. Taylor, my trunk is in the carriage. I should have telegrammed that I was coming, but do you have a room for the night?"

"I do, but even if I didn't you would still have a place to sleep." She waved to the carriage driver to bring the trunk. With the coaxing of an extra tip, she convinced him to carry the trunk upstairs to a large room with a hand-carved four poster bed and a seating area.

Kit looked at her surroundings and said, "Mrs. Taylor, I know I look like I have money, but I am just a poor as ever. Do you have my old room, the small one?"

"I won't hear another word about this; you can stay here for the night. It's my finest room, the one I reserve for my best guests – and you, my dear, are a fine young lady who doesn't owe me a red cent. Not one, do you hear me?"

"Mrs. Taylor, it's not right. At least let me pay you something."

"If you insist, you can pay the carriage driver and see to his tip. That is all the payment I will accept from you."

"Yes, ma'am. It sure is good to see you, but before I sit a spell with you, I must go and see someone."

"If you hurry, I believe you can catch that nice carriage driver. He may be able to take you on your mysterious errand. Don't forget dinner is at seven. Tonight is chicken pastry and pecan pie."

"Thank you, Mrs. Taylor. I won't be late."

Kit dashed down the stairs and convinced the carriage driver to take her to one more destination, Lawson's General Mercantile.

The carriage rolled to a stop and Kit jumped out and paid the driver. Clutching her hat onto her head in the bitterly cold winter breeze, she walked into the clean and cheerful store owned by Maggie's father. Although not as upscale as the department stores, Lawson's boasted an impressive display of cloth, laces, and nearly every type of candy or cooking implement a modern woman would want for her kitchen.

Not seeing Maggie, Kit waited in line at the counter and was greeted by a handsome young man with sandy blond hair, a mustache, and sparkling blue eyes. His manners and composure made him seem confident and in charge.

"Miss, how may I be of assistance?" he asked with a slight southern accent.

"I was hoping you could tell me where I might find Miss Maggie Lawson?"

"May I ask what is the nature of your inquiry? Perhaps there is some way I can be of assistance."

"You are kind, sir, but I'm an old friend of Miss Lawson and I would very much like to see her, if I may?"

"Yes. Is she expecting you? Who may I say has called on her?"

Kit answered in a whisper. "You may find this rude, but I would rather not say. I was hoping to surprise her as she is not expecting me."

The handsome man leaned down to Kit's height and whispered back, "Yes ma'am, I will assist you in this grand conspiracy. If you will permit me, I will only be gone a moment."

"Thank you."

Kit waited by the candy display. The smell of sugar filled the air and Kit's mouth watered as she was tempted by the bright yellow lemon drops. As promised, the young man returned with Maggie.

"Kit Lawson, I never! Why didn't you write me and tell me you were coming?"

"I didn't know myself."

"If you two ladies will excuse me, it seems that Mrs. Crawford needs my assistance in fabrics."

"Yes, thank you, Reginald," said Maggie.

The young man named Reginald nodded his head to Maggie, and Kit was certain that she saw the unmistakable lingering glance, a meeting of the eyes that signaled her closest friend was not wasting any time nursing her broken heart.

As Reginald walked away, Maggie grabbed Kit by the elbow and steered her to the back of the store. "Kit, isn't he delightful? Papa hired him in my absence and he has shown real promise."

"I know it may be wrong of me to remind you of this," Kit said, stepping around the edge of a shelf of nails and bolts, "and it's all water under the bridge, but I once saw you look at someone else that way."

"You're not wrong to bring that up, but I feel like this time it's different. Reginald is just like us – he works hard and he isn't afraid to learn something new. You'd never believe me if I told you he worked as farm hand in Johnson county only a few years ago. He's a good, honest man and the sole breadwinner for his family. His mother is a widow and he has two younger sisters."

Kit listened as Maggie described all the things about Reginald that made her forget her ill-fated affair with Joshua Smith. Watching Reginald assisting an elderly woman with her purchases, Kit was impressed by the respect and kindness he showed to the woman, who was dressed only slightly better than Kit used to when she worked at the cannery. He held the door open for the woman, and wished her a good day, unaware he was being observed.

Kit turned to Maggie and said, "What did I tell you; isn't he a saint?"

"I can't disagree with you about that, but I'm afraid that makes the second reason for my visit unnecessary," said Kit with a sigh.

"There you go, speaking in riddles again! The first reason you came here today was to see your old friend – that would be me – and the second reason you came, I cannot guess. Is it to tell me that you have left the waitressing profession and need a job? If so, I can hire you without hesitation."

"Would you hire me? I shall have to keep that in mind. I was coming here on the same mission."

Maggie pulled Kit into a small, cramped office in the back of the store, where accounting books lay open and advertisements for everything from corsets to throat lozenges lay piled on the corner of the desk.

"Sit down. Welcome to my office."

Kit sat down with a frown on her face. This trip was not turning out how she had envisioned it, not at all. "Maggie, I can see you have settled into your life here. You have Reginald and your work helping your father run the store."

"All that may be true, but I'm still curious about your reason for coming here today. You told me you are on a mission. What is it, may I ask?"

"I came to see you on my way back from home. Letty was terribly ill and nearly died, but she is much better now. Before I left Arizona, Mr. Harvey offered me a promotion."

"He'd be foolish not to offer you a promotion, as hard as you work. Don't tell me you're going to California! I'm so envious – how wonderful for you, congratulations!"

"Not exactly. There is a delay in the opening of the restaurants in California, but he's opening a new restaurant in Pueblo, Colorado. It's nicer, more modern, and bigger than any other Harvey Restaurant in that part of the country. I'm to be the head waitress and Mr. Harvey told me I could pick my own staff. I was hoping I could convince you to return with me, to finish what we started, to show that staff in Pueblo what two southern girls can do."

Maggie smiled and sighed. "Oh Kit, it does sound like a grand plan. I would have liked to join you on that adventure but since I've returned home, I think my adventuring days are behind me. Even without the prospect of the handsome Reginald, my family needs me to help with the store. Of all my brothers and sisters, I have the best head for business. I'm the level headed one, can you believe that?"

Kit whispered, "They must not know about Arizona."

Maggie giggled. "Oh no, they don't suspect a thing. I simply told them my year contract was at an end and I was homesick for the green grass and oak trees of home."

"Well, I'll never tell," promised Kit.

"You'd better not, you goose, or else you won't be invited to my wedding," said Maggie.

Kit burst out in joy, "You didn't tell me your relationship with Reginald was that far along! You are awful, Maggie Lawson."

"Be quiet! Reginald doesn't know it yet, but I'm already planning our wedding in my head."

"Just be careful. Remember what happened last time."

"There isn't going to be a next time, I can promise you that. Not ever again. I learned that lesson and I've done my homework on my dashing clerk. He isn't married!"

"Maggie, it was good to see you but I must be going, Mrs. Taylor is expecting for me dinner."

Maggie's smile turned to a frown. "Oh Kit, you've only just got here! Are you sure you can't stay for just a few nights? We can eat sweets and catch up on the gossip."

"Sadly, my train leaves tomorrow, but if you do catch this clerk on your hook, promise you will invite me to the wedding. I'll be heartbroken if you forget me."

"Oh Kit, how could I ever forget you? Tell me the truth, before you go. Don't you ever think about settling down and getting married? Isn't there any fellow who turns your head?"

Kit took a deep breath. There was simply not enough time to tell Maggie about Levi and her crisis with the man she loved. Her heart ached from the knowledge that he would not ask her to marry him, and she felt as though she would never see him again. During her train trip to Raleigh and through every minute of her conversation with Maggie, Kit had tried desperately to distract herself from the feelings she did not want to face. Those same feelings were bubbling close to the surface like boiling water, ready to tumble over the sides of her self-control.

Turning away, Kit stifled her feelings once more and shook her head. "Maggie, my dear, you know me. I'm a career girl destined to become a spinster with beautiful clothes and plenty of money. When do I have time to think of marriage?"

"You may be a career girl, but you don't fool me. I know you. I know you just haven't met the right man yet. You're going to keep working and getting promotions until that train carries you all the way to the Pacific. Maybe there you'll find your husband waiting for you."

"Maybe so, Maggie. You never can tell, can you? I mean, look at you! You traveled all the way across the country only to find the man you love right here, working at your family's store."

177

"Yes, that's just what I mean. I know your future husband is waiting for you somewhere. You just have to go out there and find him."

Kit and Maggie embraced and promised to keep in touch. Kit told Maggie she would keep an eye out for that wedding invitation, and Maggie blushed and giggled. As Kit left Lawson's General Mercantile she waved at the handsome Reginald and thought to herself that maybe, just like her friend Maggie, she didn't need to go gallivanting across the country to find her future husband. He was already at home waiting for her. All she had to do was board the train and return to Bridgeton.

"Listen to me – I love you like you were my own daughter and I'm proud of you. Do you hear me? But I will not let you go back to Bridgeton if I have to use the last breath in my body. Are you listening to me?" scolded Mrs. Taylor as she sat with Kit in the kitchen of the boarding house after dinner.

"Mrs. Taylor, I appreciate that. I do. And I know you mean well, but I love him, and what am I supposed to do?"

Kit had chosen not to tell Maggie about Levi, partly because she knew her impulsive friend's advice would be meant well, but ill-conceived – and partly because her friend looked so happy after having her heart destroyed by a man. Kit hated to upset Maggie's joy with her own troubles, but Mrs. Taylor was a different story. The older woman had bonded with Kit, and Kit felt as though she could tell the woman any secret in the world and ask for advice that she knew would be what she needed to hear.

Unfortunately, this advice was not what she *wanted* to hear.

Kit stabbed her fork into a piece of pie. The other guests had retired to the parlor, and she'd joined Mrs. Taylor in the kitchen to help clean up and to eat more pie. Sugary desserts and candy were keeping her heartbreak under control, although she worried about busting her corset.

"Kit, my dear, I am not trying to steer you on a wrong course. If I thought the young man would marry you, I would put you on the train myself, ride all the way to Bridgeton, and stand at your side as he proposed, but I cannot tell you a lie."

The tears that Kit had buried deep inside her chest spilled over at last, and ran down her cheeks as she chewed the dessert. Swallowing, she wiped her eyes with a napkin and looked down at her plate.

"I trust you. I know you would never tell me anything meant to hurt me, but the truth does hurt. I thought he loved me. After all, he told me he loved me – but he couldn't marry me, not yet."

"The question is, my dear, is not whether you believe me, but do you believe him?"

Kit wondered that same thing. Maggie had her heart broken in Holbrook by a man who'd promised her a future that he could not provide, because he was already married. Kit thought about that, and knew it had influenced her way of thinking about this subject.

"That's just it. I love him but I don't know if I can trust him. He is going to be so far away, and what if he forgets all about me and marries another girl?"

"There, there, my dear, you must not think like that. Supposing such a thing does happen, then he was a scoundrel. Be thankful you had the good sense to keep your position as a Harvey girl, and not ruin your life for a man who didn't care one bit for you."

Kit wiped her face, and folded the napkin on her leg with a sigh. "I should be happy to have this promotion and move to Colorado. It's a big city with theaters, department stores, and more churches than I have any use for, but what about Levi?"

Mrs. Taylor patted her hand. "This is going to be hard for you to hear, but until he proposes, you must consider yourself as free to pursue your career as you ever were. I will pray that he was not telling you a falsehood, but until he actually asks for your hand, you won't know his true intentions."

"But if you could only have seen how he saved Letty's life. She nearly died and he took care of her, and he never charged her family a dime – not a dime – for his services. He's a good man. That must mean he intends to keep his promise, doesn't it?" Kit asked hopefully, almost begging for Mrs. Taylor to agree with her, to give her a shred of hope.

"He does sound like a God-fearing man, a man who has goodness flowing through his veins, but my dear, as kind as he may be, when it comes to matters of the heart, all bets are off. I am not saying he didn't mean what he told you. He did; I am most assured that he meant every word while he was

179

with you. But as time goes on and the distance wears on him and you, that will be the true test of whether or not he meant those words. Then you'll soon see if he can be trusted, and if he is the one for you."

Kit listened to every word Mrs. Taylor told her. All the advice was sensible and gave her a glimmer of hope. "If he still writes to me and professes his love months after I arrive in Pueblo, then I will know his heart is true."

Mrs. Taylor cut a sliver of pecan pie and carefully laid it on her plate. Picking up the fork, she cut into the pie. "Perhaps. But don't let those thoughts drive you mad. You have your work ahead of you when you get to that fine restaurant in the great mountains. I am telling you this not to hurt you, but to remind you not to overlook any opportunities that might be right in front of you."

"But Mrs. Taylor, we aren't allowed to court, not while we are under contract."

"I'm not telling you to break any rules. All I'm trying to tell you, you silly girl, is a young lady as pretty as you are – with a fine personality and a willingness to work hard – might just meet a man who doesn't make her wait. Will you think of that?"

Kit sat in stunned silence, thinking about Mrs. Taylor's advice. "When you put it like that, it does sound terrible doesn't it? It sounds like he wants me to wait to get my wildness and adventure out of my system, like a fever running its course. He told me he was certain that I would regret marrying him, if I still have this desire to keep working and see the West in my soul. But what does he know about what is in my soul? Was it not my decision to make, whether I had seen enough and was ready to settle down? But he thought he knew better, didn't he?"

Mrs. Taylor smiled and nodded. "That is the Kit Pridgeon I know: ambitious, strong, and not sniveling over a man. I know he's good man; I don't doubt that. I know you love him and I think he may just love you. But how is he supposed to know what's best for you, as though you're a child? My dear, you are a woman and you still have a nation to conquer."

Kit shook her head in disbelief. "I do love him, that is true, but why I am going to let a man – no matter how well-meaning he may be – make decisions for me? You're right. I will write to him and pray that he comes to his senses and asks for my hand in marriage. I want to be his wife more than anything I've ever wanted in the world."

"Kit, are you sure about that? I remember a girl who, not so long ago, wanted nothing more than to become a Harvey Girl and hop on a train bound for God only knows where. Which one are you, sitting at my table, eating my pecan pie? Ask yourself that question."

"I don't know. You would have made a fine lawyer, Mrs. Taylor, because in the space of one evening you have certainly made things both clearer, and less clear. My heart still hurts like I have never felt before, but you've given me much to think about."

"Judging from that long train ride you have got ahead of you, I would wager that you have plenty of time to do all the thinking you could ever want."

CHAPTER 13

Accompanied by two hampers, one of sweets and the other filled with fried chicken and cold ham sandwiches, Kit was on a train headed West. This time she rode alone, without the companionship of a group of other young women as nervous and excited as she had been about leaving home and traveling over a thousand miles away.

Once more, Kit watched the Appalachians become the foothills, and trees grew sparse as the train left the East and steamed across the prairie. Snow many feet deep stretched as far as the eye could see in parts of Kansas, and then further west, the snow was gone once more – barely a patch on the ground as hearty pines and red rocks took over the scenery that passed outside her window.

Her book lay open in her lap, the note from Levi tucked into its pages. Her confusion about him was threatening to take over her mind and shatter her resolve. Thoughts of resigning still tempted her act impulsively, against Mrs. Taylor's advice. She wanted to be at Levi's side, to accompany him as he cared for the sick, and sit with him in the evenings by the fireside.

The memories of his lips on hers, his dark eyes, and his laugh were bittersweet as she remembered that he hadn't begged her to stay, he had not asked her to marry him. As tough as the truth was to face, he could live without her. Kit wasn't sure she could live without him.

Returning to the book, Kit vowed that she would be patient. She would resist the temptation to resign. Mr. Harvey was counting on her, and she would not let him down. It pained her to think how easily she would leave that life, if only Levi asked. She felt guilty, knowing she would turn her back on those people who were closer to her than her family, and how one-sided her affection for Levi truly seemed.

Kit stared out the window once more. She recognized the harsh and unforgiving landscape of New Mexico and felt relief that soon she would be back in Holbrook. The town was uncivilized and possessed no charm other than its desolate landscape, yet it was in Holbrook that she had made a life – a life that didn't leave her with more questions than answers. A life that wasn't filled with people who left her feeling confused and broken.

The next afternoon, the train arrived at the Holbrook station. Mr. Tate was not in his customary position on the platform to meet the hungry travelers. Instead, Kit was met by Hattie and Emma, who greeted her with a smile and a wave as they ushered travelers into the warm and inviting restaurant.

It was unusual for Mr. Tate, together with one of the cooks, not to be at the station, but Kit gave the matter no more thought as she arranged for the stationmaster to have her trunk sent to her residence. Exhausted from her journey, she wanted nothing more than a long, hot bath and a nap. Judging from the sudden appearance of Annie, who rushed towards her from the restaurant, that did not seem likely to happen.

"Kit, you're back – I'm so glad. Why didn't you telegram?"

"I meant to, I really did, but I had so much on my mind."

"We have to get back to the restaurant but tell me, how is Letty?"

"Letty will make a full recovery, thank you. I can give you back that money. Levi – I mean the doctor – wouldn't take any payment."

At the mention of his name, Kit nearly cried.

"I'm happy she is well, and I don't care about the money. There is so much to tell you! I know you want to rest, but we need you. Can you come help us?"

"I can, but I don't have my uniform on."

"I don't think anyone will tell, not this time. Come on!" Annie grabbed Kit's hand and hurried back to the restaurant.

As Kit walked in the door, she was greeted by tables full of travelers and townsfolk, the smell of steak and fresh coffee, and the noise of a bustling, busy dining room. Following Annie, she made her way through the dining room to the kitchen. Taking her jacket off and leaving her purse and hampers in the pantry, she looked down at her skirt and blouse. They were wrinkled and dusty, and she frowned.

Annie came racing into the kitchen with an order.

"Annie, I'm a crumpled mess. I can't serve guests like this."

Annie grabbed an apron off the coat hook by the kitchen door. "Yes, you can. Here, take my extra apron; it will hide the wrinkles. Come on, we have to hurry!"

It was a shock to her system at first, to be back in the middle of a lunchtime rush, but Kit soon fell back into her routine. It was late in the afternoon when she finally had a moment to catch her breath. Standing in the kitchen, she quickly drank a cup of coffee as she began to wonder why Annie was so frantic. Kit watched as Percy put the finishing touches on a cake before he turned to greet her.

"Look what the cat drug in! You are a sight for sore eyes, Kit, how are you?" he asked, with his customary cheerful smile.

Kit stepped closer to him and spoke softly. "Percy, I know I've been gone for a little while, but have I missed something? Annie was in a tizzy when I arrived and I haven't seen Mr. Tate."

"Tsk, tsk, if I didn't know better, I'd say you're trying to get the latest gossip out of me."

"Of course I am, silly."

Percy whistled. "It's quite a story, but I think Annie would prefer to tell you. She has missed having you around."

"You can tell me – it'll be our little secret," Kit said.

"No, not this time. I wouldn't want to ruin Annie's fun; she would never forgive me."

185

"If that's how you want to play it, Mr. Bryce, I will remember that you've been no help, no help to me at all," said Kit with a good-natured smile. "Enough about the news you aren't telling me, how are you and Annie?"

"We couldn't be better, and that's why I want to keep her on my good side by not spoiling the surprise."

"The surprise? That's not fair. I'm tired, hungry, and overwrought, and you won't tell me what I've missed."

"He'd better not, if he knows what's good for him!" exclaimed Annie as she rushed into the kitchen and scolded Percy.

Percy held his hands up. "I wasn't, honest! Not a word – Kit can tell you."

"It's true. He resisted all my begging and pleading, but he did say that you knew all about it, so tell me! I can't be patient, not a minute longer," Kit whined.

"Well, you will have to be, but I promise to tell you tonight after dinner. I swear it!" Annie exclaimed with a gleam in her eye.

"Very well," said Kit. "But it had better be good. Here you have me waiting tables in my traveling clothes and you won't tell me a word of gossip, not a word."

Annie's eyes twinkled with mischief. "It is good – better than good. Just you wait!"

Looking from Annie to Percy, Kit shrugged her shoulders. "What choice do I have?"

Annie took her arm. "None. Come on, the day isn't over yet! All that time away has made you lazy."

"And tired." Kit handed the empty coffee cup to Percy and followed Annie back into the dining room, her hand covering her mouth as she yawned.

~

Kit's room looked like the interior of a small ladies' shop; gloves, hat boxes, skirts, and shoes lay on every surface. Trying to sort through the outfits she

186

had not worn was tiring. The pile of clothes in need of washing spilled over the top of her hamper, and there wasn't a clean surface to be seen that wasn't covered with parts of her wardrobe. She detested unpacking, but it kept her mind occupied from thoughts of Levi and the gossip Annie had yet to disclose.

Just thinking of Levi sent Kit into an emotional abyss. The pain of his refusal to propose to her was fresh, like a wound that had not healed, and would likely not heal for many months. It was fresh and sharp, and without distractions, it threatened to consume her. If she thought too much about him, she felt like never leaving her bedroom ever again.

Fighting the urge to read his note once more, Kit was trying to concentrate on the task at hand when there came an insistent rapping at the door.

"Kit, open up. It's me," said Annie.

Kit opened the door and Annie pushed her way past several hat boxes, closing the door behind herself.

"You may have to clear a place to sit down. There is a tin of homemade fudge on the desk, if you'd like a piece."

"Delicious. I would have brought tea if I had known there would be refreshments served," teased Annie as she carefully repositioned a skirt from the desk chair and opened the tin. "Kit, this fudge is tops. Did you make it?"

"My friend Mrs. Cates did, and I'm surprised it survived the trip. Before it slips my mind," Kit reached for her purse and slid a large roll of money from its depths, handing it to Annie. "Thank you, but I was fortunate not to have to use it. You were so kind to loan me that, I won't forget it."

Annie accepted the money and absentmindedly dropped it onto the desk by the tin of fudge, "Kit, you could have kept it, but thank you."

Kit shoved her collection of gloves from the corner of the bed and reached for the fudge tin. "Annie Blyth, since you came willingly to my room I won't consider you a hostage, but if you don't tell me right now what it is I've missed, you will leave me no choice but to lock the door until you do. Do you hear me?"

"Yes, ma'am. Why do you think I came to see you?"

"You have my full attention." Kit bit into the fudge.

187

"Even though you were tired from your travels and almost delirious with fatigue and hunger, I bet you noticed that both Mr. Tate and Joshua were missing from the restaurant."

"I did notice Mr. Tate was gone, but I thought it was his day off."

"Oh, it's his day off today, all right, and it will be for the next several days as he sits at home nursing a broken nose!"

"A broken nose? What happened? Annie don't make me wait any longer, you tell me this instant!"

"It all started the day after you left. That Joshua Smith – what a no-good rake he is – he began flirting with Hattie, or at least he tried to."

"Poor Hattie, and poor Mrs. Smith. You would have thought Joshua was through acting like a lovesick Romeo after what happened with Maggie."

"As you know, his wife never seemed any wiser and Maggie, well, it was her heart broken, wasn't it? Not his."

Kit nodded. "I suppose you're right. So what happened?"

"Well, Hattie wasn't having it. She may be a country girl, but she was not foolish enough to fall for his tricks, and that was a good thing because of what happened yesterday."

"Yesterday, you mean if I'd come back one day earlier I'd know what happened?"

"Yes! It was yesterday in the middle of the lunch rush, when a girl I've never seen before, a girl from a saloon, came into the restaurant. She was dressed – I don't like to say how – but I am sure you can imagine. Mr. Tate greeted her, mistaking her for a guest."

"Was she? We haven't had any of those girls come in to the restaurant before."

"No, we haven't, but she wasn't there to eat. She was there to see Joshua."

"Oh Annie, how embarrassing!"

"Mr. Tate asked her to please wait outside and she refused. She made quite a scene. Joshua came out of the kitchen and said something to the girl. She left after that."

"Annie, you still haven't told me how Mr. Tate wound up with a broken nose."

"I was just getting to that. It was late yesterday afternoon, there weren't many customers, and this time Mrs. Smith came by the restaurant to see her husband; you know how she does. She stops by to tell him hello or some other business."

"Annie, my nerves can't take much more," said Kit, as she reached for another piece of fudge.

"Joshua came out of the kitchen and was speaking to his wife at the lunch counter, when who do you think came sashaying back in the door?"

Kit's eyes grew wide, "No, not the girl from the saloon?"

"The very same one. It was quite a scene after that. The saloon girl was jealous, thinking that Joshua was two-timing her with another woman. Mrs. Smith didn't know about the saloon girl – or much else, I would wager."

"Did they get into a fight?"

"Not exactly. Mrs. Smith was no match for that saloon girl. Joshua tried to keep her from strangling his wife and Mr. Tate asked them all to leave. Then he lost his temper and told Joshua that he'd had enough, that how he'd treated Maggie and Hattie was improper, but this was completely unacceptable. He fired him on the spot!"

Kit was shocked – she couldn't move and was barely breathing. She just sat in silence, "How did Mr. Tate get wounded, poor dear?"

"Oh yes, poor Mr. Tate. Joshua's wife began weeping uncontrollably, the saloon girl punched Joshua, Hattie ran away in tears, and Joshua broke Mr. Tate's nose in front of the sheriff, who hauled him away in handcuffs!"

"Annie, you are telling me a fib. I don't believe a word of it – it's too much to be true!"

"I swear to you Kit, on anything you like. I give you my solemn vow, and my promise as a lady, that all of it is true. Every word!"

"Is Joshua still in jail?"

"I suppose he is; I haven't heard otherwise. There's a rumor going around that Joshua was married to that saloon girl *and* his wife. What a mess! And to think you missed it all."

"I'm glad I did miss it, or I should have liked to get a hit in for poor, dear Maggie. I must write to her. She will want to hear about this, I just know it."

"You bet she would! When you write to her, send her my good wishes. Good night." Annie left Kit to her room full of clothes and letter waiting to be written.

~

It was over a week before Mr. Tate returned to work. The swelling around his nose had greatly diminished and his eyes were only faintly bruised, although he still wore a bandage over his nose. The local ranch hands who came into town chuckled and patted him on the back, accepting him as one of their own now that he'd been in a real fight.

Kit teased him. "Mr. Tate, if you decide that ranching is for you, I am sure your new friends can provide you with a good reference."

Trying to smile at Kit, he winced. "They have invited me to accompany them to the saloon this evening for a round of whiskey or beer, whatever it is they drink in those places. It was a nice gesture, but I must decline. Mr. Harvey would ask for my head on a platter if joined them."

"No, he won't. Mr. Harvey can't discipline you if he doesn't know – it'll be our secret. You may even see the other Mrs. Joshua Smith while you're there. Do give her my regards."

"Kit, I believe you are intentionally trying to make me laugh because you know it hurts."

"No, my dear Mr. Tate. I am proud of you. I heard how you stood up to Joshua and gave him your two cents, so I was only trying to cheer you up!"

"And what if I did go? I've never been to a saloon. Would you be shocked?"

"I wouldn't be shocked, not at all. Just don't gamble or play cards while you're there – I've heard rumors of the fights that break out over a hand of cards."

"Fight? I think I could hold my own," he said with a tilt of his head.

"I bet you could. If you do go and you get in trouble, send word, and the girls and I will stand your bail. Answer me this, though. What about Joshua – any thoughts about his position?"

"Not a one. Percy seems prepared to step into that role and I will recommend that Mr. Harvey give him a raise at once."

Kit beamed with joy. Percy was a nice man and a hard worker, and he deserved to move up in the company. She replied, "I couldn't agree more. How perfect!"

Kit returned to her duties, convinced that all was going to be well in Holbrook. Winter was drawing to an end, and soon she would be on her way to a new life and a new restaurant in Pueblo. As much as she wanted to go to Pueblo, to be back in a city, she felt pain every time she thought of leaving her friends in Holbrook.

Wiping the lunch counter, her mind drifted to whom she would like to take with her to Pueblo. Mr. Harvey had assured her at their meeting that her recommendations for staff would be considered. Her first choice, Maggie, was content to stay at home in Raleigh. Kit thought about sending a letter to her old roommate Lucy Barrows. Pueblo might be just the kind of place a girl like Lucy could appreciate.

As she polished the salt and pepper shakers, she thought of Annie. Annie Blyth was one of the smartest girls Kit had ever met and a real lady, the genuine article. Her genteel manner and pleasant personality would win hearts with ease, thought Kit, but she knew she couldn't ask Annie to leave Percy, not if they were falling in love.

It was strictly against the rules for the Harvey Girls to court while under contract, but in a place like Holbrook – famous for its lawlessness and far away from all the other Harvey Restaurants – the rules could occasionally be ignored or bent. Just how far they were to be bent, Kit was certain Annie and Percy were likely to find out.

Kit watched out of the corner of her eye as Annie walked out of the kitchen, a smile on her face as she hummed a cheerful tune. Kit thought about

Levi, and how she wished he was near her, in the same town, so she could be that girl – the one in love, glowing with happiness. Giving the final touches to the lunch counter, Kit tried to put Levi as far from her mind as possible, but it was no easy feat.

The remaining hours of her day went by without incident. Mrs. Hill made beef stew with cornbread for dinner that night, which was one of Kit's favorite meals. Despite her broken heart, she found comfort in the juicy beef and tender potatoes as the cold wind howled outside.

After dinner, she decided to write Lucy a letter, imploring her to come to Pueblo in the spring. As Kit sat down at the small writing desk in her bedroom, the light from the lamp dispelling the gloom, she hoped she would find the right words to convince Lucy. Kit hated to admit it, but she didn't want to face the staff in Pueblo all alone, without a companion, a friend she could rely on.

Once, before her heart was broken, her ambition was unshakable. She would have stepped off the train in Pueblo on a mission, but now she was unsure of just what her mission should be. Was she biding her time, waiting for Levi to come to his senses and propose, or was she destined to make a career and later, when she was older, find a good man and settle down? Without the distraction of work, her mind was a jumble of conflicting goals and her heart ached.

The paper lay blank on the desk as Kit tried to think of just the right words to say to Lucy. How could she ask Lucy to come to Pueblo, when she herself wasn't sure it was the right thing to do? Her concentration was broken by the sound of Annie's voice in the hallway.

"Kit? Kit, are you in there?" Annie called out as she urgently knocked on the door.

Kit could tell something was amiss, as Annie was not prone to hysterics. She jumped up from her chair and opened the door. Annie swept past her and opened the door to her wardrobe.

"Here," Annie shoved Kit's coat at her. "Put this on, and where are your scarf and gloves? And your hat?"

Kit slid her arms into the coat and fastened it. "Annie, I can tell this is urgent, but where are we going?"

"It's Mr. Tate – he may be in trouble. Percy sent word to me by way of Mrs. Hill that there has been a shooting downtown."

"Kit, there is always a shooting downtown, this is Holbrook."

"That may be true, but it seems that this time, the victim was an employee of the Harvey Restaurant!"

Kit's mind raced back to the conversation with Mr. Tate earlier that day. Panic gripped her as she wrapped her scarf around her neck. "That could be almost anyone! There are several young men on the kitchen staff, so how do you know it has anything to do with Mr. Tate?"

"Mr. Tate confided in Percy that he was going to a saloon. Percy thought it was an odd thing for Mr. Tate to do, but didn't think much about it, at least not until now."

Kit found her gloves in the pocket of her coat, and slid a crocheted cap down over her hair. "Annie, what are we doing? What can we do about it, if the rumor does prove it be true and Mr. Tate has been shot?"

Annie stopped and faced Kit. "I honestly don't know, but if we were in trouble or shot dead, I am sure Mr. Tate would be there."

"He would. He would look after us. Let's just hope this has all been a mistake."

"I hope so, but if it isn't, this is the least we can do."

Annie ran down the stairs, followed by Kit. They raced past the other girls in the parlor and out into the frigid cold darkness of a winter night in Holbrook. As Kit and Annie rushed towards the sheriff's office, Kit was overcome with guilt. If only she hadn't teased Mr. Tate and convinced him to go to a saloon, a place he had absolutely no business going to. If she had thought about her words before she said them, this might not be happening. She prayed that all of this was a terrible misunderstanding as the snow began to fall.

Annie and Kit raced through the town, their teeth chattering in the bitter cold as the snow melted against their faces. Kit could barely feel her hands and her face was numb from the temperature, steadily dropping. Approaching the area where the saloons were, Kit could hear the unmistakable sound of music, laugher, and raucous voices, even in the harsh winter cold.

Annie and Kit found the sheriff's office and opened the door. No one was inside, but a pot of coffee sat on the stove and a half-empty cup sat on the desk, abandoned before its owner could finish drinking it.

"What should we do now? There isn't anyone here; what if it was only idle gossip?" asked Annie.

Kit warmed her hands by the cast iron stove and felt the sharp prickling sensation on her face, a signal that it was no longer numb. "I pray that it was only gossip, but there is only one way to find out."

"You don't mean we should go see for ourselves, do you?"

"It might be the only way. It's either that or stay here and wait for the sheriff or one of his men to return. We don't have many choices. We can go find out what happened, or return home and wait for news, just like everyone else."

"I suppose you're right. If he was wounded and lay dying, it would break my heart to know he was surrounded by strangers at the end."

"Then our minds are made up. Let's go find out what's happened."

"And pray that Mr. Harvey never finds out we stepped foot inside a saloon."

Kit braced herself for the sting of the biting cold wind as she turned from the warmth of the stove and went back out into the night. The wind howled and the snow came down in big flakes as Annie followed her out. Kit didn't have a plan or know where she was going, so she prayed that God would be her guide.

Peering through the snowfall, Kit noticed that in the row of saloons (each brightly lit and garishly painted, advertising girls, drink, and gambling) one saloon boasted a crowd so large the people were spilling out into the street.

Kit pointed at the Silver Dollar Saloon and said to Annie, "That looks promising, what do you say?"

"If it isn't, it may be a good place to start," Annie said, shoving her hands into a fur-lined muff, an artifact of her previous life of wealth.

Kit led the way, keeping her head down as they passed the other saloons, hoping not to be recognized. Reaching the Silver Dollar Saloon, Kit noticed the lack of music; only the sound of voices could be heard in the hush. If there wasn't laughter and music emanating from the walls of this wood and glass building, then there must be something out of the ordinary happening that evening.

Kit looked around the crowd of red-faced men, some shivering in the cold. Recognizing a familiar face, she approached a ranch hand she knew from the restaurant.

"I know you may not remember me, but I was hoping you could tell me what happened here tonight?" she asked the older man. His face was as wrinkled as leather, and his eyes were dull with drink.

Slurring his words, he answered, "Miss, I don't believe we have met, but since you asked I'm obliged to tell you that a man's been shot in there, a gentleman from that fancy eating place, shot dead."

It was true, Kit thought to herself, Mr. Tate was shot. She thanked the man, and with her heart racing, she grabbed Annie by the wrist and pulled her past the crowd of men and into the saloon.

Pushing their way past the throngs of onlookers watching the spectacle, Kit and Annie made their way slowly through the assembly of ranch hands, card players, and saloon girls.

"Please, clear the way, please move," Kit pleaded as she pulled Annie behind her.

A man turned to face her and, glaring, asked, "Just why should we move for you, little lady? Just who do you think you are? You look out of place for here. This is no place for a lady, so just turn back around and go back to wherever it was you came from. Ain't no place for you, no place at all."

Kit was stunned, speechless, but Annie had an answer. "Please sir, you're right, we don't belong here. You see, it's my brother. I fear he has been shot, and I was informed of this tragedy only moments ago."

The man was mesmerized by the beautiful, stylishly dressed aristocrat, Annie Blyth. Unable to refuse a heartfelt request by a member of the deceased's family, he answered, "If you're the next of kin, that changes things. Come with me. I'll get you to your brother, darn shame, I meant no disrespect, ma'am."

"Thank you for your kindness," Annie replied as she and Kit followed the man through the crowd. Kit was faint with cold and fear, terrified that it was true – that it was Mr. Tate, shot dead on his only trip to a saloon, and his reputation forever muddied by his one night of adventure. Just ahead, the crowd parted by the stage. Girls dressed in satin and velvet, with bright feathers in their hair and rouge on their faces, dabbed at their eyes as the stranger led Kit and Annie past them.

"Coming through, I got his sister right here. Y'all show some respect, and let the lady through," said the man, shoving anyone who stood in their way.

"There you are, little lady, sorry for your loss," he removed his hat as he bowed to Annie, turning towards the tragic scene playing out only a few feet from where Annie and Kit stood. Kit stared, desperate to see any glimpse of Mr. Tate. The sheriff and the town doctor leaned over a man laid out on the floor. Kit stepped closer, not wanting to see his face, but needing to, to know if it was true.

The sheriff glanced up from the man sprawled in front of the footlights and looked right at Kit, and then Annie. He addressed them both. "What in tarnation are you two ladies doing here? You shouldn't be seeing this."

Kit's gaze drifted from the sheriff's astonished face to the face of the man on the floor, and she gasped. "Annie," she said as she reached for Annie's hand, "Look, look who it is!"

"Oh Kit, it can't be. Is that who I think that is? Is that Joshua?"

"It sure looks like him. I thought he was in jail."

The sheriff stood and was quick to answer. "He was, until he made bail. Now, what brings you two ladies here? You shouldn't be in here."

Kit answered. "Sheriff, we heard...oh, it doesn't matter what we heard. There has been a terrible misunderstanding. We thought someone else we knew was shot."

"I thought you ladies were respectable! Who else do you know who would be in a place like this to be getting shot at? Never you mind – don't answer that question," he said as he wiped his brow, a bead of sweat rolling down his face.

"Sir, I know it doesn't concern us, but we did know the man. Please, can you tell us who shot him?" Kit pleaded.

The sheriff looked uncomfortable as he lowered his voice and drew in close to Kit and Annie. "I'm not supposed to say, but since everyone knows anyway, he was shot dead by Ida – that real pretty saloon girl he was married to."

"Thank you for telling us, Sheriff, we're obliged. We don't want to trouble you anymore this evening, so we'll just be heading on home," said Annie.

"I do hope you'll take care, it's cold as a witch's – well never mind the rest of that. Ladies, if you'll pardon me, I have work to do. You'd best be getting yourselves home before you freeze or someone recognizes you."

"Yes, sir," they answered.

"Kit, Annie!"

Kit and Annie turned to see Percy and Mr. Tate standing in the crowd just behind them. Annie threw her arms around Percy. "Oh, Percy! It's Joshua, killed by one of his ladies."

Mr. Tate stared at Percy and Annie, and then he looked at Kit. "This is no place for ladies in the employ of Mr. Harvey. What brings you here?"

Percy answered for her. "It's my fault, Mr. Tate. We heard that someone from the restaurant had been shot, and thought of your comment about coming to the saloon. I'm afraid we jumped to conclusions."

"My dears, is that true? Is that why Mr. Bryce came looking for me and both of you, too? I am overwhelmed by your sentiment, overwhelmed."

"Does that mean we aren't in trouble?" asked Kit.

"Trouble? My word, no. I can see that no real harm was done. Let's get out of here and go home. This is no place for any of us, none at all," answered Mr. Tate.

With Percy leading the way, Kit walked beside Mr. Tate, his hand resting gently on her back, guiding her through the throngs of people, all trying to see what the fuss was all about. Outside the saloon, Percy and Annie walked side by side, hand in hand, and Kit and Mr. Tate followed a few steps behind. Kit took advantage of the opportunity to speak candidly with Mr. Tate.

"I am sorry that Joshua was killed. This may be wrong of me to say, but I'm glad it wasn't you. I felt terrible thinking I had convinced you to go to a saloon, that it may have been you, shot dead."

"Kit Pridgeon, I am moved by your loyalty but your guilt is misplaced. Joshua's own actions led to his unfortunate demise."

"After this evening, are you ever going to a saloon again?"

"Good heavens, no. I've had enough excitement to last a lifetime. This town has always been famous for its lawlessness, and tonight it lived up to that reputation. It is my intention to spend the remainder of my nights in Holbrook reading books, playing chess with Percy, and *not* going to a saloon."

"About Percy and Annie – you aren't going to report them to Mr. Harvey?" asked Kit.

"No. I am not. It will have to be another secret we keep here in Holbrook. He is too valuable a cook, and she is going to be my best waitress after you have gone; I would be a silly man indeed to ruin that for the sake of rule that attempts to govern people's emotions."

"Thank you, Mr. Tate, I feel better knowing that. They deserve to be happy."

"As do you, Miss Pridgeon. I hope you find happiness, wherever you may go."

Kit smiled despite the freezing cold temperature. She didn't know what was in store for her in Pueblo, but she hoped she would find happiness in Colorado.

CHAPTER 14

"Very good. You are all smartly dressed, aprons starched, and uniforms pressed. Very good, indeed."

Kit winked at Lucy and Hattie. The restaurant manager, Mr. Nathaniel Coleman, was a difficult man to impress, and she was thrilled that her staff had earned his compliments.

He turned to Kit. "Miss Pridgeon, I believe we are ready to open the doors. On this occasion, we are expecting to welcome a special guest coming from Topeka, Mr. Harvey."

The wait staff gasped and began whispering. A visit from Mr. Harvey *was* an occasion. Kit asked, "Mr. Harvey is coming to the grand opening? When are we to expect him?"

"I have it on the best authority that he will be arriving this afternoon."

"How splendid, I do hope he'll be pleased with our work here," Kit answered.

"I have the utmost confidence that he will be duly satisfied with the standard of excellence we have achieved. I must inspect the kitchen staff, if you will excuse me," Mr. Coleman bowed his head as he left the Harvey girls in the dining room of the newest Harvey House Restaurant, in Pueblo, Colorado.

199

"Kit, Mr. Harvey is coming here! I'm so excited – I hope I don't faint!" exclaimed Lucy.

"Lucy, you'll be fine. This isn't your first day as a Harvey Girl," Hattie answered.

Kit lowered her voice and quietly said to her closest allies, "Do you think the new girls are ready? Some of them have never had a job before."

Hattie replied, "You worry too much. We've trained them ourselves, and they are as good as we can make them. Kit, you're the head waitress and the best Harvey Girl in the business. If these girls are even half as good as you, you don't have a thing to worry about, not a thing!"

"Hattie, I hope you are right."

Kit adjusted her tie. It was a small change in her uniform as head waitress, and she had worked hard to earn it. She inspected the girls, clad in their crisp black uniforms and perfectly ironed white aprons. They all looked polished, poised, and ready to greet the first customers.

Kit spoke a few words to her girls, as she referred to them. "In just a few minutes, Mr. Coleman will be opening the doors and we will welcome out first customers. Some of you may be new and some of you are experienced, but we are all a team. It is our mission to work together, to make this the best Harvey Restaurant in the company. Every customer is important, from the businessman to the ranch hand. We treat them all as gentleman and we make sure they are all fed in twenty-five minutes."

Rose Perlman, a new Harvey girl from New York, spoke up. "Miss Pridgeon, isn't it supposed to be thirty minutes?"

Kit answered with a haughty air. "Thirty minutes may be acceptable at every other Harvey Restaurant, but here we strive to be the best, so we will aim for twenty-five minutes. There is no sense in having the gentlemen running for the train when we could give them five minutes to spare."

Rose smiled. "Yes ma'am. Everyone hear that? We are going to be the best."

The Harvey girls clapped and cheered, and Kit felt good about the work she had accomplished with the help of her roommate from Topeka, Lucy Barrows, and Hattie Schultz from Holbrook. Despite the personality clash she

200

had with the perpetually scowling Mr. Coleman, Kit was grateful for the opportunity to be part of this momentous occasion.

The grand opening of the newest, lavishly decorated Harvey House in Pueblo was an important milestone in her career. In a little over a year and a half, she had worked her way up from the position of new Harvey girl to head waitress of a restaurant that would serve millionaires and clerks in its gleaming, gilded dining room. Pueblo was a wealthy city, rivaling many big cities back east, and Kit considered her position as head waitress to be an honor. She did not take it lightly.

It was an honor that had come with a hefty price tag, but she promised not to let Mr. Harvey down. He'd placed his trust in her and she intended to earn that trust with every satisfied customer.

Mr. Coleman returned to the dining room, glanced at his pocket watch, and compared its time to the large clock on the wall. Facing the Harvey girls, he proclaimed, "Ladies, it is time. Trust your training, be mindful of your uniforms and manners, and always serve the customers efficiently and graciously. That is the aim of this staff."

Kit added a reassurance. "Mr. Coleman, on behalf of all of the Harvey girls, I promise that we are ready."

"Splendid. Let's greet our guests," said Mr. Coleman, as he slipped his gold watch back into his vest pocket. Buttoning his black jacket, he stood to his full height and walked ceremoniously to the door. Turning the bolt, he officially opened the restaurant.

Kit glanced at the immaculately clean white linen tablecloths, the lush green palm trees in carved marble planters, and the polished dark wood of the lunch counter, and smiled. It all seemed like a product of her imagination. It was a feeling she hoped would not prove to be as fleeting as a dream, though. How horrible it would be, to awaken from this world of opportunity and independence, to find herself back in Fish Town, gutting fish at the cannery.

Standing in a restaurant that could serve nearly a hundred diners at a time – the largest of all the Harvey Restaurants – she felt the weight of her position on her shoulders. It was due to its size and the expense that Mr. Harvey had invested in this restaurant that Mr. Coleman rarely cracked a smile or relaxed for even a minute. He was responsible for the running of the restaurant, and she was responsible for the waitresses. Although she smiled far more often than Mr. Coleman, she understood just how much pressure was on each and every staff member to make Mr. Harvey proud, and she did not intend to let him – or herself – down. Taking a deep breath, she joined Mr. Coleman at the entrance and greeted the first guests.

"Welcome to the Harvey House," she said with a genuine smile.

~

Mr. Coleman stood with Kit, Hattie, and Dina Gregory, whom he had insisted join them as they prepared to greet the afternoon train as it pulled into the station. The first few hours of business were unprecedented in Kit's experience; she had never served so many hungry patrons so quickly in all her months as a Harvey girl.

Looking down at herself, she was surprised to see that she had remained clean despite the trays of coffee and orange juice she had carried at breakneck speed through the crowded restaurant. Not a drop had spilled on her crisp white apron, a rare occasion and one of relief for Kit, who had forgotten to bring an extra apron on opening day.

"Look smart, there is the gentleman now. But you don't need an introduction, do you, Miss Pridgeon?" whispered Mr. Coleman as he nodded in the direction of a tall, well-dressed man stepping onto the platform.

Dina, a wiry woman slightly older than Kit, answered, "As much as Mr. Harvey thinks of you, Miss Pridgeon, I don't know why the rest of us are here at all."

Kit was stung by the remark, but didn't have time to think of a suitable answer as the dark haired man dressed in a tailored suit approached the small entourage. His eyes which were steel grey and matched the hint of grey at his temples. His face was handsome, but it was a face she did not recognize.

"Welcome to Pueblo, Mr. Harvey. It is an honor that you have chosen the grand opening to visit us," greeted Mr. Coleman with a smile – an expression Kit had doubted he was capable of producing until that instant.

"Mr. Coleman, the honor is mine."

"Mr. Harvey, may I present Miss Dina Gregory, Miss Hattie Schultz, and Miss Kit Pridgeon."

Kit could not understand why Mr. Coleman had chosen to introduce Dina first. It was a rude gesture and one that Kit was not likely to forget. Mr. Coleman's rudeness and Dina's insolence did not outwardly alter Kit's appearance as she smiled pleasantly, but in her thoughts, she was unable to account for their inconsiderate behavior and stinging words.

Mr. Harvey removed his hat and greeted the ladies in turn, stopping to speak with Kit. "Miss Pridgeon, it is a pleasure to make your acquaintance. I'm Guy Harvey; my eldest brother Frederick speaks highly of you."

Kit had not been aware that Mr. Harvey had a younger brother until she stood face to face with the man, there at the station. His mannerisms were similar to her employer's, and the family resemblance in his build clearly visible, but Guy was taller and his features looked rougher, less refined. His suit was expensive but Kit thought he would be just as comfortable wearing chaps and a hat, dressed as a cowboy.

"Mr. Harvey, it is good to meet you. I sincerely hope you find all is satisfactory at the restaurant," she said, with a warm smile. She met his gaze and immediately looked away. He was an attractive man and she didn't want to give him the impression that she was flirting with him.

Mr. Coleman led Mr. Harvey into the restaurant as Kit, Hattie, and Dina greeted the travelers arriving from the train. As she smiled and spoke to the men who passed, she mulled over Dina's sudden shift in attitude. It was problematic, and Kit hoped it was only a show of nerves with the arrival of Mr. Harvey, but she was not certain that was the cause. She couldn't ignore Mr. Coleman's snub, in introducing Dina ahead of Kit.

Later that evening, after the restaurant closed and the girls had settled into the dormitory, Kit invited Hattie and Lucy to join her in her private room. A tin of divinity lay open on the bed and the girls drank tea and lemonade as they talked about the events of the day.

Kit made certain the door was latched before she brought up the topic that had troubled her since the Mr. Harvey's arrival, Dina Gregory.

"Hattie, you were at the station, did you notice how Mr. Coleman treated Dina, and introduced her first?"

Hattie narrowed her eyes as she spoke, "I did! That Dina, who does she think she is?"

"I don't know. I never knew her to act like that before today. What could have happened?" asked Kit.

Lucy whispered, "You two aren't real keen, are you? Dina's worked with Mr. Coleman before, at least that's what she told me. I bet they are sweet on each other."

"Sweet on each other, Mr. Coleman?" Hattie laughed. "I can't imagine him being sweet on anyone, but that is interesting. How long have they worked together, I wonder?"

"Lucy, you might just be on to something – Dina may be jealous. Maybe she is sweet on him?" asked Kit as she bit a piece of divinity, closing her eyes as she savored the delicious candy. "Well, he's far from my ideal as a husband, but he may like her, who knows? He did insist she met Mr. Harvey, and then he introduced her first."

"That may be, but Mr. Harvey couldn't take his eyes of you, could he?" Hattie said with a smirk. "I watched him, and every time I looked, his eyes were on you, Kit Pridgeon."

Kit felt her cheeks turning red. "You must be mistaken. He must have been making sure I knew what I was doing."

"Kit, your face is as red as a cherry! You think he's handsome, don't you? I know I do!" teased Lucy.

"Lucy, hush before someone hears you. I'm supposed to be head waitress and set a good example."

"You can put on airs all you want to, head waitress, but I know the truth. You think he's handsome or else you wouldn't be turning red!" proclaimed Lucy.

"Don't be silly, you know I have a beau back home."

"You can't wait around for that doctor back home to make up his mind. If you do, you could end up an old maid!" Hattie replied, reaching for the tin.

"I don't think I'll be an old maid," Kit protested. "He has promised to ask for my hand. I just have to be patient."

"Don't wait too long – there's a difference between patient and foolish," said Hattie.

Kit smiled and sipped her tea, hoping she wasn't being foolish, but afraid that Hattie was right. She reached for a piece of divinity, hoping the sugary candy would make her feel better.

~

Kit settled into her new position without incident. Dina gave her the cold shoulder occasionally, and Mr. Coleman never smiled at Kit, although he was unable to find fault with her work or the performance of the girls under her supervision.

The conversation with Hattie and Lucy had been enlightening, and Kit noticed that Mr. Coleman only appeared to be jovial when he was speaking with Dina. Jovial as only Mr. Coleman could manage – which was barely perceptible to those in his presence. His eyes sparkled and the corners of his lips turned up in a half smile, but that was the extent of his pleasantry, and he reserved this expression only for Dina.

When she thought of Mr. Coleman's coldness towards her, she missed Mr. Tate and the staff in Holbrook. Kit was thankful for Hattie and Lucy. They were good company and her work kept her mind from drifting to thoughts of her old friends, and the recent lack of letters from Bridgeton. Kit had written letters and sent them, but she had yet to receive any mail at her new address in Pueblo.

As the days turned into weeks, she was nearly frantic. Although her demeanor was the picture of calm, in her thoughts she was on the verge of panic. She hadn't heard from Letty, Maggie, or Levi.

It was the Wednesday after Easter before she received a large bundle of mail, all forwarded from her dear friend Annie in Holbrook. Kit was overjoyed to get her bundle of letters and disappeared to her room with them after dinner.

Sorting the letters into neat stacks, she counted letters from Letty, her sister Emily, Mrs. Cates, Maggie, Mrs. Taylor, and Levi. Overcome with joy, she started with Levi's letters first, beginning with the oldest.

It was spring, the restaurant was open, and she had satisfied her duty to Mr. Harvey. If Levi asked her to come home and be married, she was certain her answer would be yes. Praying that he had finally arrived at the same conclusion, that they should be married, she opened his letters and began reading the lines, savoring every word written on the page.

The first letters were just as she expected. He wrote that he missed her, and he confessed his love for her. He wrote of his practice and his tone was encouraging, asking about her work.

As she read, the wind picked up outside. The spring weather in the mountains could be unpredictable. It had been a warm day and she could hear thunder rolling in the distance. Setting the letters aside, she crossed her small room and latched the window as the wind howled and lightning flashed in the dark sky.

Returning to the letters, she was startled to discover that Levi had hired a nurse to assist him at his office in Bridgeton. At first, he barely mentioned the new nurse at all, but in the subsequent letters her name began to appear with alarming frequency. Kit felt her heart ache as she read words singing this woman's praises.

A sudden flash of lightning illuminated the room. Thunder rumbled overhead and shook the building as the wind and rain lashed the window, rattling it in its frame. The wind made a mournful noise that echoed the feeling in Kit's heart as she read Levi's letters. Letters that were less about his plans for their future and more about his plans for his practice. A tear slipped down her cheek as she realized what Levi was trying to say without writing it – he no longer had any plans to ask her to marry him. His future was, as it had always been, centered around his work. He wouldn't marry her because he was devoted to his work, and from what Kit could tell by the letters, his new nurse shared his devotion.

Her silent tears turned to weeping as the storm raged outside. The thunder, wind, and rain were loud enough to mask the sounds of the sobbing that consumed her. There could be no mistake; Levi didn't intended to marry her, ever. He was not capable of loving anyone but his work.

A thought, as sharp as the lightning outside her window, struck Kit. Levi was capable of sharing his love only with a woman who was as devoted to medicine as he was, a woman who would not mind being second in his heart to his work. The new nurse he wrote about in such glowing terms was the woman Levi needed by his side, not her. It was a truth that Kit found hard to swallow at that moment as she cried, her heart shattering into pieces.

Kit gathered the unopened letters from her friends into a stack and carried them to her desk. She couldn't tolerate the news of weddings and happy events in her present state. She flung herself onto her bed. Turning off the lamp at her bedside, she watched as the rain fell against her window in sheets, the storm showing no sign of weakening. She wrapped her blanket around her shoulders and sobbed into her feather pillow.

She loved Levi. He was the only man she'd ever loved, and she knew he loved her. If only she didn't live so far away. Maybe he would have asked her to marry him if she had stayed in Bridgeton. It was a question she'd grappled with before leaving North Carolina and she remembered Mrs. Taylor's painful, but true, words of advice. If Levi had wanted to marry her, he would never have let her leave – he would have begged her to stay. But Levi had never asked her to stay, in fact, he had done the opposite and insisted she leave and return to her life in the west, as he returned to his life devoted to his practice. The emotion they shared in Bridgeton was love, but it just wasn't strong enough for Levi.

The truth hurt, just like the words Levi wasn't saying. He'd never really intended to ask her to marry him. The lightning flashed and Kit caught a glimpse of her freshly pressed uniform hanging on the back of her door. Illuminated by the lightning, the apron gleamed white, and she realized that it was all she had in the world, and all she could be certain of. The uniform represented her career and the life she had made for herself. Brushing away her tears, she looked at the dress and was grateful she had not chosen to resign, that she had remained a Harvey girl.

CHAPTER 15

The storm passed, and for the next few days Kit found she had very little energy. She stayed confined to her bed, not eating and barely drinking tea or water. To the house matron Mrs. Douglass, Kit appeared to have an undiagnosed illness. Her eyes were red, her color was poor, and she was lethargic. To her closest friends, Hattie and Lucy, she appeared as she truly was – heartbroken.

Mrs. Douglass tried to prevent the two young ladies from visiting their friend, fearful the malady would spread among the ranks of the waitresses in her charge. Hattie and Lucy promised their visits would be brief and that they would take precautions, as they smuggled tins of fudge and chicken sandwiches into Kit's room, trying to entice her to eat. To their dismay, nothing worked.

By Saturday, Mrs. Douglass warned Kit she would have no choice but to summon the doctor if Kit did not show signs of improvement. Hattie and Lucy assured the matron there would be no need for medical assistance, as Kit was showing signs of rallying. In private, they needed to convince Kit to come to terms with the situation, and get her back on her feet.

Friday evening Kit lay in bed, where she had lain for two days. Her face was turned to the wall, and she didn't feel like talking to anyone. Heartsore, she didn't know where she'd ever get the energy to go back to waiting on customers. She didn't even want think about facing her staff.

Sometimes, tears would fall, and she would think of the life she had imagined with Levi. She had thought he loved her. Now she felt a fool, realizing that there would be no wedding, no life by Levi's side, and certainly no little brown-eyed children to love.

A knock at the door announced the arrival of her two closest friends. Neither girl commented on the bowl of soup sitting untouched on the desk, or the sandwich which was sadly ignored on a plate at her bedside table.

"Kit, it's us. Are you still alive?" asked Hattie, as she shut the door behind her and Lucy.

"I'm here, and I'm fine," Kit mumbled, quickly wiping her eyes on the sheet.

"Kit, you have *got* to rally. If Mrs. Douglass calls the doctor and he says there's not a thing wrong with you, you are done for. How do you think it will look to have the head waitress in bed, nursing a broken heart? You're not even supposed to have a beau!" whispered Lucy.

"I don't have a beau, not any longer. Oh, why did Letty have to get sick, and why did I have to ever meet Levi?" Kit said as she sobbed into her pillow, feeling wretched and sorry for herself.

"Kit, I know you're very upset right now, but you have to pull yourself together. If you're not sick, Mr. Coleman will believe you are unable to face the responsibilities of the head waitress position." Hattie placed her hand on Kit's shoulder.

Kit turned to face her friends, pushing herself up to sitting. Lucy slipped pillows under Kit's head. "It's true. With you being out, Dina has been acting like she is head waitress, bossing us around and giving orders like we were in the army."

"Dina?" Kit raised her eyebrows. "Dina, as head waitress? She's too ill-tempered and never patient with the new girls."

"That's why we need you, Kit. You have to come back to work before Mr. Coleman decides to replace you with Dina. If we have to work for her, we'll both resign," Hattie whispered.

Lucy agreed. "We sure will – that Dina is mean as a snake and I won't tolerate it. I may not resign, but I will ask to go back to Topeka."

Kit was responsible for Hattie and Lucy being in Pueblo. They had come to the new restaurant to work with her, at her request, and she could not bear to let them down. "You're right, I know. I don't know why this has hit me so hard, I suppose it's only that I really was imagining myself with Levi. I really thought we were going to be so happy together."

"There's no shame in it, Kit," said Lucy, passing her a handkerchief. "We're just sorry to see you hurt."

Kit wiped her face and sniffled, and then squared her shoulders. "Even so, you're right. I need to put this behind me. And I promised Mr. Harvey I would make his restaurant a success."

"That's our girl. By the way, Mr. Harvey – the *younger* Mr. Harvey – will be back in just a few weeks. Maybe you'll feel better if you have that to look forward to?" asked Hattie.

Lucy chastised Hattie. "You can't tell Kit that! Her heart is still broken by that Levi fellow – she isn't ready to think about another beau."

As Kit listened to Hattie and Lucy debate when she would be ready to fall in love again, she thought about Guy Harvey, the ruggedly handsome man in the business suit, and for a moment, she smiled.

Rising stiffly, Kit walked across her bedroom. Wrapped in a blanket, her hair a tangled mess, she was certain she looked frightful, but she didn't care who saw her. Unlatching the window, she opened it and breathed in the cool night air. The cold sent shivers down her spine, but it was refreshing. It made her feel alive. Peering out, she could hear the sounds of horses' hooves and the carriage wheels, and the soft din of voices coming from people on the street.

"Kit, come away from that window this instant! You'll catch a cold and then you really will be ill." Hattie pulled Kit back away from the window.

"I just needed some fresh air, and the cold will do me good. I feel more awake now."

"Hattie is right. Get back into bed, and tomorrow you can take in all the fresh air you want. Just promise us you'll keep that window closed tonight."

Kit promised, and the next morning, much to Mrs. Douglass's astonishment, she dressed herself and sat on the front porch,. She was still pale, but she forced herself to eat a piece of toast and drink a cup of tea under

Mrs. Douglass's watchful eye. As the morning passed, she managed to convince the matron she would be ready to return to work bright and early on Monday, without the services of the doctor.

Mrs. Douglass reluctantly agreed, and Kit spent the remainder of Saturday outside in the garden, wrapped in a shawl, with a bonnet on her head. The garden was still brown from the winter but there were small green buds on the branches of the trees and bushes, green buds that would flower once more, as Kit hoped she would, when her own personal season of winter was at an end.

~

Kit's broken heart was a wound that was easily concealed, but it was still keenly felt, and never more than when she saw a young couple passing on the street, or sitting together in the restaurant, sharing a quick meal before traveling to their destination.

Her work was challenging and there was never a quiet moment at the restaurant. The demands of her position and the incessant requests of the customers filled the hours of her days and brought her solace. In a fast-paced environment like the Harvey Restaurant, Kit found it impossible to waste any of her energy on feeling sorry for herself – there was too much work to do and too many customers to feed.

She smiled for the guests and greeted each one, genuinely happy to see them. These guests, and her loyalty to Hattie and Lucy, kept her returning to work every morning. Without her dedication to her work, she knew her memories of Levi would still cause her distress. In the rare hours that she was alone, she wondered how she could have ever been so silly to fall in love with a man like Levi, a man clearly devoted to his career.

Fortunately for Kit, Hattie and Lucy did not often leave her alone, and always managed to talk her into a shopping trip, a lecture, or attending Bible study. But even their best efforts could not change the fact that soon, Kit would have to confront her feelings. Letty was getting married in the summer, and she demanded that Kit make the trip for the long-awaited event.

The letters from Levi had stopped after Kit, in a fit of despair, wrote to him asking where she stood in his heart and in his affections. The letter, mailed over two weeks ago, was still unanswered. The silence no longer pushed her into a state of panic; it now only reaffirmed what she already knew to be true. Levi did not intend to ask for her hand. If he did, he would have sent a telegram when he read her letter, but no word arrived.

She was no longer left to wonder what her future held. It did not hold Levi Kellerman, and there was nothing left for her to do but go on with her life, devoted to her work and her friends. It was the life she had lived before Levi, and it was the life she would return to, older and wiser than before.

In the weeks since her illness, Kit had poured herself into her work. The restaurant was running efficiently. Dina occasionally grumbled about taking orders from Kit, but everything was operating smoothly. Mr. Harvey was scheduled to return to Pueblo, and for the first time since she'd had to let go of her hopes with Levi, Kit was looking forward to something other than a letter or telegram from him.

Standing outside on the platform with Mr. Coleman, Hattie, Lucy, and the ever-present Dina Gregory, Kit watched for Guy Harvey. Half expecting to see him climb out of the first-class car dressed in boots and denim, she was instead rewarded by the sight of a dapper man, dressed impeccably. His jacket was the latest fashion, and his cravat matched his waistcoat.

She felt her cheeks turning pink as he approached and removed his hat, greeting the entourage of staff. For a brief moment, Kit imagined that his eyes lingered on her as he spoke to Mr. Coleman and acknowledged the Harvey girls at his side. Mr. Harvey continued to gaze at Kit as he asked, "Miss Pridgeon, I was sorry to hear of your recent illness. Are you recovered?"

Kit answered, "Yes, Mr. Harvey, I am recovered. Thank you."

"You had Frederick and me worried. You are valuable to this family."

"Mr. Harvey, thank your brother for me, and thank you for the kind words."

"My pleasure, Miss Pridgeon. I do hope we will have an opportunity to speak later this afternoon," he said, as he joined Mr. Coleman.

Kit felt an elbow in her ribs as she turned to face Hattie and Lucy. They were both smirking at her in a way that suggested she was not the only one to notice that Guy Harvey had his eye on her. Her heart, which for some weeks had felt dead inside her, fluttered slowly back to life, though it was with some apprehension that she watched Mr. Guy Harvey walk into the restaurant.

As the hours of the day slipped away, Kit remembered his request to speak with her and soon realized that she would be unable to escape her duties for a chat. Guy apparently came to the same conclusion as he oversaw the operation of the kitchen and every aspect of the restaurant. Kit saw him timing her girls as they served customers, and hoped they were beating the required time of thirty minutes.

When the lunch rush was over the traffic decreased only slightly. In the afternoons, Kit would take a fifteen-minute break in the kitchen to eat a quick bite. Often, a sandwich or a bowl of soup was all she had time for, before she was needed back in the dining room. This afternoon was no exception, especially with Mr. Harvey in attendance. As she sat on a wooden chair by the pantry door, out of the way of the staff, she bit into her ham sandwich as Guy came into the kitchen.

The staff acknowledged him as they went about their duties. Kit stood to return to the dining room, her sandwich nearly intact on the plate.

Guy walked towards her. "Miss Pridgeon, don't stop eating on my account. After your recent bout of illness, you need your appetite. Frankly, I am pleased to see you have regained your appetite. When I inquired as to your health, Mrs. Douglass said that you were not eating for a time."

Kit did not know how to respond. "Mr. Harvey, thank you for your concern. It just goes to show how good a company this is, for you to worry over the illness of one of your wait staff."

Guy laughed, and it was a heartwarming sound. "You, Miss Pridgeon, have a sense of humor! And here I thought you were all work."

"Sense of humor? Mr. Harvey, I wasn't trying to be funny."

"You may not have been, but I don't believe you understand how highly regarded you are by my brother...and by me. We both hold you in the highest esteem."

Kit nearly choked on her sandwich as she swallowed a bite of ham and bread. "Both of you? But you only just met me."

"That may be true, but judging from what I have already seen, you have earned our respect. Are you aware of the average serving time for this restaurant?" He stepped out of the someone's way.

"I have trained the girls to do it in under thirty minutes."

214

"Twenty-five and a half. With your training, they have shaved over *four minutes* off the required time. Yet the customers do not seem to be rushed in any manner. In a restaurant this size, an efficient wait staff is vital."

Kit beamed with happiness. After so much bad news, good news was a welcome change. "Mr. Harvey, do you mean it? Tell me truthfully, are we the fastest? I will work hard as I must until we are the best and the fastest."

"Miss Pridgeon, there can be no doubt, your girls are the fastest team I've ever seen. Well done."

"Thank you!" she exclaimed as she tried to contain her excitement. There was no reward or accolade, but knowing they were the best was all she needed. "I can't wait to tell the girls."

He cleared his throat. "Actually, I had a different idea. Please allow me to share it tomorrow morning, before we open the restaurant."

"Oh, Mr. Harvey, would you? Hearing it from you would mean so much to everyone."

"I will be staying in town this evening, and I would very much like to speak with you. May I convince you to accompany me to dinner? If you already have plans, I understand. I apologize for the short notice."

Kit's eyes widened, and her heart raced as she repeated the word. "Dinner?"

Guy nodded. "Yes, dinner. I'd planned to speak with you this afternoon, but there seems to be no time available for our meeting. Perhaps at dinner, we could converse without interruption."

Kit's rising pulse rate quickly returned to normal. Mr. Harvey was asking her to dinner to discuss business; she was foolish to think his intentions were romantic. Trying to hide the disappointment she felt, she replied, "Dinner would be fine. What time shall I be ready?"

"I will send the carriage for you at half past seven." He turned to go, and paused. "Miss Pridgeon, I look forward to this evening. I am grateful you have agreed to accompany me."

Guy left the kitchen and Kit stared at the half-eaten sandwich on her plate. A rich and powerful man like Mr. Harvey could not find a girl from Fish

Town to be interesting company. As she finished her sandwich, the fluttering in her heart returned to the state of dull pain it existed in these days.

Chiding herself for imagining that Guy Harvey could think of her as anything other than a good employee, she slid the plate into the sink, straightened her apron and returned to the dining room.

~

Hattie and Lucy disagreed with Kit about Mr. Harvey's intentions, and they were only too quick to tell her how vehemently they did so as they helped Kit to dress for the occasion. Lucy stepped in to fix Kit's hair in the latest fashion, and Hattie scrambled to select the perfect perfume and jewelry for the evening.

"Kit, this is important. You must look your best," Hattie said, poring over the contents of her jewelry box. "You don't have much in the way of jewelry, do you? I'll lend you my marcasite ring and earrings; they'll match the dress you are wearing."

Kit was dressed in a crimson dress, embroidered with black flowers. Her hair was arranged in a high pompadour with black ribbon, and Lucy had loaned her a black cape for the evening. Wearing the jewelry Hattie had carefully chosen, Kit looked every inch the fashionable woman, she just didn't feel fashionable on the inside. Deep down, she was certain she would be an old maid someday.

"Kit, you are beautiful. That color makes your complexion glow – you should wear red more often!" exclaimed Lucy.

"Hattie, Lucy, thank you," Kit said as she held their hands. "Oh dear, is that the time?"

"Hurry, Kit, you don't want to keep Mr. Harvey waiting. You know what the rules say about tardiness!"

Kit hugged both her friends, and grabbing her black embroidered purse, she rushed down the stairs, careful not to trip on her petticoats. The carriage was waiting for her at the curb when she stepped onto the sidewalk.

Kit had neglected to ask Mr. Harvey where they were dining, and she hoped her dress was suitable to the restaurant he chose; she did not want to be underdressed. She fretted about her hair and dress all the way to the

216

Wicklow Hotel, a place Kit had only walked past, never daring to venture inside.

A footman greeted her at the door and escorted her inside. The lobby was elegantly appointed with red velvet settees, crimson and gold drapery, gigantic palm trees in gilded pots, and a marble fountain as the centerpiece. Mr. Guy Harvey stood by the fountain. He turned to face Kit, and she felt his gaze fall on her face. His eyes met hers.

"Miss Pridgeon, you look delightful. Have you dined at the restaurant in this hotel before? I have been told it has a fine selection of fish and clams brought in fresh from the Gulf of Mexico."

"No, Mr. Harvey, I have never dined at the Wicklow before this evening, and the last time I had seafood was this winter in Bridgeton."

Mr. Harvey offered his arm, and Kit walked beside him into the restaurant. Gilded chandeliers and golden candelabras gave the dining room a luxurious ambience. The head waiter escorted them to a table, past well-dressed patrons festooned in peacock feathers, beading, and strands of pearls. Kit looked down at her dress as Mr. Harvey complimented her. "Your dress is lovely. That color suits you."

"Thank you," she answered, as they were seated.

Kit didn't say much, shyly listening as Guy made small talk. She watched with fascination as the light from the candles bathed his features in a warm glow, and his eyes sparkled in the light. She was unsure what to say, choosing instead to listen. Disappointed that he was not romantically interested in her, she tried to remain impervious to his charms, his easy laughter, and his sense of humor. But he made it hard for her not to feel attracted to him, try as she might to be polite but unmoved.

After the fish course, Guy was quick to change the topic of conversation to business. As the waiter cleared away the plates and brought the meat course, rack of rib with roast potatoes, Guy asked Kit a question she was unsure how to answer.

"Miss Pridgeon, this may seem like rather a pointed question and it may not be my business to ask, but what are your plans for the future?"

Not long ago, Kit could have answered that question with ease, knowing exactly what she wanted, but after Levi she was no longer sure. "Mr. Harvey,

217

I hope to continue working for your company. After that, if there is an after, I'm not certain."

"Do you have dreams? Goals you want to achieve? When I first met you, I must admit I saw you as an ambitious woman. Perhaps my opinion was shaped by my brother's impression of you."

Kit understood what Guy meant, that something had shifted. "Mr. Harvey, do you mean to imply that I am no longer that woman, that you no longer believe me to be ambitious?"

He sipped his water before answering. "I believe you are ambitious, that you are unafraid, and ready to take on any challenge. I just wanted to tell you, in private, that I sense a change in you. Are you being treated well by Mr. Coleman? Do you not like the new restaurant? If you do not wish to discuss it, I understand. I don't mean to be intrusive."

Kit tried to understand why Guy Harvey would be interested in her ambition, or her happiness. He was a stranger, and he was her employer, so she wasn't sure how much she wished to reveal to him. Across the table, his eyes were kind and his smile, sincere. She felt she could tell him secrets that lay in her heart, but she wasn't certain she trusted herself to reveal them to him, a man who could only see her as an asset to the company. She was struck by the similarities between this conversation with Guy and her conversation with Levi – both men had invited her to a beautiful restaurant and asked her about her future.

Choosing her words with care, she said, "You are observant, I must admit. I have been treated well at the restaurant. Mr. Coleman is not as amicable as Mr. Tate in Holbrook, but he seems to be a good manager."

"Miss Pridgeon, perhaps I spoke out of turn, which was not my intention. We've only just met, and I had no right to pry into your personal affairs. I had rather hoped to find you as excited about your prospects as I am."

Kit looked at Guy with a quizzical expression. "Excited about my prospects, whatever do you mean?"

"Fred knew your heart was set on California, so he wasn't pleased to have to delay the opening of his restaurants in that state and he was disappointed that he was unable to keep his promise to you, Miss Pridgeon. He's been impressed with you ever since you convinced the staff in Topeka to make charity their number one priority after serving the customers. Your work ethic and dedication to the company has not gone unnoticed, and I would like to discuss your future."

Kit was intrigued. "What future might I have with the company, other than remaining in Pueblo?"

"Fred has placed his trust in me to lead the expansion west. Our plans to open restaurants in California are once again being discussed, and I wanted to determine your interest in that venture."

"Would I be a head waitress at a restaurant? Is that the position you have in mind for me?"

"Miss Pridgeon, in our company we see women as more than wait staff. With your ability to lead by example, train, and teach, I was rather hoping you might work with me as we prepare to open the new restaurants. The dormitory and training facility at Topeka are not large enough to accommodate the staff and the girls we will need to hire and train." He paused while the waiter cleared their plates once again. "You don't have to make a decision this evening. If you are content here as head waitress, then I don't want to persuade you to make a move you might regret."

"In California, I'd no longer be a head waitress…but what would I be, exactly?"

"You would be a staff member, rather like a professor at a university. With our company growing at such a rapid rate, I'm afraid you and I are in uncharted territory. I can offer you a substantial raise, and you would no longer wear the uniform of the wait staff. Your living arrangements would be of your choosing, although you are welcome to take a room in the dormitory."

Kit blinked, and smiled thoughtfully. "Well, this is unexpected. I wonder, what about Hattie and Lucy? They came to Pueblo to work with me, and I don't believe they'll want to stay under Dina Gregory as head waitress."

"Miss Gregory is a hard working woman, but her leadership skills are not as developed as yours. I do not believe we would make the decision to promote her, regardless of how forcefully Mr. Coleman tries to convince me otherwise."

"He has tried to convince you to promote her, to my position?"

"Yes, regrettably, he has. I suspect his motivation maybe less than professional, but I am not at liberty to discuss that, and I am confident you won't repeat it." Guy gave her a meaningful look.

Kit suppressed a smile. "You have my word. And Hattie and Lucy? What of them, if I should choose to accept your offer? And what of me – what if I want to marry in the future?"

"Hattie and Lucy may stay in Pueblo or be assigned to a different restaurant of their choosing, although I did consider Lucy as a possibility to fill your position once you have joined me in California. As to the subject of your marrying, that would be entirely up to you. You would not be a Harvey Girl, and therefore not subject to the strict rules. I don't see any reason why you couldn't marry if you like."

Kit was delighted. The dinner was not romantic, but it was memorable, and it was just the medicine she needed to heal her broken heart. California was once again her destination. She'd thought it no longer held any magic for her, that the Pacific Ocean was just a dream – but at the mention of it, her cold and wounded heart yearned for adventure and the smell of salt water.

Kit thought of the possibilities of her new position, and realized she already felt more energetic and more positive than she had in a while. "Mr. Harvey, when would I begin as a member of your staff?"

"This summer. We are projecting the opening of the restaurants in the early autumn, and will need to hire and train girls during the summer months."

The waiter brought the dessert course, a triple-layered chocolate cake. To Kit, the cake seemed like the perfect end to the dinner, and she was in a celebratory mood.

"You asked me earlier if I was still ambitious. To be honest, I did have some bad news recently in my personal life, but that is behind me. I am confident that by the summer, I will have recovered from the incident fully and will be able to devote myself to the success of this venture."

Guy smiled. "Miss Pridgeon, I don't think I'll have to wait until summer. You seem to have made a sudden recovery at dinner this evening; perhaps I should ask you to dine more often."

"Perhaps you should." Kit blushed. "But as I do not need any time to consider your offer, I accept."

"Very good. I'm delighted, and I give you my word – once we are settled into our offices in San Francisco, I promise to dine with you as often as you will allow."

CHAPTER 16

Spring passed into summer and Kit prepared to journey to California to begin her new position as staff member to Guy Harvey at his San Francisco office. Lucy decided to stay in Pueblo and accept the head waitress position and Hattie remained at her side; the two had become inseparable. Kit promised that she would not forget them, and that positions waited for them in California any time they chose to transfer.

Before she traveled to San Francisco she made a trip back home to Bridgeton to see her best friend become Mrs. Letty Pridgeon. It was a bittersweet journey. She saw Mrs. Cates and Letty, her sister Emily, and her brother Thomas. Her parents attended the wedding in the parlor of Letty's house, the same parlor Levi had used as an operating room only months before. The memories of Levi haunted Letty's house like ghosts, and made Kit's decision to avoid seeing him even more difficult.

She was no longer in love with him, but she wished they had said goodbye as friends. Still, she stuck to her resolve and did not seek him out. She knew this was the right decision when Letty's mother confided that Levi had married his nurse only a week before Letty's own wedding.

Kit returned to Colorado, leaving her past behind her. The trip back home had given her an opportunity to say goodbye to the people and the place that had made her the woman she was, the woman with ambition and a sense of adventure. As the train left the station, she was not sure when, or even if she would ever come back, a fact that made her wistful for days gone by – but not for the hardships and poverty that came with them.

She stayed in Colorado for a few days to pack her belongings and give Lucy all the last-minute advice Kit wished she had received. Lucy appreciated every word, and promised to make Kit proud. On her last night in Pueblo, Kit treated Hattie and Lucy to dinner at the Wicklow, a treat that was an extravagant splurge but one that would live in their memories. Tears were wept and stories shared as the Harvey Girls promised to stay in touch and always be as sisters. Kit realized that it was her last night as a Harvey Girl, the last time she could call herself that. As Guy had explained, she was in uncharted territory.

The following morning, Mr. Coleman wished Kit a safe journey, Hattie and Lucy cried, and Kit climbed aboard a train heading west. This time she was headed as far west as she could go. Leaving Pueblo, she was overcome with excitement. She was finally going to see the Pacific Ocean – she was going to California, and living a dream she'd had since she became a Harvey Girl.

A book lay unread in her lap, and a hamper full of delicious sandwiches and sugary confections sat beside her, unopened. Kit peered out the window, her eyes glued to the changing scenery. With a smile, she recognized how she felt; it was the same trepidation and joy she felt when she left North Carolina. She was reminded what it was like to be a brand new Harvey Girl – unsure of what the future held, and fearful and happy all at the same time.

Outside the window, she watched the mountains turn into red rocks, the red rocks become flat brown desert, and the desert become green and lush once more. California was a wild place and yet it held the fascinating city of San Francisco. Spanish missionaries and conquistadores had settled California, and were followed by the pioneers and seekers of gold. It was as thrilling as any place she had ever imagined, and she could hardly wait to step off the train and see it for herself.

The journey to California was long, much longer than Kit had imagined it would be. Arriving at the station in San Francisco, she was exhausted but not interested in sleep – there was too much to see and too much to do. Stepping onto the platform, she held her hand up to shield her face from the morning sunlight, her parasol forgotten at her side.

"Miss Kit Pridgeon, allow me to welcome you to California!" said the familiar voice of Guy Harvey.

"Guy, it is so good to see you. Have I made it? Am I really in California?" she asked with a wink.

"Yes Kit, you are. I have a carriage waiting."

Kit did not immediately move from the platform. Instead, she took a deep breath. She was in California and she wanted to savor every second. Kit turned to face the handsome man at her side. Although it was a secret kept from everyone but Hattie and Lucy, Kit and Guy were on a first name basis. They had become friends and spent much of the spring in each other's company, planning every detail of their venture out west.

Kit was afraid to put into words how she felt about Guy. Memories of the last heartbreak haunted her, but she enjoyed his company and the friendship that had grown from their mutual respect and dedication to their work. If Guy never returned her feelings she would be content with his friendship, or so she told herself.

"I will arrange to have your trunks brought to the carriage. I have a delightful afternoon planned…or you may rest, if you prefer."

Kit answered, "Rest? I don't need rest – I did my resting on the train. No, I'm in California, a place I never believed I'd ever see, and I want to see the ocean. Can you arrange that?"

"As a matter of fact, that was precisely what I had in mind, unless you would prefer to remain here at the station?"

Kit patted Guy on the shoulder in a good-natured manner. "While the station is lively, I am certain it cannot hope to compete with the majesty of the Pacific. Lead on, sir!"

"I'd better show you all there is to see today, because we start work tomorrow. Are you quite sure you would rather not rest?" His smile was mischievous.

"If you say 'rest' once more, I will climb back on that train and never return!" said Kit.

"No, you won't. You would miss me terribly, admit it."

Guy teased her as though they were more than friends, but she refused to allow herself to fall in love with him. His sense of humor was due to his warm personality, and she promised that she would not make the same mistake again, by listening to her foolish heart. That very heart fluttered uncontrollably every time she was near Guy and every time he looked at her with those steel gray eyes, sometimes as stormy as seas in November.

225

Guy escorted her to the carriage, and pointed out important buildings along the way to the Pacific Ocean. As the carriage approached the water, Kit could smell the familiar scent of salt water, a scent she found comforting.

From the window, she watched as the small strip of blue she'd glimpsed in between the buildings became a large expanse of ocean stretching to the horizon. Enormous ships and small fishing boats shared the waters, and Kit's heart raced with happiness. She turned to Guy and said, "Oh, this is beautiful. I can't believe it, there it is, the Pacific Ocean. Thank you, thank you for everything." She flung her arms around him.

As she embraced Guy, she suddenly remembered she was embracing her employer, and drew back in embarrassment. "Goodness, I apologize. I didn't mean to...I'm just so happy."

"There is no need to apologize, none at all," he said with a warm smile.

The carriage came to a stop at a hotel overlooking a narrow strip of beach. Climbing out of the carriage, Guy reached up to help her down. "I hope you like it here, until we can make more suitable arrangements."

"Yes, this will be perfect. But Guy, didn't you tell me you have a day planned?"

"I do. Check in to your room and change out of those traveling clothes; we have a special afternoon waiting for us."

Kit followed his directions. The room he'd requested for her use had a magnificent view of the ocean, with the breeze blowing gently in the window. Kit changed into a pale blue cotton summer dress, leaving her heavy traveling suit on the bed. She tied a blue ribbon in her hair and selected a straw hat for the occasion. Breathing in the heavenly ocean air, she left her hotel room and joined Guy in the lobby.

"Kit, the color blue suits you. You look like a vision in that dress."

"You are much too kind. May I ask what have you planned for us?"

"Follow me, and you shall see,' he said, as he held out his hand. Kit was unsure whether she should take it. It was a romantic gesture, and one she'd sworn to avoid. Looking into his gray eyes, she felt her resolve to not fall in love melt away. She placed her hand in his and let him lead her outside, to a beautifully set table under a white tent. There, a waiter stood patiently and brought a bottle of champagne and fresh seafood for luncheon.

226

The sand of the beach under her feet, and the sound of the waves crashing on the shore was overwhelming for Kit. A tear of joy slid down her cheek as she looked at the man across the table, this man who had arranged all of this just for her.

"Guy, this is so beautiful. You've made this day far more special than I could ever have hoped."

He blushed, and cleared his throat. "Kit, there is something I've been wanting to say to you since the first day I saw you, at the station in Pueblo. I think I knew it then and I know it now – I love you. If you don't feel the same as I do, tell me, and we'll be friends."

Kit stood from the table, carefully placing the linen napkin down. She walked to the water's edge. The waves roared as ships glided past on their way to Asia. From the white sand of the beach, she looked at the fishing boats and remembered once, when she sat on a dock wanting a different life, and praying that something more than Fish Town waited in her future.

"Kit? Have I upset you? My darling, have I said too much?" Guy asked as he stood beside her, his eyes on her face, Kit's gaze drawn to the water.

"Guy, if you only knew how far I've come in my life, how many miles I've traveled to find you, to be here with you. I don't know what to say; I can't find the words to express all that I feel, all that I want to tell you."

Guy gently touched her cheek, turning her face to his. His eyes gazed softly into hers. "You don't have to tell me how you feel using sentences and lengthy explanations. One word will be all I need from you. Miss Kit Pridgeon, will you marry me?"

Kit's heart fluttered happily. The scene of natural beauty faded from her perception as she saw only Guy, his soft smile, his ruggedly handsome face. The words he asked were the most beautiful words she had ever heard. She nodded, and said, "Yes."

Guy did not respond with words. Instead, he leaned close to Kit, and embracing her in his arms, he kissed her long and passionately, as the waves lapped at their feet and seagulls called overhead in the blue sky. As he held her in his arms, Kit smiled and thought about all her dreams that had come true, every one of them, because she had dared to answer an advertisement in the newspaper to become a Harvey Girl.

It was a story she hoped she would tell her granddaughters one day, that she had been young and adventurous and once, she had worn the uniform of a Harvey Girl. Standing beside Guy, she wondered if her granddaughters would believe it, but it was true, every word.

A NOTE TO MY READERS

Thank you so much for reading my book. I sincerely hope you enjoyed it. I had an amazing time researching and writing about the Harvey girls and imagining Kit's journey. Harvey girls were strong, independent, and courageous. I have the upmost respect for these one of a kind pioneers of the wild wild west!

If you enjoyed the story and have time, please leave a review where you purchased the book. You'll be helping others make a decision on their purchase and I appreciate your effort, so will other forthcoming readers.

If you would like to be the first to know about my new releases, promotions and giveaways, please sign up for my mailing list on my Facebook page, Katherine St. Clair author. If you have any comments or questions about my books, please do not hesitate to contact me at katherine@maplewoodpublishing.com.

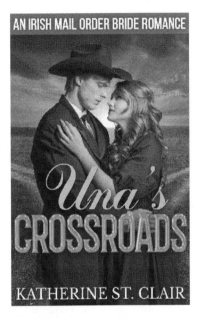
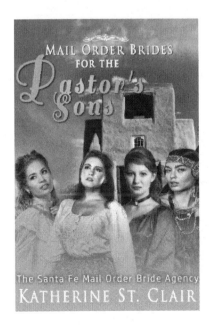
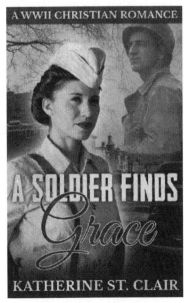

Made in the USA
Columbia, SC
04 July 2017